CW01624042

This book is dedicated to Elaine Everest.

Acknowledgement

I'd like to thank all the golf courses I've played at, the other golfers trying to get to grips with the game, and the glorious wildlife. All of which gave me the seeds of ideas to build this story on.

As always the mutual support of my writing friends has been a real morale boost to me while writing this book, and managed to keep me sane. As has the confidence of Paul Hilton and the team at Rampart Books. I'd also like to thank family and friends for keeping me energised to write more books. And finally my gratitude, as ever, to you the reader for your continued interest and enthusiasm in my work.

MURDER IN THE ROUGH

NICK STUART

This Edition
Rampart Books

ISBN 978-1-915778-81-9

Rampart Paperback

Murder in the Rough

PROLOGUE

About two hours before a spring dawn in the verdant Kent countryside, a timid young female fallow deer grazed cautiously on fresh grass in the darkness of a small copse. The alert doe's head lifted and her ears twitched as she checked for unexpected sounds or movements. All the while her well-developed sense of smell was constantly checking for unfamiliar scent. A momentary shudder went through her white spotted gingery brown body as she turned her head from side to side to scan the area with exceptional vision. Satisfied her senses hadn't picked up anything hostile, she gave a flick of her short black and white tail bowed her head downwards and took another mouthful of the sweet tasting wet grass.

The person had no right to be in the doe's domain at that time, and no right to be measuring distances with a rangefinder from behind a mound to where she stood, or to be using sophisticated night vision equipment. But they had clear instructions from their employers, and they never failed to carry out instructions. It was an unpleasant business they were in but it paid extremely well, and they had long since learned to switch off to the consequences of their actions and remain professional. This was an unusual commission, generally they applied their particular skills to human targets. But the preparation was done, crosshairs aligned, and a bright red laser dot positioned precisely on their prey. In an instant there was a soft swoosh and the muffled thud of impact as the shot from the weapon found its quarry and the young unsuspecting doe fell dead where it stood. This was an accomplished hunter, careful to be downwind of the animal, using an almost silent weapon and ensuring it was an instant kill. They couldn't afford a squealing wounded creature alerting anyone to their presence, nor the sound of a shot on a still night, or a waving flashlight that could carry for miles in the dark. The crossbow bolt entered the high shoulder of the doe and from around twenty yards it was guaranteed to be fatal. This is the point where the shot breaks the spine and causes central nervous system damage. That paralyses the deer instantly, and the trauma means the animal will expire in a matter of seconds. The assassin knew their stuff and had good quality equipment, so mercifully the doe didn't suffer, but the job wasn't finished there. The hunter rose from behind the mound then removed a rope and a large serrated double sided hunting knife from a camouflaged backpack. They lashed the doe's hind legs together with a rope at the hooves, threw the rope over a low branch of a sycamore tree and hoisted up the dead animal so that its head was suspended at waist height. Under the head was placed a plastic tub to catch the warm deer's blood as the predator hacked through skin, flesh, sinew, and bone to remove the head and place it in a black refuse sack. This part of the operation had to be over with quickly, before the light arrived. The Hunter's employer wanted both the blood, and the head retained. They didn't know why at that time and didn't much care, it was just another instruction. But they knew, as with any commission, nothing incriminating could be found at the scene and any evidence had to be destroyed without a trace. They could do that. It was nothing new in their world. But suddenly in their sharp peripheral vision they noticed the headlights of a small vehicle heading across a grassed area towards the copse, obviously something electric because it was almost silent. It had to be an over enthusiastic worker getting ahead of their day's work, but the hunter didn't want a confrontation or to have to take another life that morning. So they carefully gathered their spoils and left in more of a hurry than they had intended. So much of a hurry that they uncharacteristically made an error and left the crossbow bolt inside the deer's carcass—a mistake which might lead to their undoing.

1

The sun was rising on an unseasonably cold late April morning, a light spring frost covered the grass and the crisp air was biting into exposed skin. The smell of wood smoke was drifting from nearby houses and a stiff breeze was animating long grass in the natural hollows of the landscape. Further down the valley three young fallow deer with clouds of vapour pulsing from their nostrils bounced and scampered to find better grazing, while a pheasant clacked loudly in the distance. This place was only eighteen miles from central London, but a million miles from the hubbub.

The day heralded a contest between two perceptive minds pitted against each other, their roles changing back and forth to gain tactical advantage. These were men once used to catching villains, arsonists and even murderers. They had spent a lifetime exposing people trying to deceive them and become attuned to the criminal psyche. Together they had put away some of the country's top fraudsters and now they were competing with no quarter given—on the golf course.

This was ex-major insurance fraud investigator Charlie Flint, an average height square jawed handsome older man with a full head of greying hair in his late fifties. And his only slightly younger, best pal, recently retired Detective Chief Inspector Tim Featherstone from London's Metropolitan police fraud squad. Tim, by comparison was a more rugged character about six feet two and thickset, with a face that bore all the scars of a man who had played competitive rugby in the scrum for many years. They were known to each other respectively as Flinty and Fev. And now they both had time on their hands to meet for their favoured pastime at least once a week, always at *The Sycamores*, a club where they were both founder members.

'Your honour Flinty,' his old friend said as Charlie loosened up with a few practice swings. 'I'm coming for you this week. It's about time you bought the beers.'

'Hah,' Charlie said sarcastically. 'I think my money is safe matey.' He bent forward and pushed a fluorescent pink tee into the ground and balanced a pristine white golf ball on top of it.

Just as Charlie had committed to his stroke and was about to connect club with ball, Tim blurted, 'I'm convinced that head professional is dodgy you know.'

Charlie spectacularly sliced his ball into the woods to the right and cursed loudly. 'Yeah, thanks mate,' he said testily, snatching his tee from the ground.

Tim stepped up to strike his ball, he took his backswing and with immaculate timing on the down stroke Charlie said, 'What dodgy bent, or with some strange sexual preferences?'

Tim hooked his ball straight into a bunker, grimaced and they both smiled as they knew their regular first tee gamesmanship was over. He slid his driver back into his golf bag and hoisted it onto his shoulder laughing as he said, 'Touché my friend.'

The pair started off up the lush green fairway together

before they peeled off to find their respective balls. As the sun moved higher in the sky and the temperature rose pleasantly Tim said, 'You're the one with the sixth sense for these things Flinty. And as you've told me a million times, you are never wrong, so what do you think? But I suppose right now I'm probably more concerned about that decapitated deer found hanging from a tree and drained of blood the other week.'

Charlie's face distorted with a pained expression as he adjusted the position of the golf bag on his back. 'Yes, as much as the whole gruesome affair sickens me, I can understand that some low life might want to kill an animal quietly with a crossbow for free venison and let it hang for a while. But there has been no attempt to take the meat, only the blood—and the head. There was hardly any spillage on the ground beneath the carcass so what would someone want with a severed head and a couple of litres of deer blood?'

Tim gave a fake shiver. 'All a bit barbaric mate, but I'm sure the boys in blue will get to the bottom of who shot Bambi eventually. Probably some weirdo cult wanting to dance naked in the woods with flowers in their hair and smarm blood on themselves. Not good for the club at all though, and I'm sure they will want it kept quiet as the locals are all getting very twitchy about it. But I don't think it's got anything to do with Willis Martin, not really the style of a world-famous golf professional. He strikes me as more of an out-and-out crook.'

Charlie nodded, 'I agree, but I'm trying not to get involved in that stuff anymore—never goes down well at home with Ruth since I've retired. Wouldn't want to upset the old girl now. She's stuck by me and my crazy job for a lot of years.'

Tim burst out with a laugh, 'Know what you mean mate Louise is the same, I wouldn't have put up with what she has, guess they must love us eh?' His eyes widened and he grinned as his face filled with enthusiasm. 'But we just can't leave that natural sense of justice alone can we, it's in the both of us and must be satisfied? The rush of adrenalin when you are onto something, and the thrill when you finally get a case buttoned up and take a villain off the street. We're like peas in a pod us two.'

A rabbit scampered as Charlie hacked his way out of the woods, and Tim made a hash of playing out of the bunker. Neither had advanced much further up the fairway.

'So, what have you picked up that's bothering you about Willis Martin?' Charlie asked.

'Well, there is just something not kosher about him. He's hardly ever here, almost never gives lessons, and there are often strange people turning up to the shop at all hours to see him when he gets back from his trips. But according to Craig Galbraith, the Japanese owners insisted on Willis having the job.'

Charlie looked at the first green and considered the distance and club he would need to get him there as he located his golf ball. 'Well, we don't need the course manager to tell us Willis is a top-class pro, played on the circuit for years, been on TV and competed in all the major tournaments. He's pretty much a household name in golf circles, but gone off the boil over the last few years. Still, it's hard to believe he's here on our little course really. Probably made a lot of money and can obviously still trade on his name in retirement.'

'Precisely. So how did the Japanese convince such a big name in the golf world to become the head professional at a tin pot course on the outskirts of London. When he could have gone almost anywhere in the world Flinty?'

'Hardly a tin-pot course at these prices,' Charlie chuckled.

'Well it probably is when he's been used to places like Augusta and St Andrews.'

Charlie smiled, 'He married a well to do English girl didn't he, and they live in the wilds of Surrey somewhere. Perhaps he's had enough of the golf circus and wants to settle and be nearer his wife Adriana. I know I would be—she's a lovely little thing from what I've seen.'

'Lovely, but apparently very strange Flinty. Bit of a wild child by the sounds of it.'

Tim assessed the club he would need for his next shot, took a pitching wedge from his bag and made a practice swing. 'Yeah, I get that convenience stuff, but he still spends half his life in the U.S. or Thailand and leaves the other two professional boys to do all the work. And, let's be honest, apart from being loud and full of crap, he does have the kind of arrogant face you just want to smack, doesn't he?'

Charlie gave a wry smile. 'He is a bit of an acquired taste I agree Fev. Probably he's just a figurehead—you know, someone famous to put on literature and the website. That might be enough to earn him his money.'

Tim peered through his rangefinder device and checked the distance to the green before he took his shot. 'And I'm guessing those strangers that come to see him could be buying some of his sponsorship stuff through the back door. You know just traders after a cheap set of clubs or golf shoes that he's been paid to use. Think he's got the kind of remit that lets him do whatever he wants. If the owners were that insistent to have him on board, then perhaps Craig just had to get him at all costs.' Tim eyed up his shot and aligned himself. 'Question is Flinty, are we going to leave it alone, as we know we should, or get involved? After all, we only play golf here. So why should we care?'

Charlie took another practice swing further over on the same fairway. 'Well my old mate, as you quite rightly deduced, my sense tells me Willis is up to no good, and getting amongst it might help keep our razor sharp minds from going dull. And neither of us are ready for that pipe and slippers thing yet are we—as much as our wives might want us to be.'

'No. And neither of us are ready for that divorce thing either Flinty, so we need to watch ourselves and be fair to the girls.'

'Agreed.'

They both started to concentrate on the game and put their third shots on the green. Charlie and Tim fist bumped walking down the fairway and Tim said with a satisfied tone to his voice, 'Think we can safely say the old firm is back together then, eh. Don't know where this will take us Flinty, but something is very wrong here and we're going to find out what it is.'

2

The Sycamores was a parkland course that had taken two years to construct, and had been awaited by the golf fraternity in the southeast of England with great anticipation. The new course was set on the edge of the north downs and bordered a forest which gave it the added attraction of a managed fallow deer herd roaming freely through the grounds enjoying the unlimited lush grass. It was set to be one of the best golf courses in the county, and also ranked highly in national listings. But more importantly it was right on Charlie and Tim's doorstep. The Japanese owners had made it clear this was to be a prestigious course to attract the best clientele and therefore had designed and staffed it accordingly. To Charlie and Tim this meant only one thing —it was going to be expensive to become a member. But they had both retired on good pensions, golf was their hobby and also the thing that cemented their enduring friendship every week. So they made sure to attend all the impressive marketing events and took advantage of the founder member joining offer. But they knew the second year was going to be a different story and far more costly. As the club's first year end approached Charlie spoke to Tim over a beer in the club's lavishly appointed bar after one of their weekly contests. 'You know I love this place Fev, even though it's a bit flash I get a real sense of belonging here but...'

Tim interrupted, 'Come on Flinty, you know that everything before *but* is bullshit. Are you trying to tell me that now we have to pay full price this course is going to be too dear for a couple of old rough diamonds like us?'

Charlie laughed, mainly because his friend knew him so well. 'Kind of,' he replied. 'I was going to say exactly that, but I have an idea that might let us play golf at The Sycamores very cheaply. And also give us a way to get under the skin of what's going on here.'

Tim gave Charlie a dubious look but was very much aware of his friend's cerebral capabilities. 'Sounds brilliant Flinty. If you can pull that off, I'm right behind you, if not in front of you. Can't help thinking there's a catch involved somewhere though.'

'Just a little one, we might have to do some work. Do you trust me Fev?'

'I think that's what they call a rhetorical question, mate.'

'Ok then, follow me.'

There were three loud and confident, but somehow polite, knocks on the polished wood door of the course manager's office deep inside the large mock Tudor clubhouse. 'Come in,' Craig Galbraith said in a soft educated Scottish accent. Craig was an affable man in his early fifties, slim and well dressed in a casual designer golf kind of way, always professional in his outlook and very focused. He had been headhunted by the Japanese owners from a well-known course in Berkshire, the kind of high-profile world renowned course that would have needed an exceptional package to attract him away. As the senior man at *The Sycamores*, he had the best office in the building, with sweeping views of the fifth fairway through large picture windows and suitably luxurious furnishings for entertaining large corporate clients with money to spend. His office, like his mind, was well ordered everything in its place and a clear desk. With the exception of two filing trays and a silver framed professionally posed photograph of his wife and two young boys taken some years earlier. The oak veneered office door swung open and into the warm carpeted room stepped Charlie Flint and Tim Featherstone. Craig looked up from his computer and smiled warmly at the men he knew as members and people he regularly enjoyed passing banter with. 'And what can I do for you boys this bright morning?'

Charlie grinned cheekily and said, 'More what we can do for you Craig.'

Craig burst out with a laugh. 'Go on.'

'Well, Tim and I have been thinking and wanted to put a proposal to you.'

'I don't like it when you two start thinking, somebody usually ends up in prison, don't they?'

The men had a definite connection with Craig, and Charlie recognised the hidden compliment. He smiled. 'Once upon a time, maybe.'

Craig sat upright in his leather high backed chair and leaned his elbows on a shiny oak desktop. 'Come on then, what's this proposal boys, I'm all ears.'

Charlie pointed to a cute picture of a fox cub on a wildlife wall calendar behind Craig's head and said, 'Nearly subscription time isn't it, and we thought that as you very clearly can't seem to hang onto course marshals, we could do that job for you free of charge—well apart from letting us play for nothing when the course is available that is.'

Craig roared with laughter, 'Come on boys, what are you up to? You both retired at the top of your professions. So why would you want to be chasing round a golf course making sure people are behaving themselves and following the rules? It's a thankless task and you might end up getting a load of abuse.'

'Don't worry about abuse. We've had a lifetime of that,' Charlie said as he turned towards Tim, 'And would you want to abuse that face? Anyway, it'll give us a focus, and you some professionalism on this course. Plus, who better than an ex-chief inspector and a senior fraud investigator to police it. Especially while we have this bloody awful deer business hanging over us—it might just give the members some comfort.'

Craig shook his head. 'I think I'd have got less grief if it had been a human hanging upside down from that tree. It's really whipped up a storm.'

Tim said cynically, 'I can see that. According to the papers, the Police seem to be putting it down to a group of illegal immigrants they found camped out nearby. Hah, they're just trying to pin it on anyone to calm the locals.'

Charlie joined in the conversation of disbelief. 'Yeah, so when they smuggled themselves into that fully loaded lorry in Calais with ten others and jumped out somewhere between there and here, they managed to escape with a crossbow tucked up their jumpers. And they've probably not eaten for days either. Think I would have been building a fire and cooking myself some venison. If you're going to get caught for it, you might as well have a full belly. And what would they want with deer blood, for goodness' sake? The boys in blue are going to have to try harder than that, no-one is going to buy it.'

Craig breathed heavily and seemed uncomfortable. 'I hear what you're saying, but just for your information, the police have picked up four of those illegal Syrian immigrants hiding out in the woods at the back of the course. It's about the third lot they've found hiding there in recent months.'

Charlie nodded. 'They choose here because we're so close to the coastal motorways. Somehow they jump on at Calais and either get dumped by a corrupt lorry driver or escaped at the transport cafe a couple of miles down the road. Then wait for their mates before giving themselves up and claiming asylum.'

'What is it you always say Flinty?' Tim asked. 'Never jump to conclusions and always look beyond the obvious. Well, that's not what the police are doing, is it?'

Craig was prepared to cling onto the smallest snippet of positive news about the situation. 'Well, it's a bit of a coincidence, isn't it? Four starving Syrians with free roaming deer in the area.'

Charlie's sense of justice meant he had to disagree. 'Well, I'm sure it's helping the police pacify the press for a while and everyone will think the immigrants are guilty until proven innocent.'

'Well, that's for the police to establish while they are in custody, isn't it?' Craig said, turning his head away.

'Still all the time they are in custody, the members are happy, I suppose,' Tim said sarcastically.

Charlie looked Craig squarely in the eyes, 'You don't believe those immigrants are guilty any more than us, do you?'

Craig gave a huge sigh. 'No, of course not. But it suits me to go along with it, especially when they have been catching and eating fish from a nearby lake and one of our neighbours have reported a cat missing. Fact is neither me nor the police have a Plan B at the moment, and that's going to be a problem when the Syrians are released.'

Craig's body visibly shivered. 'This whole sick business smacks of the occult to me, and we don't want that kind of thing anywhere near our course. We're trying to attract members, not drive them away.' He looked disturbed, drifted off in deep thought and then chuckled, 'But let's get back to your proposal chaps. I agree it would be a perfect solution, and it might help to get the club captain off my back. But quite frankly I still don't believe your motives.'

'OK then,' Tim said, 'We're bored senseless and need to get out of the house.'

'That's more like it,' Craig said, smiling broadly. He leaned back in his chair, looked at the ceiling, and pondered for a moment. 'Ok, you've got yourselves a deal. Let's give it a try and see how it works for both of us. Maybe you can do weekdays, and Gerry will carry on with weekends, but I really don't mind, just work it out between yourselves and I'll get the HR people to draw up a contract for your protection.'

'Great, thanks Craig.' Charlie hesitated. 'Oh, and you could feed us too when we're working,' he said as he opened the door to leave.

Craig grinned, 'Alright, now get out of here while you're still ahead. Talk to Gerry and work out a rota, and you can use Nathan if you need to. Gerry will give you the lowdown on him.'

As they left Craig's office and walked down the corridor, Tim's fist bumped Charlie and winked. 'Now people will open up to us and we can really start finding out what's going on at this club.'

3

Gerry Barber was an engineer by profession who had retired early on a generous redundancy package and became a marshal at *The Sycamores* for beer money and free golf. He was a good marshal in an encouraging, rather than demanding, sort of way and knew Charlie and Tim well as players. They were both very much aware he was desperate for help and run ragged on his own after the resignation of his two colleagues. The men had made a point of sharing their plan to become marshals with Gerry and club captain Mike Goddard before speaking to Craig, and gained emphatic support from both.

'How did you get on lads,' Gerry asked impatiently as Charlie and Tim met him at the practice area where he had been hovering in the pleasant warmth of an early May morning. He was anxiously hoping to catch them fresh from their discussion with Craig.

A broad smile crept across Charlie's face, 'The man from Del Monte—he say yes.'

Gerry's eyes widened and he looked delighted. So delighted that his legs became animated and they thought he was going to break into a dance. 'That's brilliant news, my missus will be so pleased that I don't have to be here seven days a week anymore. It was taking all the joy out of golf for me. Hope your wives are on board?'

Charlie and Tim gave each other a look that said, We stupidly hadn't given that much thought.

'Ah, they'll be fine,' Tim said, waving a hand across himself dismissively. 'Now, you need to show us the ropes Gerry, then we have to sort out a rota.'

Gerry couldn't keep the elated grin off his face. 'Absolutely, just a few basics I have to tell you first. As you well know, this club has got some real snobs as members who are quick to complain about the slightest thing. So there must be no changing clothes or shoes in the car park. No golf shoes in the clubhouse, and make sure you know what the dress code says and be prepared to have a word with people if they are wearing the wrong thing.'

'We know all that Gerry,' Tim laughed. 'We've been members here since it opened.'

Gerry grinned, 'Yes sorry lads, I'm still excited by the news. The important thing is to keep everyone moving, and if there is an event on I generally let the members police themselves. We have been allocated golf buggy number twelve to use. It has its own parking bay next to the others, there are three keys to it, so I would put one on your key ring so you can use it first thing if you need to. But if you are playing, you'll have to walk, unless you can use your charm on Craig, of course. Oh, and don't let the buggers intimidate you. I'm afraid the two marshals that left took some of the criticism to heart.'

Tim grinned. 'I was a policeman for far too many years to let anyone intimidate me, Gerry. I'll take it as a challenge.'

Charlie said, 'Got it, thanks, mate. Oh, and Craig mentioned to talk to you about Nathan.'

Gerry nodded, then frowned as he moved them further

down the path, and away from the swoosh of clubs and the crack of balls taking flight up the driving range. As golfers practiced their swings, uttering the odd profanity when it didn't go well, he said, 'Yes, Nathan, you do need to know about Nathan. You must have seen him around the course though, right? He's the lad who always wears green overalls, whatever the weather.'

'Yes, of course,' Tim smiled, 'he looks a bit—'

'Simple?' Gerry interrupted. 'Well, he's not the sharpest blade on the mower. I'll grant you that. I had to explain to him that a society was a group of golfers in a club that could play anywhere—he thought they were singers, bless him. But he more than makes up for his deficiencies with enthusiasm and willingness. I think he's a lovely boy. He will do absolutely anything for me, and with a smile on his face, too. Not like some of those lazy bloody green keepers. Do you know the story of how he got here?'

'Something to do with Willis?' Charlie suggested. 'He seems to be behind most things that happen here.'

'Yes, Nathan used to work for Willis. He asked Craig, as a favour, for the club to employ him. Apparently, his wife Adriana couldn't tolerate the boy and didn't want him living on site at their big house. Ha, little miss fancy pants.' Gerry raised the side of his hand to his mouth and whispered, 'That she can't keep on.'

Tim's eyes widened. 'You'll have to tell us about that, too. This is all new to us.'

Gerry gave a scornful shake of his head, 'No shame that girl. Anyway, they inherited Nathan as a gardener with their place in Surrey. Seems she couldn't deal with his slow wittedness, or ability to know one plant from another, and demanded Willis get rid of him. I'll be fair to Willis though he did find him another job with accommodation, otherwise the boy would have been out on the street—literally.

Funny thing is he seems to have no bad feeling towards Adriana but come to that, he doesn't seem to have any bad feelings for anyone. Craig was very good too, even though the cynic in me thinks it helped him be seen as a caring employer, but he genuinely felt sorry for the lad. Besides, Nathan had a driving licence and he could run guests to and from the railway station. As well as clearing up around the place and working with the groundsmen and me.'

Charlie looked surprised, 'So he lives on site then?'

'Yes, he's got a poky little flat above the clubhouse. You wouldn't know it was there, get into it by the back of the kitchens. Don't think he likes to spend much time there though, he's never happier than when he's busy working.'

'Can't argue with that,' Charlie said.

Tim was curious, as an ex-policeman would be, 'So what about his family, where do his mum and dad live?'

Gerry sighed loudly. 'He came from an orphanage. But much as I've tried I can't get him to talk about his parents or his past. From what I can make out it seems he's had a sad life, always in care.'

Charlie was moved by Gerry's revelation, 'It's amazing how he stays so positive with a background like that.'

Gerry gave a warm fatherly smile. 'You'll figure him out. I'm quite protective of him and we even have him over to dinner now and again. Just a couple of things you need to know, though. He loves animals, seems to have claimed the club's cat, and is really upset about this awful deer business.'

Charlie grimaced. 'Aren't we all—and what was the second thing?'

Gerry burst into a fit of laughter. 'He's a bit of a pyromaniac.'

'Oh great,' Tim said, 'saved the best until last, eh?'

Still laughing, Gerry explained, 'No, I mean he loves a bonfire. Jason, the head green keeper, gets him to gather any fallen tree debris from the course and burn it now and again. Just need to keep your eye on him that's all, he doesn't need much of an excuse.'

'Now back to Adriana,' Tim said in a half jest.

Gerry pulled a distasteful face and seemed irritated by the mere mention of her name. 'She's nothing but a little trollop that's what she is. Now come on boys, you must have heard the rumours about her and James the golf pro? But she makes no bones about it. Seems she'll do a turn for any man, especially if they are rich or important enough.'

Tim laughed, 'Better start saving up then Flinty eh, bit out of your league though.'

Charlie glared at his friend. 'But surely Willis must know what she's up to then, Gerry?'

'Of course he does, but he's just as bad. He has girls throwing themselves at him all the time and takes full advantage of his fame. Him and Adriana seem to have some kind of weird arrangement where anything goes in their marriage. But Willis does what the hell he likes at this club anyway, and if Craig doesn't like it he'll go above his head to the Japanese owners. He's a virtual pro, just a big mouth with a huge ego who swans around hoping to get recognised and does nothing.'

'Not a fan then?' Tim suggested.

Gerry's face grew angry. 'No, I'm bloody not a fan, and you won't be either when you get to know him.' He took a breath, and put a hand on each of his new colleagues shoulders and said, 'Come on let's sort that rota out, then I'm going to buy you two a drink to celebrate.'

They all walked down a concrete pathway towards the green-keeper's buildings and a large steel shed that was shining brightly as the sun reflected from the grey metallic surfaces. 'This is your new home,' Gerry said proudly. 'We have the bit on the right, not much more than a cupboard really, and Jason has the rest. Gets a bit hot in the summer and cold in the winter, and it can be noisy when the lads next door are moving their vehicles in and out, but you won't be in here much.'

'Great sales pitch Gerry,' Charlie chuckled.

Inside their new domain they discussed rotas, daily duties, looked at the diary of events for the year and established where Gerry kept everything. After their brief but informative meeting Charlie and Tim headed for the clubhouse bar while Gerry locked what was to be their shared but very austere new office.

Tim said, 'I'm sensing you were right Flinty, and even more convinced something is very wrong here. It seems that both Willis and his wife could get away with murder at this club and the Japanese would back them.'

'Exactly Fev, and I'm beginning to think I might know why that deer had to die.'

4

As founder members, Charlie and Tim knew all the professional golfers at *The Sycamores,* but were keen to establish themselves in their new roles as marshals. Famous head professional Willis Martin was out of the country, looking after business interests either in the states or Thailand. As he did at least once every month, and seemingly with the full blessing of his employers. When he was playing on the circuit, Willis would travel with an army of coaches, phycologists, nutritionists, medical and admin staff plus a full security team. But since a shoulder injury forced him to give up playing competitively, Willis chose to travel alone, and the lack of an entourage helped him keep a much lower profile.

While Willis was travelling abroad his number two, and senior professional, James Cole was responsible for providing most of the golf lessons, dealing with members' queries and representing the club on any golfing issues. But he was a competent professional and completely up to the job, when he put his mind to it. James was twenty-eight years old, tall and lithe with a mop of blond naturally wavy hair. He was sharp featured and handsome standing at six feet two he looked like he might be a Scandinavian. James wore all the designer golf clothing very well and could easily have been a male model. He effortlessly had the look and aura of a stereotypical young successful golfer. And he was very much aware of the presence he had with most of the ladies at the club or female visitors. However, James was an overconfident and slightly immature lothario who thought all he had to do was smile, which often led him to lose sight of his work responsibilities. His father was something big in the city and as well as having a gift for golf, he was an only child who enjoyed a privileged background. His father had paid for everything and even set his son up in a luxury flat, so James had really never experienced the struggles of the real world. Junior professional Ben Tilman by comparison was from a working-class family in his early twenties, five feet nine and stocky with a prematurely receding hairline, but he was a natural golfer. Outside of golf Ben was a keen DJ and martial arts enthusiast but was constantly plagued by low self-esteem. Nonetheless he was always pleasant and a hard worker who all the staff at the course had taken to.

Charlie and Tim walked through the fully glazed swing doors of the professional golf shop on the ground level of the impressive clubhouse at *The Sycamores*. It was built in the style of a mock Tudor mansion externally but bright and modern inside with contemporary materials and equipment, contradicting the architectural illusion. The shop smelt of new clothes, leather shoes, and the thick wool blend carpet covering the floor. There were racks of polo shirts, sweaters, trousers, and waterproof clothes. Stands with winter and summer golf shoes, woollen hats and baseball caps. Around the walls were freestanding displays of golf clubs by all the major manufactures with endorsements by famous players on cardboard exhibits. Ben looked up from checking competition scorecards that were laid out on the glass-topped counter and smiled. 'Morning Gents, what can I do for you today?'

'On your own mate?' Tim asked.

'Yes, I seem to be on my own most of the time these days, but probably best we don't go there.'

Charlie chose not to probe Ben's strange comment that was probably prompting one of them to ask a question in response. 'Well we thought we'd drop in to let you know we have just signed up to become course marshals. We'll be splitting the work with Gerry.'

Ben's face lit up, he almost slammed his pencil into the glass worktop and rushed around from behind the counter thrusting his hand towards each man in turn, 'That is just fantastic news and will really help Gerry, and us in here too. What a relief to have some of the pressure taken off.'

'Do you get a lot of pressure then Ben?' Tim asked, suddenly wondering if he was going to regret his decision to become a marshal.

'Oh, just niggly bits you know, simple stuff since the other guys left. But things I can well do without when I have everything else to deal with. I've been here all hours recently and even had to turn down DJ work in the evenings because I'm so knackered. Haven't used the studio at home for weeks either.'

This was Charlie's opportunity to start exploring, 'So where does James fit into all this?'

'That's a very good question Charlie,' Ben said, moving back behind the glass counter and losing all of his previous enthusiasm.

'Strikes me as a bit of a ladies' man,' Tim said, picking up some golf shoes to examine, finding the price tag and putting them back quickly.

Ben nodded his head, 'Yes, he's that alright. But it was

better when he was chasing anything female with a pulse, at least he was here most of the time.'

Charlie gave a thin-lipped smile, already knowing the answer to his question but keen to hear Ben's take on it, 'Ahh I see, he's got himself a new girlfriend and it's all a bit intense—eh?'

'Well, that's partly right Charlie. He's got himself someone else's wife to be precise. Someone who is currently out of the country.'

'You're kidding?'

Ben frowned, 'I wish I was Charlie, and it's all going to end in tears. But right now as a golf professional the bloke is a waste of space. In fact it's worse than that, I have to cover for him every day and keep apologising for his mistakes.'

Charlie shrugged, 'Well now we're on the team we are happy to help you wherever we can, but relationship advice is not really a strong point for either of us.'

Tim was irritated by the obvious injustice and far less diplomatic than his friend. 'That boy is the senior man when Willis is away, and he should be showing some leadership and stepping up instead of dropping you in it. Someone needs to tell him his fortune.'

Ben glanced around the shop furtively to make sure no-one was lurking who might hear what he had to say next. 'I shouldn't be telling you this but James is really pissing me off.'

'It's ok Ben,' Charlie said with a smile, 'We obviously have the type of faces that people think they can tell their innermost secrets to.'

But from the relieved look on his face Ben had clearly been itching to get the source of his frustration off his chest. 'James is particularly upset because he feels locked into The Sycamores. When he was given the senior professional job here, he thought he had great prospects and might succeed whoever was head pro. That was until the Japanese owners insisted Willis was brought in and given a huge salary. So now James has all the responsibility of a senior pro but no chance of taking over from Willis, or ever getting the respect or pay that he gets. James feels trapped and angry because working under someone like Willis looks really powerful on his CV. But he thinks if he ever left people would wonder why he would give up such a prestigious club. And also it might prove difficult to convince prospective employers he wasn't just looking to trade on Willis's name. So he thinks he will forever be stuck as Willis's dogsbody.'

'So does James see screwing Adriana as some kind of payback?' Charlie asked.

'Well, I think that's how it all started, but she is in complete control of him now.'

'Really?' Tim said with astonishment. 'So James actually is knocking off the famous Willis Martin's wife?'

'At every possible opportunity Tim,' Ben said with a deadpan expression. 'Morning, noon and night. But he is totally obsessed and getting weirder with it by the day. He can't think about anything else but her, he's lost all concentration. Not turning up for lessons, failing to book tee off times for people and forgetting to record competition entries. Everyone is losing patience with him. And to make things worse he's badmouthing Willis all the time. And love him or hate him the man is a brilliant golfer and we're lucky to have him here. I can't help but think this will turn nasty because Willis is going to kill him when he gets back.'

5

In a quiet and desirable semi-rural close, near Sevenoaks in Kent, and inside a very comfortable four bedroomed 1960s detached house—provided by a senior career in insurance. It was seven thirty and breakfast time. 'You seem to be spending a lot of hours at that golf club recently Charlie Flint,' his kind natured wife of thirty years Ruth said as she reached into the refrigerator for a carton of milk. She walked to the table wrapped in a light grey silk dressing gown with her blond bob tousled after a night's sleep. Ruth had perfected the art of making something that was bothering her sound like a throwaway comment. But after so many years of marriage, Charlie was wise to it and knew whatever it was wouldn't rest there.

Charlie had never lost his defining sense of humour and Ruth had never stopped finding it one of his most endearing features, even though he always used it to his advantage. 'Well Mrs Flint, you were the first to remind me how expensive it was to join, so I'm getting my money's worth. Besides all that exercise is keeping me fit, and of course you know that absence makes the heart grow fonder, don't you.' He leaned over and kissed her cheek.

Ruth grinned. 'Don't give me that old flannel, what are you up to—it's written all over your face.'

'I'm enjoying my early retirement dearest. That's what I'm up to.'

Ruth laughed out loud. 'You and Fev are as thick as thieves. You can't play golf for eight hours a day and several days a week.'

Charlie lifted a spoonful of cornflakes from a china bowl slipped it into his mouth and said casually, 'Ok then I'm having a wild passionate affair.'

Ruth laughed even louder. 'What's so funny?' Charlie asked pointing to his face, 'You think that another woman wouldn't find these mature good looks irresistible?'

She pinched his cheek gently and shook it. 'No, not at all Mr Flint. I'm sure all the old girls in their pink Pringle jumpers, check shorts and sun visors are swooning. But you like your life far too much to disrupt it, plus you and Fev can't both be having an affair.'

Charlie reached over and patted his wife's bottom. 'And I love my wife far too much.'

Charlie was born with an inbuilt honesty, which had made him so good at his job as a senior insurance fraud investigator for one of the country's biggest companies. But it also made him an awful liar, and from the very beginning of their relationship, Ruth had always been able to see right through him. 'So, are you going to tell me Charlie, or shall I ring Louise to see whether Fev has come clean to her yet?'

Charlie tried to play it cool by taking another spoonful of cornflakes. 'Are you familiar with the term course marshal, my dear?'

'No. It sounds like someone with a cowboy hat and big droopy moustache who captures baddies.'

'You've got it,' Charlie said as he leaned forward and did his best to enthuse to someone who had absolutely no interest in golf. 'Well, they've asked Fev and me to be course marshals when they have events on or it's busy.'

Ruth looked sceptical. 'Right.'

'But here's the clever part.'

Ruth blurted another laugh and Charlie frowned at her premature mockery. 'As I was saying, the clever part is that we don't have to pay our extortionate annual subscription anymore, and we can play whenever the course is quiet for free.'

'So what do you have to do for this remarkable deal?' Ruth said with more than a hint of sarcasm.

'Just make sure that everyone moves along, doesn't hold up play and sticks to the rules.'

'So you and Fev are now the golf police at one of the most exclusive courses in the county.'

'Exactly. Well, the way I look at it, despite me drawing them both explicit diagrams, our two girls still haven't got the message about producing grandchildren. Fev's girl is the same and his boy is too young for all that nonsense, so demands on our time are fairly low right now.'

'Hmm, grandchildren,' Ruth exclaimed with a thoughtful expression on her face. 'Maybe one day we'll have little ones crawling all over us and wearing us out. Then your time won't be your own Charlie Flint.'

Charlie slipped an arm around Ruth's slender waist. 'But until that time Mrs Flint—there's golf.'

Charlie and Tim's friendship had been steadfast since their early working days when they quickly realised there was a natural chemistry that existed between them. And their closeness had spread to their families. They would often holiday together on the island of Minorca at a villa they rented in Santo Thomas and were godparents to their respective children. All the kids had grown as friends, stayed in touch and the families had lived reasonably close to each other. And as a longstanding arrangement, Ruth, and Tim Featherstone's wife Louise would meet every week for shopping or coffee and, naturally, to discuss their husbands' shortcomings.

Ruth stood up and began to clear the dishes from the breakfast table. 'Well it won't surprise you to know Mr Flint that Louise and I have already discussed this very topic.'

Charlie swallowed hard, he sometimes thought that Ruth was a better detective than he was. 'Luckily for you, Fev's story is pretty much the same as yours, and we get the saving money bit. But we have both reached the conclusion there is more to it, and you are both doing this to get closer to what's going on at the club. Maybe even to start investigating that awful deer business. And also to stop yourselves getting bored with retirement.'

'Well kind of,' Charlie said cautiously. 'But mainly for the golf.'

Ruth's attitude changed and she looked uncharacteristically cross. 'The golf is fine Charlie, and I understand that both you and Fev are taking more of an interest in The Sycamores. But we don't want to hear it's any more than that. We know what you are both like, you've spent a lifetime chasing criminals, but now is not the time to be putting yourselves in danger. And there are some bad people at that club.'

6

'Bugger!' was Tim Featherstone's frustrated cry as the golf ball he had just struck with his nine iron fell well short of the firm manicured sixteenth green at *The Sycamores* golf club. He was a powerfully built man with a reasonable technique but was still not able to get the kind of performance out of his clubs he wanted. And on a warm still June day he couldn't blame the wind holding his ball up either. He shook his head, 'Just not getting the distance that I should with these clubs Flinty.'

'Don't think it's the clubs mate, they haven't changed. I think it's operator error. Don't forget you're nearly a veteran now,' Charlie laughed. 'Why don't you buy yourself a new set you must have had those for twenty years. Think of all the money you'll be saving on subscriptions with our new deal. And besides, it's not very becoming for a course marshal to be playing with museum pieces is it?'

'Yes, I suppose you're right Flinty, and the technology has improved a bit since I bought these,' Tim said as he glared curiously at the battered metal head of his golf club.

Charlie hoisted his golf bag onto his back, slipped his arms through the straps and prepared to walk down the fairway with his friend. 'Willis seems to be shifting sets of golf clubs like they are going out of style. He always says he will bring you back a set on one of his visits to the states at a discount. Why don't you take him up on it and that will also give us a chance to see how he operates?'

'Yeah, I often wonder how he gets several sets of clubs every time he goes, probably something dodgy going on over there.'

'I very much doubt that Fev, they are always from the same manufacturer, and the one that sponsored him throughout his playing career. And someone as famous as Willis must have some kind of lifetime arrangement with them.'

'You're right of course Flinty, and he wouldn't risk his reputation on selling moody golf clubs would he?'

'He's not that stupid.'

Tim slid the club back into his bag shaft first, gazed forlornly at his ancient set of irons, and chuckled. 'They have seen better days, haven't they—maybe you're right Flinty and I'll soon get my money back from beating you every week.'

'It's a nice concept mate, but unlikely.'

'OK then,' Tim said, 'let's strike while the iron's hot.'

Charlie winced at the joke. 'Oh, please.'

'Yeah, sorry it was a bit lame wasn't it. What I meant was, as Willis is in the country I'll speak to him when we finish here and while you are in the clubhouse buying the beers.'

Charlie won the round by five strokes so was somewhat reluctant to buy the beer, as it was the loser's privilege. So he decided to accompany Tim into the pro shop to meet Willis and discuss the purchase of a new set of irons.

Willis Martin was approaching fifty, but still in good physical shape. He was around six feet tall with a permanent tan, dark hair that was receding across the top of his head and greying at the temples. His features were strong and distinctive, especially his green eyes, and he had a real aura about him. In the pro-shop he was busy being charismatic, and very loud, with a small group of sycophantic members. But Willis caught eye contact with Tim who was inspecting a golf bag he had no intention of buying. 'With you in a sec guys,' Willis shouted across the room.

Charlie smiled and whispered to Tim. 'Let's see if he is as good as his word with these clubs, eh Fev.'

Willis said, 'Enjoy your round guys,' to the members, signalling to them their conversation with him was now over. Then he turned grinned and lurched deliberately across the carpeted floor like John Wayne and thumped down a hand on both Charlie and Tim's shoulders. 'So what can I do for you two reprobates today? Don't tell me. You've upset someone out on the course and want me to repair the damage for you. Or maybe you need me to give you some lessons on how to sink fifty-yard shots from the rough.' He laughed as though it was hysterically funny.

'Not exactly,' Tim replied sedately. 'But I think the time has come for me to change my set of irons, Willis.'

'And you want to know if yours have any antique value, huh?' He gave a sickly sweet smile and squeezed Tim's shoulder, 'What you really want to know is can I get you a set from back home like I said I would isn't it buddy?'

'That's about the size of it Willis,' Tim replied.

Willis shook his head in a defeated kind of way—like a used car salesman about to negotiate on the price of a car. 'Well, all the stuff I just bought back from the states has gone. I get them to order you see bud. You might have to wait until next time.'

Charlie gave a discrete and sarcastic *I told you so* kind of smile to Tim as Willis said. 'But I tell you what Tim, there may be a chance. The guy I sold a set to last week bought them as a gift for his dad, but his pop can't get on with them. So I can maybe buy them back off him, only problem is the old guy has some kinda skin condition so I'm gonna insist on changing the grips for you. I change the grips anyway, the original ones are garbage. I'll fit you a new set of Nielsen Blues. I wouldn't use anything else. Played with them on tour, great for feel. So the thing is Tim, if I can do a deal, the clubs are hardly used and I'll probably get them for around half the new price—does that work for you buddy?'

Tim looked at Charlie for his endorsement. 'Don't look at me mate,' Charlie said. 'You should be taking his hand off.'

One week later, Willis had worked some magic and Tim's new set of clubs arrived. And the American was right they didn't look used at all, especially with new top of the range grips fitted. Tim was delighted that he'd got such a good deal and was keen to put his new equipment to the test. So on a day when he and Charlie weren't supervising play, they went out onto the course at dawn with only the resident wildlife for company.

'Huh, don't seem any better than the old ones,' Tim said disappointedly as his ball dropped short and well to the right of the first green startling a young grazing deer.

Charlie laughed out loud. 'Give it a chance Fev, you've got to get used to them.'

Then the new club head technology started to work for Tim and he began to hit the ball further and straighter than before, causing him to develop a distinctly euphoric bounce to his step. 'Yeah—not too bad at all these Flinty, good idea of mine to change them. I feel a winning streak coming on. Hope you've got your wallet.'

In the early mornings, locals would often walk their dogs across the golf course using the public footpath that crossed the fifth fairway. As marshals, Charlie and Tim got to know the regular dog walkers, and their dogs, acknowledging each other as they passed. Up ahead of them they spotted a familiar waggy tailed black and white springer spaniel diving in and out of the long grass in search of interesting smells and rabbits. It was Oscar, and on the other end of the long lead was his master a grey bearded older man wearing a green gilet, flat cap and walking boots. This was retired police dog handler Don Moore, not an ex-colleague of Tim's, but someone from the same force with a lot in common and always worthy of a chat when their paths crossed.

'Morning Don,' Tim said. 'Has Oscar found anything interesting this morning, good to see he's still not lost the impulse to work.'

'Morning boys,' Don replied. 'No. Even though he stopped working before me he will never lose the will to work. Once a sniffer, always a sniffer.'

As was normal when they met, Oscar bounced over to them enthusiastically to say hello and look for a treat. But on this particular morning he had more of an interest in Tim's golf bag.

'What have you got in there?' Don asked as Oscar circled the bag repeatedly.

Charlie laughed, 'He's got new clubs and the grips that have been fitted smell decidedly fishy. He must think they might be edible.'

But Don wasn't laughing. 'It's not fish Oscar is interested in. Trust me, there is something dodgy in that bag—he is never wrong.'

7

Suddenly, becoming course marshals gave Charlie and Tim kudos they hadn't expected at *The Sycamores*. They became more recognisable around the clubhouse, particularly with bar and kitchen staff, along with Craig's administrative team. All of which they had encountered before, but never as colleagues, only as club members being given due regard. This meant they were now included in all the sordid gossip and wild speculation that ran around the club on a daily basis. All of which they were far too professional to engage in, but helped enormously in their mission to get under the skin of the club.

At the end of a busy morning out on the course with a golf society, Charlie and Tim were talking to Craig Galbraith over a coffee in the main clubhouse bar. By this time they had started to develop a close working relationship with the course manager, and any formal barriers were fast breaking down. Apart from being comfortable in Craig's company, they soon realised he was an excellent source of valuable information. And Charlie blatantly prodded for intelligence. 'So come on Craig, what's your take on Willis and his wife—we're hearing all kinds of stories?'

In his mind, Craig had quickly made a personal connection with Charlie and Tim. He considered himself a good judge of character and regarded them as men he could trust. But the truth was, he didn't really have anyone else at the club he felt comfortable enough to confide in. He checked around the bar to ensure no-one was in earshot and lowered his voice. 'Well, Adriana is a socialite, privately educated and mixes with the Sloane Square set. Her father is a member of the British aristocracy fallen on hard times. Lost most of his fortune through gambling debts it would seem. He has disgraced the family and they've disowned him apparently. But it left Adriana a bit high and dry financially and unable to keep up her image.' He leaned towards them and whispered. 'Call me bitchy boys, but Willis is much older than her and I believe she saw him as a meal ticket and a chance to keep her lifestyle. I think they are just using each other but they keep it together well for their public personas. There's no doubt she is an attractive girl though, real model material, and she often wears very risqué clothes to prove the point. They have no children and seem to lead separate lives most of the time. She swans around the golf club as though she owns it and runs all the events here. And Willis... well, you know about Willis, he can walk on water.'

'Do I detect a hint of bitterness Craig?' Charlie asked.

Craig sniggered, 'Whatever gave you that idea, but you can make your own minds up boys. Here she comes now, I'll introduce you.'

Adriana Martin breezed into the bar with her always obedient assistant Kate in tow. Adriana's entrance was in a raving extrovert kind of way, designer clothes, short skirt, gaping white blouse and high heels, look at me boys. She was shapely, in her mid-thirties, well made up and a striking beauty with immaculately cut shoulder length dark hair, porcelain skin and deep hazel eyes. She also possessed a natural sense of style that would have made her look good in a bin liner. In complete contrast was Kate, a frumpy girl who wore steel-rimmed glasses and very little makeup. She was slim with her dark hair scraped back into a ponytail, wearing sensible flat shoes and a grey trouser suit. But it was clear who was doing all the work as Kate followed Adriana with a clipboard like an eager puppy, waiting for an instruction.

'Ah Adriana, Kate, I'd like you to meet our new course marshals Charlie Flint and Tim Featherstone,' Craig said proudly gesturing towards the two men.

Kate was the closest. She smiled and thrust out a hand to Tim and Charlie in turn, 'Pleased to meet you chaps. Welcome aboard.' she said very formally.

Adriana was an overtly sexual creature and looked at both the men with a promiscuous glance. She leaned in towards Charlie, allowing her blouse to gape and expose expensive underwear. Then said in her softly spoken seductive plummy tones, 'Well Charlie I look forward to working with you,' as she pressed her breasts into his chest and gently kissed his cheek leaving a perfectly formed bright red imprint of her lips. Tim was soon in for the same treatment with, 'I hope to get to know you much better,' tagged on with a knowing smile.

The two retired men were dumbstruck, young attractive women just didn't speak to them like that or behave in such a way towards them. Especially as they both had children almost as old as her. If they didn't know better, they would think she was either offering sex or toying with them for amusement.

Adriana disappeared off towards the kitchen, and her sweet, classy perfume wafted behind her like a vapour trail.

While Kate busily scribbled down clipped instructions to action as soon as she got back to the office.

Tim was still dazed. He turned to Craig and said, 'Bloody hell, what was that all about?'

Craig roared and said, 'I told you. That's Adriana for you, she's a one off and doesn't care what anyone thinks of her. I'm not entirely sure if she's a nymphomaniac, boys. But my advice is to stay well clear. As you can see she is very beautiful—and very strange. Nonetheless, her and Kate make a great team and bring us in loads of money from events. Mind you, Kate does most of the work. She was here before Adriana arrived and I'm just lucky that they get on.'

Charlie asked, 'So how did Adriana get here then Craig? Seems like she is doing little more than fronting the operation up.' He remembered Gerry's words about her treatment of Nathan. 'And I sense an underlying spite about her?'

Craig shrugged his shoulders and gave a submissive smile. 'Seems like Willis insisted on her having the job as part of his package. He has the Japanese eating out of his hand. And you're right, Adriana is not one to upset, she is well aware of the power she wields.'

'Interesting,' Charlie mused.

'Very, but thank goodness we've got Kate, she's a really switched on girl,' Craig replied

'And no doubt she makes Adriana look good,' Tim added.

'Sadly, that's the case Tim. But I have to be fair. Adriana does seem to charm a lot of work out of people—mainly men I'll grant you,' he chuckled.

As they walked away from Craig, Tim said to Charlie, 'I'd seen her from a distance before but hadn't realised she was quite so striking. I can see why any man would be mesmerised by her.'

‘Yes, she’s hardly plain is she?’ Charlie replied. ‘But she’s the kind of woman who would suck you in and blow you out in bubbles. And there’s definitely an ugliness beneath the surface that she wouldn’t hesitate to show to anyone who got in her way.’

8

'You know this is going to cost you a beer and a bag of dog treats boys don't you?' Don Moore said, as he ushered waggy tailed Oscar into the empty pro-shop and Charlie bent forward to make a fuss of him.

Tim frowned. 'It's a small price to pay Don, but it's going to cost me a lot more than beer and treats if you and Oscar find something here. Let's get on with this while it's quiet can we. Charlie has convinced Ben to grab some lunch while he minds the shop and it seems James is out filling his boots again so he won't be back for hours.' He turned to Charlie, 'Flinty you keep guard at the door while everyone is out. Follow me Don.'

Don looked confused. 'Blimey, it all goes on here doesn't it.'

Tim led Don and Oscar into an untidy office area at the back of the shop with papers strewn across two unattended desks, and then beyond into a small workshop kitted out with a wooden bench and a golf club vice. He stopped and closed the door once they were inside. 'Ok, here's how I see it Don. This is where the club pro Willis fitted the new grips to my clubs, and he insisted on doing it himself. Weird when he normally considers himself far too important to do any menial work, isn't it? I've found the box with the new grips in and they're the same ones as on my clubs. So I'm going to put that box on the floor and see what reaction we get from Oscar.'

Don looked mildly disinterested, 'I can tell you now what his reaction will be, but yes, I understand the logic Tim, carry on.'

'It's a process of elimination Don,' Tim said as he lifted the rectangular cardboard box from the wooden bench placed it on the floor and flipped open the leaves on the top. 'You will notice there is a definite fishy whiff about them. I'm also going to put the bottle of solvent and some tape down that he uses for re-gripping—just in case.' He looked at Oscar and said, 'Here you go boy, see what you make of these.'

With his tail constantly wagging and head down, Oscar completely ignored the bottle of solvent and the roll of tape, but sniffed the cardboard box vigorously and reached inside. He clamped his teeth around one of the new grips, pulled it from the box and took it to Don. Tim gave an exaggerated sigh of relief and said, 'well, that looks pretty conclusive to me.'

Don removed the golf grip from Oscar's soft mouth and patted his head. 'Sorry Tim, I'm afraid the only thing that's conclusive is he wants me to throw this for him to chase. There's nothing in here that interests him. Otherwise he would have been on it like a shot.'

Tim gave another sigh, this time out of frustration. 'Right. Well the next stage in the process is to let him have another look at my clubs. I'll get them from the car.'

'Alright,' Don said with an air of inevitability in his voice. We'll wait outside with Charlie. We've no need to be in here now.

Just as they were about to leave the pro-shop an unexpectedly early and flushed looking James walked up the corridor and stared disapprovingly at Oscar. 'It's alright James,' Charlie said. 'Don is a friend of ours and Oscar is a working dog.'

'What kind of working dog?' James enquired.

'A guide dog for the blind,' Tim interrupted.

James smiled sceptically. 'I don't think so. They are normally Labradors, or Golden Retrievers.'

Don had quickly latched onto the joke. He bent forward and pretended to feel for Oscar, then exclaimed. 'Good grief, what have they given me then?'

Everyone roared with laughter and James walked further into the shop shaking his head, exhausted and unable to compete with the witty swordplay. While Tim left for the car park and his golf bag.

'Let's do this somewhere discrete,' Don said. 'I don't think it's a good idea to have people witnessing a drug dog at work in a public space.'

'Agreed,' Charlie said as Tim arrived back with his golf bag. 'Let's go to the buggy storage area. There's a patch of grass there that's out the way, and we'd better not hang about as it looks like rain.'

All the golf buggies were in use out on the course, so the area at the rear of the clubhouse was quiet. Charlie took a last panoramic scout around for people, and at the darkening sky. 'How do you want to play this Don?'

The ex-drug squad man immediately dropped into his former role and took charge. 'I want Tim to take every club and item out of his bag and lay it on the ground, then I'll let Oscar off the lead and if there is anything there, he'll show me where it is.'

Still with his tail wagging Oscar excitedly bounced and skipped past hats and gloves, tees and balls, scorecard holders and pencils. He ignored Tim's driver, fairway woods and putter, heading eagerly towards the new set of irons.

Don called Oscar back and gave him a treat. 'Ok now I want you to spread out those new clubs so he can sniff them one at a time,'

Sure enough, when he was released again, Oscar indicated at each of the seven iron clubs laying on the grass verge. 'There you go,' Don said. 'There are traces of drugs on every one of those new clubs—and we now know it's not the grips or anything used in changing them.'

'What kind of drugs do you think, Don?' Tim asked.

'Now bear in mind that Oscar is no longer a bona fide working drug dog.'

'But he can still do it, can't he?'

Don seemed offended by Tim's insensitive implication. 'He's the best bloody dog I've ever had. Of course he can still do it. He's just getting on a bit like the rest of us.' Then he smiled affectionately at his happy little dog and ruffled his head playfully between his hands. 'Oscar has a hundred percent hit rate on cocaine, so I would bet my pension on him—he's still the best.'

Tim scratched his chin. 'Question is, are those club shafts full of cocaine. And if so what are we going to do about it? What's your view Don, this used to be your area?'

Don had a confident smile. 'Not a chance they are full of cocaine now. I would think that's why he insisted on changing the grips. But they may never have been either. It could simply be that Willis, or the previous owner, if there was one, had traces about them—that's all Oscar needs.'

Charlie asked, 'So where do we go from here, because all my senses are screaming at me that Willis, our club professional is up to no good.'

Don answered succinctly. 'Fact is lads, you've got nothing but a feeling and a positive indication from a retired sniffer dog on what could be simply random fingerprints. Hardly enough to convince the police to pay someone a visit in the early hours and ransack their homes, especially a world-famous golfer. You are going to need solid evidence and perhaps you should get Oscar back when your man ships in some more clubs.'

Tim nodded in agreement. 'Yeah, Willis goes abroad about once a month and if we can get a look at the clubs before he sells them, we might have a bit more of a clue.'

Large spots of rain began to strike the ground. Don looked to the leaden sky and knew it was time to leave. 'Ok let me know when you're ready. But for what it's worth, Oscar indicated on every one of your new clubs, and quite distinctly. So if I had to put money on it, I'd say your superstar golfer is also a drug smuggler.'

9

Charlie and Tim were enjoying a sandwich at lunchtime in a corner of the steel shed they shared with head greenkeeper Jason Crosby. The space multi tasked as their office, workshop, dining room and store. It was no more than a square sectioned off area within a large industrial building. The shiny shed was one of a group of functional buildings that were partially hidden behind tall shrubs at the top of the entrance drive. And Gerry's warning had been right. In the summer months it suffered from oppressive heat gain through the metal sheet cladding, and when it rained it sounded like a drummer pounding on the roof, and throughout winter it was impossible to keep warm. But despite its architectural shortcomings it was home for them while they were marshals at *The Sycamores*. On the large metal door came a polite tap and the sound of someone nervously clearing their throat to gain attention. It was new recruit, Nathan, gingerly venturing inside and paying an impromptu visit to check if anyone was at home. Nathan was in his early thirties about five feet ten tall and with a muscular build. He had thick, dark unkempt hair and was in the same green overalls he always seemed to wear since the day he arrived. The startled expression on his kindly boyish face suggested he wasn't expecting to find Charlie and Tim in residence and he was very apologetic when he saw they were having lunch. 'Oh, I'm sorry, I didn't know you were eating.'

'It's Ok Nathan,' Tim said. 'Come in and grab yourself a seat we're just finishing anyway. Gerry has told us all about you. Do you want a coffee? Charlie was just about to make one.'

'Was I?'

Nathan sat on a workbench and looked uncomfortable with their banter, thinking he was imposing on their time. He spoke with an anxious edge to his voice, 'Err, no coffee thanks. I only came in to see if Jason had left me anything to do. I've done all the normal stuff and the course is too busy to get onto now.' He shuffled nervously on the bench. 'I like to keep busy see, don't like doing nothing.'

Charlie moved around some loose papers on the desk looking for any handwritten instructions from Jason, while the sad and vacant look on Nathan's face hadn't escaped him. 'Can't see anything here for you Nathan. Tell you what, if you're free why don't you come and help us this afternoon. We've got to set up a drinks tent alongside the ninth green. Need to get some tables, drinks and glasses out there and serve all the old farts refreshments while they tell us how badly they've been playing. Then listen to them telling us their playing partner is a bandit, and clear away when they've all gone. What do you think, are you up for it mate?'

Nathan suddenly looked excited. 'It would be great helping you, Mr Flint and Mr Featherstone, but what's a bandit?'

Charlie chuckled. 'Oh, it's just someone who is a better player than they say they are.'

Tim moved across the room and slipped an arm around

Nathan's shoulders. 'It's Charlie and Tim and don't look so worried,' he said as both men made a point of shaking Nathan's hand. Which felt rough and hard with callouses.

Nathan smiled uncomfortably. 'It's just that I'm not very good at talking to people. I'll move all the stuff for you, no problem, but I'm not one for chatting see, I get nervous.'

Charlie and Tim were fast establishing Nathan's limitations. 'You've got yourself a deal mate. Anyway, Tim's got enough old chat for all of us.'

Nathan gave a relieved grin and almost leapt from the workbench towards the door. 'Let's go then. I'll get the small truck from the green-keeper's workshop and bring it back here and pick up whatever you want.' Then he was gone like a man on a mission.

'Blimey, he's keen isn't he Flinty?' Tim said. 'He'll have to pack that up.'

Charlie was reflective for a moment. 'Great to see that kind of enthusiasm in a youngster though, isn't it Fev. But I can now see how he wouldn't fit into Adriana's perfect world. What a bitch though, that kid is a grafter and just wants to please.'

Nathan worked like a Trojan for hours and was constantly looking for the next thing to do. At the end of the afternoon when everything was stored away, Charlie said, 'You've worked really hard today, Nathan, thanks for your help. Come on I'll buy you a beer.'

'Oh, that's alright, I like working with you and Tim. But I don't drink Charlie, don't like the taste of it, that's why Mr Galbraith likes me driving the minibus. But I'll come and have a coke with you if that's ok?'

'Of course it is mate, you can have anything you like,' Charlie said waving him in the direction of the clubhouse. 'That's an interesting accent you've got there Nathan. Do I detect a hint of Irish?'

'Oh yes, my first foster parents were Irish—they had me from when I was a baby for a few years, so maybe I picked up something from them. But the orphanage I lived in most of the time was in Surrey.'

Charlie could see that Nathan was physically uncomfortable discussing his childhood, just as Gerry suggested he might be. He vowed never to mention it again, thankful that his children had been blessed to have a normal upbringing. 'Alright then mate let's get you that drink, and if you're really lucky I might throw in a bag of pork scratchings, that's if this club isn't too upmarket to sell pork scratchings.'

The three men sat in a small room at the back of the clubhouse that staff used at break times or after work. The club had strict rules about manual staff taking up tables in the main bar—and especially when they were wearing overalls.

'You're a little bundle of energy aren't you?' Tim said. 'What on earth do you do with yourself in the evenings stuck upstairs in that flat?'

'Oh, sometimes I go to Gerry's house. And sometimes Ben takes me to his gigs and I help him move all his DJ stuff. Now and again I stock up behind the bar, or move furniture for a function. Most nights I just watch TV.' He smiled broadly, 'but I love to watch old cowboy films, you know, from back in the sixties.'

Charlie sensed an opportunity to probe. 'You used to work for Willis and his wife, didn't you Nathan. Did you like it there?'

'Oh yes,' he replied, 'but here is better.'

Charlie pushed a bit harder. 'Did you get on with them, she can be a bit funny I hear, can't she?' He leaned forward and grinned. 'You didn't upset her, did you?'

Nathan shrugged and sipped on his drink. 'Oh, she's ok, moody sometimes and shouts a lot, but maybe I was a bit slow for her. I don't mind though, because Willis got me this job from Craig, which is great, and I still see everybody.'

They finished their drink and cemented a relationship. An arrangement Nathan seemed very happy with, but he couldn't offer much in return, apart from an occasional lift in the club's minibus. 'I can always pick you up and take you home anytime if you want to have a drink. Craig won't mind. I do it for Gerry and the professionals sometimes.'

Tim smiled. 'Do you know what Nathan, we might just take you up on that. It sounds like a great idea.'

Although Charlie and Tim felt sympathy for Nathan's plight, the fact was Craig had rescued him from Adriana, and probably the street. He liked nothing better than to work and feel he was being useful, and they were sure they could put him to good use and give him some self-esteem in the process.

As Charlie and Tim left for the car park, they saw head green-keeper Jason walking towards his car and Charlie waved him over. 'We've had young Nathan helping us this afternoon with the drinks tent. That boy can work, can't he?'

Jason nodded knowingly. 'I could do with another couple like him in the mornings. He's not the quickest on the uptake but once he knows what to do, he just keeps going and never complains. But annoyingly some of the lads have started calling him Neanderthal Nathan behind his back.'

'Better not let me bloody hear them,' Tim said angrily. 'I hate that sort of behaviour and he's worth two of any of them.'

Jason grimaced. 'Yes, I know he is. I've offered him training on all our equipment. He seems to love anything mechanical. I can see by the look on his face he just wants to get at it, but he always turns me down.'

'Do you know why?' Tim asked.

'Well, I can guess Tim. I don't think he can read or write very well, and he'll have to do both to get the safety certificates.'

'Ahh, that's such a shame, isn't it?' Charlie replied. 'Ok, we'll continue to use him in the afternoons if that's ok with you.'

'Yes, of course, keep him busy. He laps it up. Catch you tomorrow.' Jason walked back to his car and drove off down the twisting driveway and towards home.

Charlie looked at Tim and they knew each other well enough not to have to convey their inner feelings in detail. 'I know we can't right the wrongs of the world Fev, but we'll do what we can for the boy. Makes you wonder what on earth is going on in that bloody Adriana's head and what other kinds of evil she's capable of doesn't it?'

10

The working rota for Gerry, Charlie, and Tim as course marshals was quite simple. Charlie and Tim would do weekdays, working together, and Gerry would do weekends, covering as necessary. Gerry liked to do weekends because he didn't have any children or grandchildren to take up his time and energy. Plus, he could keep his eye on Nathan, who he seemed to be assuming some kind of parental responsibility for. And, of course, Nathan was content to work every day of the week.

Charlie was both concerned and curious when he asked Gerry ahead of a sponsored tournament why Nathan worked constantly. 'Surely the boy must want to rest sometimes.'

'No, not really,' Gerry replied. 'He doesn't know what to do with himself and is quite happy to come round in the buggy with me at weekends. He empties the bins, runs people to the station, and pretty much does anything I ask him to do.'

Charlie frowned. 'But he doesn't get paid for that. A boy of his age should be chasing girls, watching sport or even his cowboy films.'

Gerry said uncomfortably, 'I know, and I've tried to tell him, but he just likes to feel useful and seems as happy as a pig in shit all the time he's busy.' He mused for a moment. 'Having said that, he does seem to be rather taken with that new young blond waitress with the stud in her nose.'

'You must mean Tina,' Tim said. 'Yes, I've seen him talking to her. I think she's a local girl.'

Charlie gave a curious sideways look to his friend, 'How do you know her name is Tina, and she's a local girl?'

Tim smiled. 'I'm an ex-detective and now a marshal. I have to make it my business to find these things out Flinty. Well, let's hope it's looking up for him on that front and maybe he might start getting less free time.'

Gerry laughed at the witty exchange between the men, 'Well no-one would be happier than me, and I can only hope it takes his mind off bonfires for a while—he's a bugger, isn't he?'

The men all seemed pleased that something positive might be happening to Nathan, who didn't seem to have experienced much joy in his life. And even though some of the grounds-staff still referred to him as Neanderthal Nathan, out of Tim's earshot, everyone admired his work ethic—especially Craig Galbraith.

Charlie's naturally inquisitive and caring nature compelled him to seek out the young waitress to confirm if she had a mutual interest in Nathan and he wasn't going to make a fool of himself or become the butt of any unkind jokes. During the course of a lunch break, a couple of days later, he saw a slim and petite girl serving in the busy club-house bar. From a distance, he could just see the artificial light reflect off a tiny piece of crystal on the left-hand side of her nose. Got to be her, he thought, so he carefully slalomed his way through noisy golfers waiting to be served at the bar and caught up with her on the way back to the kitchen with a tray full of empty plates. He took a less than discrete glance towards her name badge and said, 'Ahh, so you're Tina?'

The girl was in her early twenties with bleached blond hair pulled into a ponytail and dark roots showing across the top of her head. She didn't smile sweetly and enquire after his question as Charlie had expected. At closer quarters Tina seemed a little earthier than he had anticipated, slightly shabby around the edges with a disinterested, bordering on intolerant, expression on her face. And she was clearly not impressed by his interruption. As the girl turned to face him, Charlie was shocked to notice several bite marks on her chest beneath the semi-transparent white blouse of her uniform.

'That's right, I'm Tina,' the girl said in a very clipped, almost aggressive fashion, taking the wind out of Charlie's sails. 'Do I know you?'

Charlie was taken aback by her directness, 'Err, well I'm sure we've seen each other around Tina, but I've heard Nathan mention you. We work together sometimes.'

'Don't talk to me about 'im, wot's ee bin sayin,' she snapped back.

Charlie was keen to avoid any kind of public confrontation that might be brewing in the girl's head, so he chose his words carefully. 'Oh, nothing bad, just that he likes you.'

'Well, I don't like 'im no more, ee's a bloody animal. You tell Nayfun to stay away from me, or I'll tell me dad and he'll kill 'im stone dead.'

As the girl turned and moved rapidly towards the kitchen swing door, Charlie noticed more red and angry marks through the back of her blouse. She backed through the door and out of sight as Charlie mumbled under his breath, 'Yup, I'll be sure to pass the message on Tina.'

Outside the clubhouse in the late June sunshine, Tim

was talking to Nathan on the pathway by the putting green and Charlie joined them, looking thoroughly confused. Tim knew his friend well enough to know something was troubling him. 'What's wrong Flinty?' he asked.

After recalling the damage Nathan had inflicted on the young girl's body, Charlie looked at him in an entirely different light. 'I've just been speaking to Tina in the bar, Nathan. Seems like you two have had a bit of a falling out?'

Nathan looked ashamed and hung his head. 'Yes Charlie, I don't see girls very often and…' He stumbled over his words. 'Well, you know, I get a bit excited sometimes and can't help it, but I really liked Tina. She don't like me now though.'

'I got that distinct impression, mate.'

'I still like her though.'

'Mmm,' Charlie declared in a highly judgmental way. 'I would make a point of giving her a wide one for a while.'

'What do you mean?' Nathan asked.

'Give her some space,' Tim said

'Oh, ok. Think we're finished anyway,' Nathan said, backing up the path and raising an arm to wave at one of the green keepers over near the practice bunker. 'Got to go. Someone needs my help, have to get some sand, probably.' Then he ran up the path and away from more advice he didn't want to hear.

'Who'd have thought it Flinty,' Tim said.

'Yes, but what you don't know Fev, is that he's really had a go at that poor girl. She is in a mess and must be so embarrassed.'

Tim mused, 'Obviously a tiger lurking beneath that placid exterior of his.'

Charlie was still not amused by Nathan's behaviour. 'It's not funny Fev, you should see her and you wouldn't be impressed if it was your daughter. Plus, she says she's going to tell her dad if he doesn't stay away from her. Well, to be precise, she said her dad would kill him.'

Tim looked worried. 'Yes, you're right Flinty. I would probably want to kill him too. But we've got to hope Tina doesn't tell her dad, because I've just realised who he is. He's a member here. He's that bloke with the shaved head and arms like tree trunks who owns the scaffolding company and looks like a thug in a Pringle jumper. Lenny, I think his name is. Always holding court in the bar at ninety decibels. Like a tattoo covered uncultured fish out of water at this club. But apparently got designs on becoming captain next year—could be interesting.'

Charlie looked equally worried. 'Yes, I know who you mean, and he's the sort who would take on a rampant tiger with his bare hands. Or even worse, get Nathan the sack, and where would he ever get another job like this one?'

Tim started to shuffle anxiously on the pathway, 'I've seen Lenny's type plenty of times when I was in the Met, typically using the company as a front for criminal activity. He'll know people who can arrange for all sorts of unpleasant things to happen. Things that normal people would only read about in newspapers or see in films. Maybe my suspicious mind is going into overdrive Flinty, but I've got a nasty feeling that Tina's dad may have a link to the Japanese owners.'

11

On a cloudless August morning, with the day set to reach thirty-two degrees, Charlie and Tim got a local golf society underway with an early shotgun start. So called because golfers positioned at each of the eighteen holes all commence playing on the sound of a shotgun being fired. Except health and safety requirements dictated a shotgun was no longer used. It was now a very loud compressed air klaxon that Tim activated at exactly eight a.m. startling all the animals and sending birds scattering from the trees for miles. The logistics of the event were complicated particularly that early in the morning when very few staff were on site. But everyone got away at Tim's signal and the golf societies invariably policed themselves. This meant that after a chat with the organisers about how best to play the course, and a friendly reminder on sunscreen and staying hydrated, the two marshals could look forward to an easy few hours. So they slipped back to the clubhouse for a coffee and to check their messages.

In the main admin office Charlie pulled a few papers from the pigeonhole allocated to Course Marshals. 'Anything interesting?' Tim asked.

Charlie shuffled through the papers in turn, 'Just a few flyers for discount in the pro-shop, a playing schedule for the next month.' He pulled the last sheet to the front. 'Oh, and Craig wants us to pop in when we've got a moment. You got a moment, Fev?'

Tim jokingly checked his watch. 'Yes, I think I've got a moment to go and speak to Mr Galbraith, Flinty.'

'Ok let's do it now then.'

Craig Galbraith's days were constantly busy, but even without an invite he would always find time for Charlie and Tim, and the respect was mutual. Charlie rapped the knuckles of his right hand gently and politely on the oak panelled door of the club manager's office. From the other side of the door they heard Craig's soft Scottish tones utter, 'Come in.' Spoken in a way suggesting an interruption wasn't really appreciated but wouldn't be declined.

Charlie eased the door open and caught the familiar smell of wool carpet and linseed oil that never seemed to have left that room since it was first furnished. He witnessed Craig's grinning face come into view. 'Hello boys, thanks for dropping by,' he said with real warmth.

'So you've decided to send us on that two week training course in The Maldives after all then Craig,' Tim said flippantly.

Craig chuckled, 'If you mean the reef fishing course, then I'm afraid I've already had all the Marlin and Tuna taken out of our little lake, so no, sadly not. But do take a seat. There's something I need your help with chaps.'

Charlie sensed bad news. 'What's wrong then Craig.'

'Oh, nothing's wrong. I just want to make sure that everything is right, Charlie.'

'Sorry. not with you.'

Craig pulled a handwritten note from one of his desk trays and held it out in front of the men. He sighed and shook the sheet of paper softly. 'Late last night I had a call, and this bombshell dropped on me. The Japanese owners have decided they want to come and look at their golf course next week.'

'That's not unreasonable, is it?' Tim asked.

'On the face of it, no,' Craig replied. 'But with the backdrop of them asking for our accounts, which are just about breaking even. And that whole deer business is still unsolved. So I'm not sure it's going to be a very comfortable visit.'

'So what do you think they're going to do on this visit then Craig?' Charlie asked.

Craig shrugged. 'Truth is Charlie, I don't know. You see for people with their sort of money this course is just a plaything. But they'll suddenly become interested if we start losing them money hand over fist.'

Tim interrupted, 'And you believe they might just want to cut their losses before they start making them?'

Craig abruptly stood up from his high backed leather chair and pushed his palms firmly onto the polished wooden desktop. 'Well, I want to make bloody sure that thought doesn't even cross their inscrutable minds, and I need you to help—are you with me?'

'Yes, of course,' Charlie said. 'What do you want us to do?'

Craig strutted around the room like a commanding officer about to issue battle orders. 'Well, I can't change our accounts or the order book, they are what they are. But I can do my best to make sure that everywhere looks good, there is a positive atmosphere about the place. And finally, have the owners leave here believing we are on the up.'

Tim frowned. 'But there's no getting away from that deer being slaughtered and mutilated is there. The press are still all over it and the locals constantly talking about it on that social media stuff—well, so my wife tells me.'

'No, you're right Tim,' Craig replied. 'But I'm playing that down as a one-off incident and the subject of a full-blown police investigation. If they look at the local newspapers, and I'm sure they have, they'll see that all the journalists have been judge, jury and hangman. Once the police let the illegal immigrants go, the press moved their attention to the Kosovan car cleaners. Who they're now increasingly convinced are to blame.' He shook his head in despair. 'I can only hope the owners don't want to dwell on the subject.'

'So where do we come in?' Charlie said, eager to establish his part in the exercise.

Craig dropped back into his chair and said in a voice full of nervous excitement. 'Well, I'm going to take care of everything in here, and I'd like you two to keep an eye on everything out there on the course. We'll meet every morning at eight between now and the owners arrival to go through what's happening on the day, and I'll invite Jason the head green keeper. I will speak with the clubhouse people separately. I just want to know that when the Japanese folks go out on the course it's the best it can be.'

Charlie smiled, relishing the thought of a new challenge. 'Better give us some detail then.'

Craig slid an A4 sheet of paper from a filing tray across the polished desktop and stopped it in front of him. He slipped on his reading glasses and moved the sheet into focus. 'Their people sent me this e-mail today confirming they are coming over to London for business meetings starting next Monday for four days. They are basing themselves in a Park Lane hotel and planning to jump on a train at Victoria on Wednesday morning to spend the day with us before heading back to town. They are saying they don't want a fuss or any special effort, they just want to see a normal day. And they also want to experience the rail network for themselves.'

Tim laughed, 'Well that's not going to be a great start to their day is it?'

Craig shook his head and smiled. 'Positive Tim, let's stay positive. So I'd like one of you to go and pick them up at the station in the bus. Can you ask Nathan to clear all his crap out of it and I'll get the Kosovan boys to give it a thorough clean—if they're still talking to me. And speaking of Nathan, it's probably best to keep him out the way on the day.'

'That's not fair Craig,' Charlie protested.

'No, I know it isn't.' Craig paused ruefully. 'He's just a bit clumsy and not my favourite person today. This morning he was collecting a group of people from the station and backed the bus into a concrete bollard, damaging the rear light cluster. I really don't need it at the moment and haven't got time to get the flaming thing fixed.' He sucked in a breath, 'Ok let me rephrase that statement then. Make sure Nathan is busy on the day - and definitely not with bloody bonfires.'

'Understood,' Charlie said, choosing not to dwell on Nathan's unfortunate lack of coordination.

Craig adjusted his glasses and went back to studying the printed off e-mail. 'There will be three of them, Mr Kenzo Tanaka, Mr Osamu Hangai and an interpreter that they are picking up over here. They should arrive on the nine-thirty train, then coffee and introductions in the boardroom before having a tour of the course and meeting the golf professional staff before lunch. Then a wrap up meeting with the accountants and me before heading back into London on the train. Fortunately Willis will be here, so golden boy can suck up to them for a while and we'll get Adriana to come for lunch as a distraction. But we can't get away from them looking at the course, even if it's pouring with rain they'll want to do it. So I'm suggesting the three of us take one person each around the course in a buggy procession. That should be the easy part, because the course is looking good and playing well. Now they are adamant we don't change anything in the diary because of them. But they will doubtless want to speak to players as they go round. Fortunately there are no societies, league matches or club events on. So we need to make sure that, purely coincidentally, the right members are playing golf at the right time - if you get my drift. You know who these people are boys, so can I leave it with you to arrange that little piece of jiggery pokery with young Ben. He's a switched-on boy with that sort of thing. Unlike James, who seems to be away with the fairies at the moment.'

Tim nodded vigorously. 'Gotcha, we know exactly who we need to be playing on the day—and more importantly, not playing. And we'll let them know the owners are around and might want to talk to them.'

'Great, thanks. I need the Japanese to leave here thinking this is a place that people love, and we have the potential to be really successful, even if we haven't quite got there yet.'

The three men all shook hands to seal the arrangement and Craig breathed far more easily knowing he had his best staff on the case. As they walked slowly out of the clubhouse and up the concrete path Charlie seemed troubled by the meeting. 'Craig's got the wind up about something, Fev, I can sense it, and it's something he's keeping from us.'

'I agree Flinty, but when you think about how much the owners must have paid to tempt him away from his last club, he won't want to put a foot wrong. Anyway my friend, dust off your deerstalker this will give us an opportunity to watch how that reptile Willis is with the owners, and what they might be involved in together—how's your Japanese?'

'Never been better Fev, it's completely non-existent. And

as much as Craig won't like it, we are going to have to make sure that Lenny the scaffolder is around too, so that we can check out that little connection he might have.'

Tim chuckled, 'He'll love us for that as an aspiring captain, a tipoff that the owners are coming.'

'That's if he doesn't know already.'

The following Wednesday morning, Tim collected the three men in the sparkling clean mini-bus, with the still damaged light cluster he tried to keep out of their sight. They were not the kind of Japanese moguls he had anticipated in dark suits, white shirts, sombre ties with lots of nodding and bowing. They were casual in American designer clothes, both in their forties, sophisticated, polite and respectful. The interpreter was a slim and smiley young man with dark hair named Riku. Born in southwest London, the product of an English father and a Japanese mother.

Charlie and Tim were waiting at the front of the clubhouse with three fully charged and cleaned golf buggies when the visitors emerged from the clubhouse with Willis and Craig. Willis quickly disappeared off into the pro-shop with his normal sickly sweet toothy smile and said, 'See you at lunch guys, have fun.'

Charlie had half expected to be muscled out of driving one of the guests around by Willis. But he strangely seemed happy to avoid the employers who had given him probably the best golfing contract in the country. Craig was to drive Kenzo, Charlie, Osamu, and Tim was going to take Riku the interpreter. They were just getting their pictures taken by a photographer Craig had hired when out of the clubhouse burst Lenny in a bright orange polo shirt and black shorts. He lumbered up the pathway in a laboured fashion with an outstretched, heavily tattooed hand. 'Mornin' gents pleased ta meet ya, Lenny Jackson, decent golfer, entrepreneur and next year's captain with a bit of luck—eh.'

Everyone cringed at Lenny's barefaced cheek and Craig muttered under his breath, 'Over my dead body.' But the special guests smiled graciously and shook Lenny's hand before being whisked off quickly towards the first tee.

The Japanese visitors spoke better English than anyone expected, but always chose to have an interpreter in tow to pick up on any nuances that might impact business discussions. Craig was doing his best to make polite and positive conversation in his buggy. While Charlie wasn't making much headway with his passenger outside of enthusing about the course, and any references to Willis were simply met with a gregarious smile. So if any intelligence was going to be forthcoming, it had to be from Tim, via the Englishman who was in his buggy. 'So Riku, have you worked with our guests before?' he asked.

'No never Tim,' he replied. 'It was a special concession for me to get this assignment because I'm a keen golfer and a huge fan of Willis Martin. I don't know how they managed to get him to work at this course, but what a coup—eh, he's an absolute legend.'

'Yes, that's always interested us Riku, seems strange that a man like him would come here doesn't it.'

Riku nodded in agreement. 'Yeah. My colleague back in the office who normally does this Japanese company's work says they wanted the best, and she was at the contract negotiations. She wouldn't tell me the details but apparently Willis wasn't headhunted, he put himself forward. Yet still insisted on total flexibility, and she was amazed he didn't seem to show them much regard. You know sort of, if you don't like me then go and find yourself another golf superstar to work at your little club.'

'And you still like him?' Tim asked.

'They're all a bit strange these people with enormous talent, aren't they. I'm just delighted to have met the man.'

He took a mobile phone from his pocket and held it up to Tim, 'And I got a brilliant selfie to show off to my golfing mates.'

On the day of the visit things couldn't have gone much better. The forecast showers stayed away, the course was immaculate and they got some great feedback from carefully planted playing members. As expected, despite his apparent bravado, Willis was a complete sycophant, and the owners seemed suitably taken by Adriana, who had dressed for the occasion. But the Japanese men were far too smart not to know that the whole thing had been stage managed, and the main event was always going to be the meeting with the accountants.

Tim dropped the party back to the station and waved them off on their grubby graffiti covered train into central London. Then he spoke to Charlie before they went into a de-briefing session with Craig. 'Sounds like Willis isn't particularly tight with the Japanese after all, thinks they are lucky to have him by all accounts.'

'Yes, and I'm not entirely convinced that Lenny is on their team either.'

As Tim nudged the half-open door to Craig's office, he whispered, 'Unless it was all an elaborate show for our benefit.'

'Thanks for your help today, boys,' Craig said, squeezing the shoulders of both Charlie and Tim as they entered the room. 'I really couldn't have done it without you, and your part went like clockwork. The Japanese were tight-lipped about everything, but they seemed to enjoy the course.'

'But did they enjoy the accountant's figures?' Charlie asked with emphasis.

Craig frowned and twisted his palms upwards, 'Your guess is as good as mine Charlie, they didn't really pass comment, only asked about membership numbers.'

Trying to remain positive, Tim said, 'But that's good, isn't it? At least they didn't rip into you and tell you to do better. Did they mention the deer, by the way?'

'Yes, they did. But I had a call from the police earlier today to say they had taken one of the Kosovans in for questioning again, which kept the owners quiet.'

Tim looked at Craig sceptically. 'That's highly coincidental timing, isn't it. Just right to take the heat off while the Japanese boys were here?'

Craig shrugged and ignored the comment. He looked strangely distracted, both relieved and anxious at the same time. Charlie attempted to settle him. 'It's over Craig, they'll decide whatever they decide, and you can't influence it any more today.'

'No, you're right. Come on, I owe you two at least one drink. Sorry to seem so distant, it's just there are pressures here that you may never understand.'

12

It was early afternoon at *The Sycamores* on a hot July day and Ben Tilman was working alone in the air-conditioned pro-shop surrounded by new clubs, clothing and golf paraphernalia for sale in Willis's franchise. He was answering the phone taking bookings for the course, checking people in and dealing with queries from players. And in his spare moments, he was setting up competitions for members and updating past results on the club's website. Meanwhile, Willis was away again visiting his business interests and James was predictably missing.

'On your own Ben?' Charlie asked as he entered through the large aluminium framed glass door walking into the shop that smelt like a clothes store.

'No change there then,' a disgruntled Ben mumbled. 'Willis is swanning around the world, James has disappeared again, and muggins is left to do everything as usual.'

It was a rhetorical question, but Charlie felt he needed to ask it to show some support. 'So James must be out giving lessons then?'

Ben laughed sarcastically, 'Yeah, he's giving something,

but I think the lessons are coming from Adriana—always the same when Willis is away.'

In a deadpan fashion Charlie commented, 'He's probably demonstrating an in-to-out swing path then.' But Ben's sense of humour had long since evaporated and he seemed thoroughly depressed.

'Yeah, probably,' Ben said, not lifting his gaze from the counter. 'Whatever it is, he's winding me up a treat. For a top-class golf course we're giving a crap service.'

Charlie had cleverly manipulated the conversation and used Ben's negative impetus to his favour. 'Listen Ben, my mate Tim and me have been thinking that after the early morning rush, or when the weather is bad, we usually have spare time on our hands. And when Willis is away, you are obviously up against it, so we wondered if there's anything we can help you with.'

Ben looked up and smiled graciously, 'It's very good of you to think of me Charlie.'

'That's the kind of guys we are,' Charlie joked.

Ben finally managed a grin. 'Yes, I know, but there probably isn't anything I can give you to do that doesn't need training. And, no offence, it would take me longer to train you than to do the jobs myself.'

'Well, there must be something, we are quite practical blokes, and no-one needs to know that we're helping out, and you look like you need a break.'

Ben scratched his head and thought for a moment, then the tension began to drain from his face. 'Well, you can't give lessons. I've seen you both play,' he laughed.

'That's hurtful Ben.'

'And you can't add up properly, your scorecards are always wrong.'

'That's just ageist.'

'Mmm, I tell you what though, I've got a pile of clubs to re-grip out the back and members beating me up every day because they are not ready. It's an easy job I could teach you in fifteen minutes.'

'Bingo!' Charlie thought, I might be old, but I haven't lost my touch. The smart young boy has walked straight into my trap. 'So what about James, won't he object if he finds out?'

'Make me laugh,' Ben retorted. 'James doesn't know if he's coming or going. He's so busy shagging himself senseless and lovestruck with Adriana that the Martians could invade, and he wouldn't notice.'

Good answer, went through Charlie's head. 'OK, I'll come in with Tim a bit later and you can run through it with us.'

'Great. But leave it until after four will you.' Ben rolled his eyes theatrically. 'We have to go through this charade of bollocks with James. He rushes in looking red and flustered at three o'clock, giving all kinds of pathetic excuses for being late when everyone knows where he's been. He stays here for about an hour, pretends to do work in the office, while sending Adriana a million text messages and e-mails, then disappears off home in a trance.'

'Not bitter then,' Charlie mumbled as he walked towards the door. He turned back and called out, 'We'll be back just after four then.'

'Brilliant, see you then, and thanks again for thinking of me Charlie. I really appreciate it.'

'It's a pleasure,' Charlie shouted, grinning as the glass door clicked closed behind him, knowing that very soon he and Tim would be able to inspect Willis's next consignment of clubs from America, and find out what was really going on.

In the quiet tiny workshop at the back of the pro-shop within half an hour, Ben had got both Charlie and Tim fully trained. They were adept at cutting off worn rubber grips from golf clubs, removing old adhesive tape, applying new, then squirting on a coat of solvent and sliding on a brand-new grip. 'We'll hang on and do a few tonight while we're in the swing of it,' Charlie said. 'Get yourself home Ben, you look exhausted. I'll drop the key into the bar later.'

Ben didn't argue. He just left with a tired smile, a thank you and a wave as he walked out of the shop towards the car park and an early night for once.

'Well done Flinty,' Tim whispered sarcastically. 'Have you seen the enormous pile of clubs over there that need re-gripping—a bloody master stroke.'

'Shut up, you old woman. This is indeed a master stroke Fev, because when Willis arrives back with more clubs from overseas, we will be able to open one up without him ever knowing. We know he changes the grips anyway, and he only ever uses the Nielsen Blue stuff, which he has a stock of here. Plus, we'll be trusted to hold the key to his workshop so we can do it when the place is empty, but we'll have to be quick before he ships them out.'

Tim put a gentle hand on his friend's shoulder as an unspoken apology. 'Yes, you're right of course Flinty, but I can just see us getting stuck with this flaming job forever.'

'Get a grip.'

'What?'

'Pass me one from the box.'

After about two weeks of James being constantly worn out, Ben covering all the work, and Charlie and Tim getting him out of the mire with the members waiting for their clubs, Willis returned to *The Sycamores*. As was normal on the day of his mid-morning arrival in the UK, he dumped four sets of golf irons, in separate cardboard boxes, into his workshop. Then quickly checked his post and e-mails, before leaving for home to sleep and recover from jet lag.

'Can I borrow the keys to the pro shop please Karen,' Charlie asked one of the bar staff at about five thirty with a well-rehearsed worried look on his face. 'I've lost my car keys somewhere, house keys and everything on the bunch. I was in there earlier, but everyone has gone home now.'

'Oh dear. Yes, of course, Charlie,' she said, handing a small bunch of keys across the wooden bar top. 'I'll switch off the alarm for you. Hope you find them.'

'So do I. Thanks Karen, I'll bring them back in a while.' He leaned on the counter and whispered, 'Oh, and could you do me a favour and not mention this, I just feel so stupid.'

Karen gave a sympathetic smile and then winked. 'Mention what?'

'Thanks.'

Charlie met Tim in the corridor outside the glass fronted pro-shop, unlocked the door and promptly locked it again once they were inside. They slipped quietly through the office and into the workshop. Charlie closed the door and switched the lights on. 'Right, let's get on with it. The first challenge is we have to get one of these boxes open without it being obvious.'

Tim smiled, 'Leave that to me Flinty, I used to be in the fraud squad, remember. I'll carefully slit the packing tape down the side with that Stanley knife, take out a club and use Willis's superglue to stick the cardboard back together when we've finished. He'll just lose patience with the box when he wants to open it, rip it apart and won't even notice, or blame whoever packed it. Well, that's the theory, and in my experience, it usually works.'

'That's ingenious Fev.'

'Do you think I learned nothing from the villains Flinty?'

Tim pulled a golf iron from the box after performing his

own brand of cardboard surgery and handed it to Charlie. 'Interesting, that confirms he must have changed the grips in the states, and they are all Nielsen Blue, the same as the ones we have here.'

Charlie sliced the rubber grip up its length with a sharp Stanley knife and peeled it off the club's shaft. Then he started to scrape off the double-sided adhesive tape while Tim hovered over him anxiously. 'Pull on that piece of string hanging out of the shaft will you Fev,' Charlie said, pointing to the now open end of the hollow steel club.

As Tim gently eased the string from the club's shaft out slid a long slender clear plastic bag packed solid with white powder. 'Gotcha!' he said, punching the air.

Charlie quickly put the club in a vice and began the process of refitting an identical grip from stock. He said, 'Well, we don't need Oscar now, unless this is very expensive, and very illegal talcum powder hidden inside these clubs, and I'm sure every one of them is the same. Now find yourself a bag to put it in so you can take it home.'

'Take it home!' Tim exclaimed loudly. 'Are you serious? Louise will go completely ape shit if I walk in with this. And why me?'

Charlie huffed, 'Well firstly I wasn't suggesting that you walk through the front door and tell Louise you have a lovely bag of fresh cocaine for her. And secondly, I'm the brains of this outfit and you take the risks. That's how it works.'

'Since when?'

'Since I got us trained and in here tonight to uncover Willis's little game.'

'Ok, I'll keep it in the car for now.'

After ten minutes, Charlie had replaced the grip and slipped the club back into the box, leaving Tim to glue the cardboard edge shut. 'Whoever this stuff is going to will be wanting Willis's blood when they find one of these clubs is empty, Flinty.'

'Well, with any luck he'll be banged up by then.' Charlie said. 'And now you know why your new clubs were so cheap.'

13

Cedar Avenue was the kind of quiet tree lined street that you might find in the better residential areas of most suburban towns or villages. Despite the name, the avenue had no cedar trees at all but was dotted along its length by tall poplar trees with roots that over the years had forced up paving slabs. The houses were all built in the 1930s during a mass building programme fuelled by an economy coming out of recession. The avenue was a mix of desirable semi-detached and detached properties, of which most had been progressively improved over the years. Number 16 was a perfect example of a four-bedroom detached dwelling that had been tastefully face-lifted and had a double width driveway leading to a single garage. This was the home Craig Galbraith had rented while he was based at *The Sycamores*. When he first arrived his family was wife Kirsty and 22-year-old twin boys, but now one was travelling in Australia and the other away studying at university. So Craig and Kirsty predominantly lived there alone.

Cedar Avenue was in the centre of the stereotypical English village of Denesford. Idyllic, with its duck pond, cricket green, two pubs, grocery store, and a thirteenth century church. It was about a twenty-five-minute drive for Craig, but he considered that was a small price to pay for such a perfect setting. And Kirsty was happy volunteering at the local Citizen's Advice Bureau three days a week.

It was four a.m. on a still and dry morning when a white vehicle turned into an unadopted and unlit lane about a mile away from Craig's house in Denesford. The driver had given careful consideration to the weather and their movements that day. They had an important job to do and needed to be in and out of the village quickly without drawing unwanted attention. Parking away from the reach of the lights from the main road, they leaned across to the passenger footwell and gently lifted out a plastic supermarket bag containing the purpose of their night's work. Then they carefully stepped out onto the hard, dry, uneven ground. Wearing a light coat to ward off the night chill and a beanie hat pulled low across their face, the stranger leaned on the driver's door until it gave a controlled click shut. There was no point locking the vehicle at that time in the morning and the electronic beeps and flashing lights would have only telegraphed their presence. The thirty paces to the main road were quick and easy on the compacted soil and gravel surface that after days without rain, made no sound underfoot. Then came the walk on public pavements, hugging the hedges and walls of houses and always keeping the carrier bag concealed on their inside. On a few occasions they were caught by car headlights. They looked away, guessing the drivers would think they were a night worker, and would be too sleepy to pay attention anyway. The visitor finally crossed the main road before reaching a small parade of shops, to avoid the scrutiny of security cameras. Then crossed back again a hundred yards further up at the entrance to Cedar Avenue. The sweet smell of jasmine hung heavy in the air like some kind of surreal welcome. A quick scan of the first front doors of the avenue told them the odd numbers were on the left, so number 16 had to be eight houses up on the right-hand side. The avenue was deathly quiet without a soul in sight. The dull glow of moonlight was only disturbed by an occasional wispy cloud or the high branches of poplar trees moving in the light breeze. Suddenly the red glimmer of a car's taillights appeared at the top of a slight incline in the road. There was the cough of an engine starting, then a saloon car backed off its driveway and stark white headlamp beams swung around to face the stranger. They leapt over a low brick wall into the nearest garden and crouched behind a large laurel bush. The perfume of lavender rose in the air after they brushed a border, and their movement triggered the sensor of house security lights. The car passed quickly, stopped at the junction, turned left and its glowing rear lights soon disappeared from sight. The visitor moved quickly from their cover not wanting to trigger the light with a second movement. But urban foxes that patrolled the street every night would surely get the blame if anybody bothered to glance through twitching curtains or blinds.

Number 16 Cedar Avenue was in complete darkness as the foxes had already done their sweep scavenging for food at this end of the street and were working their way up the hill, as automatic house lights being activated in the distance testified. Craig Galbraith's sleek and shiny black Jaguar XF was parked on the drive next to an immaculate silver Range Rover Evoque. They were cleaned every week by the Kosovan cleaners that worked out of the golf course car park. Both cars were pointing inward towards the house and shielded by a six-foot privet hedge from the nearest neighbour on the left-hand side. Even though Craig's car seemed unmistakable a quick check that the Jaguar's number plate tied up with the one the visitor had memorised confirmed they were at the right place. Sliding between the passenger side of the Jaguar and the hedge to get to the front of the car they lifted up the carrier bag pulled open the handles, untied a black plastic sack and carefully placed its contents to rest in the gap between the top of the bonnet and windscreen. The two bags were screwed into a ball and wedged firmly into a coat pocket. Then the stranger eased themselves backwards into the street. They started walking with haste, following the same route back to their vehicle, and then reversed down the unadopted lane into the main road. The next element of the night's strategy was to drive to a 24-hour supermarket. En route removing the beanie hat and smoothing their hair with spit and the flat of their hand for the waiting shop cameras. The whole exercise had taken them little more than half an hour. At the brightly lit supermarket, they parked in the middle of an enormous empty car park under the glare of floodlights. Walking to the shop the driver took a trolley from one of the Perspex shelters and strode confidently towards the entrance. Outside the main door, they discreetly dropped the screwed up plastic bags from their pocket into an empty waste bin that would be overflowing by mid-morning and have its contents disposed of. Right now, they wanted their every movement to be noticed, because this was to be their alibi for the night should they ever need one. They would say that they couldn't sleep and went grocery shopping while it was quiet. There would be a receipt and camera footage as proof, perfect. This was a professional and their task had been successfully completed to the letter, and there would be no doubting who the calling card had been sent from. Craig Galbraith had received a classic message he would never forget—there was no mistaking the meaning of a severed deer's head.

14

Sitting in the privacy of the shiny shed's office at the start of what was going to be a busy day, Charlie and Tim were quietly pleased with their detective work from the night before. Particularly as they now had compelling and hard evidence against Willis that would surely put him away for several years and end his illustrious career in shame. But they had no compunction about sending him to jail. The man was a crook abusing his position by fuelling a violent and sickening trade and he needed to be taken off the street along with his cocaine. Charlie also felt justified in that following his senses once again had been the right thing to do. But there was just one detail spoiling all their virtual back slapping. They had a highly illegal packet of white powder concealed in the boot of Tim's car with a street value of about £10,000—and they desperately wanted to get rid of it to the authorities. Charlie looked to Tim as the ex-policeman for a solution. 'My suggestion Flinty is that I give Don Moore a ring. His team used to do this sort of thing and he's not long retired and still has mates in the job. Taking this down to the local nick would just be too much of a faff, too many questions and too much paperwork.'

'Yes, sounds like a plan Fev, but sooner rather than later, eh, because Louise is going to kill you if she finds out you've been hiding a bag of cocaine under your spare wheel. And Ruth will kill me for letting you do it.'

'You'd better believe it Flinty, especially after I was ferrying my boy and his mates around in the car last night.'

Tim agreed to call Don Moore early that afternoon when the course would be quieter. 'Hello Don, this is Tim Featherstone from the golf club. Just to let you know that we don't now need Oscar's expertise. We took one of the pro's latest imported clubs apart yesterday and pulled out a bag of what we believe is cocaine, which we've kept as evidence.'

'Well, it's got to be something dodgy hasn't it,' Don said. 'Why bother going to all that trouble concealing it otherwise, and it is almost certainly cocaine. Great work, well done Tim, but you and Charlie must be careful, don't ever underestimate the kind of people involved in the drugs business. Your life means nothing to them.'

'Understood Don and thanks, and that's one of the reasons I need to pass this bag of drugs onto someone sharpish. And ideally hand the whole case over to the police so that they can stop Willis in his tracks. Trouble is, I don't know who to speak to anymore.'

Don didn't hesitate for a moment. 'No, but I do. Leave this with me, Tim.'

Tim was conscious of the likely fallout once the news about Willis reached his supply chain, several people would be losing a lot of money and be looking for retribution. 'Look Don, you were just walking your dog across the golf course, and we got you involved, so I don't want you troubled with all of this. Can you get your contact to phone me?'

'No problem Tim, us ex-coppers never quite hang up our truncheons, do we. But I'll make a call. My contact is Detective Inspector David Evans in the National Crime Agency, a

Welshman, but don't hold that against him. He is a smart detective. Expect a call soon.'

'Thanks mate and give Oscar a treat from us—outstanding work.'

At around five o'clock, Tim's mobile phone rang, with the default ring tone that Charlie always told him was old and boring, like its owner. 'Hello, Tim Featherstone,' he answered.

A confident Welsh accented voice came at him. 'Hello sir, Detective Inspector Evans here. I've had a call from Don Moore who tells me you may have some information for me regarding the activities of an American citizen Willis Martin. And I understand you were once a DCI in the Met's fraud squad?'

'That is correct, inspector, and I also have some evidence I need to pass over to you.'

'Yes, Don explained. Are you able to get to London tomorrow? It might be easier than us descending on you and causing suspicion. We'll pay your expenses.'

'Absolutely, and expenses won't be necessary,' Tim said, feeling excited to be part of the organisation again. 'And I'll bring my colleague, who has been a crucial part of this exercise.'

'Of course, sir.'

Tim agreed the time and location for a London meeting and arranged cover for the day with Gerry. He and Charlie took an almost empty mid-morning train still dirty from the commuter runs into Charing Cross station. And then they got a hot and sweaty Northern Line underground journey to get within a half mile of an old-style red brick police station in South London. It had wide Portland stone steps at the front entrance leading up to double leaf solid wooden doors with an antique blue police sign hanging over. A short and overweight, middle-aged balding man in a polo shirt, jeans and brown brogues greeted them at the public entrance. He shook hands and introduced himself as DI David Evans. 'Thanks for coming in. Nice to meet you both. Found us alright then?'

Tim replied, 'Not many nicks I haven't been to in the Met area, but I think this might be one of them.'

The detective inspector grinned, 'Aren't many left quite like this in London. We use it from time to time. Just thought it would be easier for you to get to. Anyway, if I can get you to sign in, we'll have a coffee and a chat. Follow me.'

Tim was expecting a quiet room somewhere on the top floor that had been refurbished and belied the tiredness of the building. Something that might be used by senior officers for meetings, with thick carpet, reasonable furniture, freshly brewed coffee and biscuits on a china plate sitting on a highly polished wood table. Instead, he and Charlie were ushered into a grubby interview room on the ground floor that smelt of stale mops with a stained vinyl floor and a yellowing fluorescent light. 'Have a seat chaps,' Detective Inspector Evans said, indicating towards a metal table surrounded by four black plastic chairs. 'Coffee is on the way. You must be used to this environment, Mr Featherstone—eh?'

Tim smiled through the disappointment, but was pleased the detective had done his homework. 'Yeah, they're the same the world over, aren't they?'

A young PC in uniform entered the room backwards, carrying a tray of instant coffee in plastic cups with milk and sugar in pots and packets. 'Thanks Tom,' the inspector said as the constable slopped the coffee while depositing the tray on the table, then left the room without speaking. Evans must have seen the look of disdain on Charlie's face. 'Sorry it's not the Ritz,' he said with a hint of sarcasm. He looked towards Tim for moral support. 'But you know how it is.

These rooms are not normally used for entertaining and nothing else is available today. Think yourself lucky you weren't offered any of our rancid custard creams,' he laughed, but no-one else did. 'Now in your own words, tell me what you know and how you obtained the item Don has briefed me about.'

Charlie and Tim proudly relayed their story of guile and ingenuity, then Tim slid a supermarket carrier bag across the linoleum covered table. Inside, looking like a white snake, was the unopened long, thin plastic bag full of cocaine wrapped in newspaper. 'Here's your evidence inspector,' he said with an air of satisfaction in his voice.

Evans looked astonished. 'You took a risk bringing that with you into this part of London.'

'Not as much of a risk as leaving it at home with my family inspector,' Tim replied.

'Yes, point taken.' Choosing his words carefully, the detective examined the long clear bag. 'Well done chaps, I don't need to check this. It's obviously cocaine and gives us absolute proof of a drug trafficking operation that we were already onto.'

'You knew about it?' Charlie asked incredulously.

'Yes Mr Flint, Willis Martin has been on our radar for a while. It's not by luck he keeps getting drugs into the country unchallenged, but this gives us what we need to categorically prove what he's up to.'

Both Charlie and Tim were astonished. 'So, are you going to nick the toerag now?' Tim asked.

'I'm afraid not, gentlemen. Your evidence and information has been incredibly helpful, but I must ask you to back away from this now. Leave it to us.'

Tim was indignant, 'But the bloke is bang to rights. And he's going to keep doing it unless you stop him.'

Evans slid his chair backwards, screeching on the hard

floor as if to back away from an argument. 'Yes, I understand sir and you are of course, correct.' He cleared his throat and took a sip of cold coffee. 'Now only because of your background and involvement I can tell you a little more. The fact is, we are working closely with the American Drug Enforcement Agency and this case has far wider international implications than simply importing a little cocaine into the UK. But we have more work to do before taking any action. We can't risk divulging our interest in Willis Martin at this stage. There is a much bigger picture to consider.'

Charlie couldn't contain himself any longer. 'Look inspector we've got our fingerprints all over this, and we are now exposed to a network of killers who won't take long to figure out we are involved. So don't just thank us for our bloody help.'

Evans stood up to indicate the conversation was over. 'I appreciate your concern, Mr Flint, but I have to stress this meeting never took place, and Willis Martin must be allowed to operate as normal, albeit we are watching his movements from a distance. Your involvement will not be obvious to Mr Martin, and we won't be poking around at the golf club either.' He held the carrier bag aloft. 'And I suspect that someone in the states will be blamed for losing this. But you know how this works, Mr Featherstone. These people don't have rules or respect, and we can't absolutely guarantee your safety. So I would strongly advise that however frustrating you find it, you both behave as though nothing has happened and keep a low profile. Now, as I say, I want you both to leave everything to us and do not discuss the situation with anyone else. We need you to remain professional. But be assured that Willis Martin will be bought to justice in due course, until then leave it alone. This is now a matter of national importance.'

15

Even though they took comfort in their instincts being right, Charlie and Tim found it hard to face Willis Martin after their frustrating meeting with the police in London. It went against the grain to have caught him red-handed, and then allow him to escape without him ever realising he'd even been caught. But they understood there was a much bigger prize to be had somewhere, which they could only speculate on. But it just made things worse for them, knowing Willis was a far more significant villain than either of them had realised. Their similar natures made them both completely disillusioned with the injustice of the situation, and eager to know what else the golf club's famous head professional was up to. Still, they just had to trust the police, accept the situation for now and keep quiet, grudgingly hoping that every day would be one nearer to Willis's comeuppance. Yet all the while, his smug and comfortable life seemed totally charmed and unaffected.

Oblivious to what had gone on with Charlie and Tim, Willis quickly settled back into a routine at *The Sycamores* after his latest trip abroad. Well, what most people saw as his version of a routine at least. This meant doing very little work, being on permanent charm offensive while lauding it around the golf course and taking an obscene salary. When he was publicly visible, Willis was often to be found out on the practice range with his latest prodigy from overseas, a young fresh faced Thai lad named Pom who followed him around like a puppy.

One late warm July afternoon when the course had emptied, and the terrace bar overlooking the eighteenth green was full of golfers enjoying a post round drink, Charlie and Tim moved along the concrete pathway to the practice range. They stopped and were watching the activity with great interest, particularly as Willis was working with Pom on his swing. 'Is this the kid that Willis reckons is going to be the next big thing on the circuit?' Charlie whispered, half covering his mouth.

Tim mumbled his reply. 'Apparently that's why he brought the boy over from Thailand. But if that's the case Flinty, you and me are going to get picked for the next Ryder Cup. The boy has a long way to go, and from where I'm standing, he doesn't seem to have any natural ability at all. In fact, I'd say he was bloody hopeless.'

Pom was probably eighteen or nineteen years old, but looked younger because of his slight frame, jet-black hair, and unblemished skin. With a golf club in his hands, he looked decidedly ungainly, but Willis was still persevering with the kind of expert guidance that serious golfers would pay a high price for. 'Get through the ball buddy and make sure you end up facing the target after you've taken your shot. Keep working on it and don't forget that grip I showed you.'

Charlie and Tim were still full of contempt for Willis, and Charlie couldn't resist taunting, 'He's coming on a treat,' after a ball went sideways from Pom's golf club.

Willis didn't miss the sarcasm, and suddenly became

defensive over his student. 'Give him a break. He's getting there, guys. Just having one of those off days today that we all have,' he shouted.

Willis adjusted Pom's grip on the club and said, 'Keep practicing bud, just gonna speak to the marshal guys,' then started trotting towards the pathway. He was wearing another garish designer golf outfit that he'd been sponsored to wear by one of the famous golf equipment manufacturers. This consisted of black and white checked trousers, a flamingo pink jersey, white shoes and an orange baseball cap.

'Do you think he knows he looks like a complete pratt, or shall we tell him Flinty?' Tim murmured to his friend.

Charlie uttered from the side of his mouth just before Willis reached them, 'Well, on the basis he gets to choose the clothes he is paid to wear, I guess he must already know.'

'Hey guys,' Willis said with the kind of friendly bouncy attitude that told them he was after some kind of favour.

Tim's frustration with Willis's fake charm was getting the better of him. He was struggling to be nice when he knew he was in the presence of a drug trafficker—and that was the best case. 'What is it Willis, you obviously want something.'

'Don't be like that buddy. I was your pal when I got you the cheap golf clubs—huh?' Willis gave another false smile, and Tim bit hard on his tongue. 'I've gotta go make some calls and I wondered if you guys could spend an hour with Pom on the putting green. You know how the training routines work.'

'Love to help Willis, but I've got a shampoo and set booked,' Charlie said.

'And I'm taking the dog to have his anal glands cleared,' Tim quickly followed.

'Aw come on guys, just an hour, then I'll owe you an hour each of coaching. That's a fantastic deal—isn't it?'

As much as Charlie and Tim were growing to detest Willis more by the minute an hour's coaching with a world-famous international golfer was definitely a coup.

'Okay,' Charlie said, before Tim could answer. See you in an hour.

Willis disappeared into the clubhouse and Tim waved a decidedly nervous looking Pom towards the tranquil and empty putting green two hundred yards to their right. It was bathed in sunlight, but pleasantly dappled by the surrounding trees. The men had met Pom before in passing and as much as they could remember about him was that his English was limited, so consequently he didn't say much. They introduced themselves again and shook Pom's small, soft hand, now starting to get blistered from so much golf practice. Pom seemed uncomfortable as they went through the basic putting stroke with him and got him to do a few practice shots. And when they set up a circle of golf tees three feet from one of the holes on the green, he looked perplexed and wondered what was coming next. Tim placed a golf ball down at the first tee on the immaculately manicured grass surface. 'Ok Pom, now I want you to putt a ball from each of these points into the hole. When you miss one, then go back to the start again. Keep doing that until you get them all in first time, then we'll move the circle further out. OK?'

'No problem,' Pom said as his nervousness seemed to evaporate and he got on with missing the first putt.

'So where are you from in Thailand Pom?' Charlie enquired.

Pom didn't look up from his next putt. 'I from Patong in Phuket Island, sir.'

'And is that where Willis has his golf course?'

'Close to there. On North of island, sir.'

Charlie and Tim were straight into detective mode while they had Pom to themselves for an hour. He was concentrating on putting like an excited child and not thinking about what he was saying. 'So did you to play there and Willis saw your promise?' Tim asked, trying not to laugh.

Pom was returning to the first tee peg in the circle for the fourth time patiently trying to get it right. With head bowed over his putter and concentrating on his shot he said, 'No sir. I no play golf, I work in hotel bar.'

'I thought you wanted to play golf?' Charlie enquired.

'No sir, I no like sport. Only like watch Manchester United on TV. Mr Willis say to try because I am good, but no good.'

'Manchester United, eh?' Tim grimaced. 'Not Tottenham Hotspur or Chelsea?'

'No sir, Manchester United very big in Thailand.' Pom punched the air and smiled broadly as a ball dropped into the cup.

'Yes, I'm sure they are,' Tim replied cynically. 'Now get back to your putting.' He looked at Charlie and whispered, 'Strange oriental customs.'

'So how did you end up in England with Willis then Pom?' Charlie asked.

Pom was missing most of his putts, but still getting excited when he fluked one in. 'I get drinks for Mr Willis every night at hotel, and he say he would help me make passport to England. Say he will give me job.' He was suddenly distracted by a group of Canada geese noisily flying overhead in formation. He had clearly never seen such a spectacle before and was bewitched by them.

'Oh, they are just flying back to their home for the night after feeding in our lake,' Tim said.

Charlie and Tim exchanged an inquisitive glance. 'So where do you live in England Pom?' Charlie asked.

Pom leapt off the ground as a golf ball rolled around the cup and dropped in. 'I live in house in garden near Mr Willis house. He has big house.'

'Yes, we know Pom. so do you live there on your own?'

A brief sadness crept into Pom's eyes. 'Oh no sir, I with many other Thai people who work for Mr Willis, some cleaning, some gardens, some cooking. He nice, but madam, she not so nice.' Pom pulled a scornful childlike face then put a hand to his mouth as he realised what he had been saying. 'You no say I tell you this, Mr Willis he no like.'

Tim patted him on the shoulder, 'Don't worry Pom, we will say nothing about this.' He moved closer to the young Thai and lowered his voice, 'You can always come and talk to us if you want to.'

Before Pom could reply, they heard, 'How's it going guys,' as Willis bellowed from the entrance of the clubhouse to announce his pending arrival at the putting green.

Charlie was quick to say, 'Oh he's getting the hang of it,' before Pom confirmed his inadequacy by prodding his putter clumsily at the ball and missing yet another putt.

Willis put an almost over friendly arm around Pom's waist, and they started off down the path towards the car park. But not before Pom turned and placed his palms together as if in prayer, then bowed slightly towards Tim and Charlie in turn using his traditional Wai gesture. Willis was keen to leave and ushered Pom away, saying—'Thanks, good job, guys. Catch ya later.'

'Hmm,' Tim said, scratching his chin, 'sounds like Willis has several Thais living in the grounds of his house and all of them brought in as hired domestic staff.'

'Well, much as I dislike the bloke, I suppose we could maybe give him the benefit of the doubt for something. I know he's getting cheap labour, but they are probably having a better start in life. And we have evidence he does have a heart. Look what he did for Nathan.'

'Yes, I'll give you that Flinty, but I'm still not sure I'm convinced a drug smuggler would be that benevolent—how about you and your famous intuition?'

'Knowing what we know about him, I don't believe a bloody word of it either, Fev.'

16

Mike Goddard was a large ruddy faced balding man in his sixties, with a personal hygiene problem that everyone but him seemed acutely aware of. And on a clammy July day, it was particularly evident. He was still furious about the deer killing back in April but had seen the appointment of two ex-professional detectives as course marshals a highly positive step. Nonetheless, after three months of his club captaincy, he was not convinced *The Sycamores* management were doing enough to push the police to find the culprit and remove the negative stigma surrounding the club. He was witnessing people refusing to play on his course, and players threatening to cancel membership on a daily basis. Let alone the constant derogatory comments from the press and local community. And this was the day he was going to let the course manager know that his patience was exhausted.

At around midday, Mike stomped out of Craig Galbraith's office in the clubhouse breathing heavily, looking sour faced and angry. He was heading for the bar, having given the club manager that little piece of his mind that was shouting—for god's sake, stop faffing about and get something done about this—I am sick of your excuses.

In the confines of Craig's office, there was still the distinctly human smell that seemed to follow Mike everywhere, and a lingering tension that was almost palpable. Craig knew Mike was right, and he hated having to say, 'I'm waiting for the police to get back to me,' because it implied he didn't care enough and nothing could be further from the truth. He threw open a window to clear the acidic air, gave a deep and troubled sigh, picked up the receiver on his desk phone and tapped in a number he had memorised.

The phone rang four times and a man with a faint west country accent answered. 'Hello, Detective Constable Lee Watkins speaking.'

Craig was relieved he didn't have to wait for a return call or go around the houses to find the policeman dealing with his case. 'Ah, great, hello Lee, it's Craig Galbraith from The Sycamores golf course here. Just wondering if you have made any progress on our case yet. As I've just been reminded it's running into about three months now.'

The policeman took a second to take stock and seemed strangely defensive, 'Oh hello sir, yes, I know, and I was due to give you an update but it's been frantic here, we seemed to have had a spate of illegal immigrants to deal with for some reason. But let me reassure you we haven't been sitting on our hands.'

Craig didn't really want to hear about how difficult life was at the local station. He was impatient for news on the deer killing, especially after the broadside he had just received from Mike Goddard. With some irritation in his voice and determined to lay it on thick, Craig said, 'It's just getting very uncomfortable here, Lee. The members are becoming very anxious and want this solved, with some threatening to leave the club, and you know the kind of members we have here. And as if that weren't bad enough, visitors are giving us a wide berth. We've had functions cancelled and the locals are out searching for people dancing and chanting in the woods. We're even generating deer vigilantes who are patrolling the course at night, for goodness' sake. I get dozens of e-mails and calls every week and I'm afraid very soon something is going to kick off. Especially as the club captain has just ripped me a new arsehole.'

The detective, without a hint of emotion or humour, calmly said, 'I fully understand sir, we are getting those calls and e-mails too. But let me explain what we have done so far, which might give you some comfort, and you are free to pass it on. We've checked the deer carcass, crossbow bolt and immediate surroundings for any useful DNA. And as you know a painstaking search has been undertaken of the area looking for a crossbow or the knife used to butcher the animal, or even any footprints we can lift casts from. We are also trying to trace manufacturers and retailers of crossbow bolts, and who they might have supplied them to. Sadly, we have failed to come up with anything conclusive yet, but that in itself tells us a lot.'

'Really?' Craig said quizzically.

Lee Watkins ignored the obvious sarcasm. 'Yes, it tells us quite clearly that this wasn't just some random event by an opportunist, because we would have found some kind of evidence by now. Whoever did it clearly didn't want to get caught, as they must have worn overshoes, gloves and probably disposable overalls to stop them getting covered in blood - all of which have doubtless been thoroughly disposed of by now. The crossbow bolts are so far untraceable, and our killer is someone who has killed a deer before, most likely a hunter who knows how to kill an animal quickly and cleanly. But that doesn't happen in

England because of the Deer Act, unless there is a legal cull when rifles would be used. So whoever it is may well have picked up their skills in a country where hunting deer is legal.'

Craig stood and gazed aimlessly out of his office window across the course. 'I know I've asked this before, Lee, but why would someone want to go to such lengths to kill a deer in that manner?'

'That's what is eluding us at the moment, sir. This was like a professional killing of an animal, precise, controlled, and so far, untraceable.'

'So that rules out the immigrants you were questioning, then?'

'Yes, we released them quite quickly and they've claimed asylum, now all their mates are arriving. And before you ask, I've run a check on the car wash people that operate from your car park at the course. They are all perfectly legal as far as I can see. I'm not sure whether their pay and how they live is though. But that's another matter. They are Kosovans so we're currently looking into any criminal records from their country. But this crime really doesn't fit with them, only gets the press excited for a while. No, this is far too sophisticated.'

Craig dropped back into his chair and said scornfully, 'Thanks Lee, you've made me feel ten times worse. It would have been better if it had been some passing poacher we couldn't catch. Wait until this gets out.'

'Yes, I know, sorry, sir. But we have the media crawling all over us too, so we are going to ramp up the pressure. You will see much more of us and we'll be asking lots of questions and maybe even visiting people in their homes. Oh, and by the way, is your head professional around?'

Craig quickly checked his desk diary. 'Willis? No, not right now. He's home from the states, pops in now and again, he'll be back in tomorrow morning—why do you ask?'

'Oh, it's just that Americans hunt deer for sport in some states, don't they—just wondered if he's ever done it?'

Craig fell silent in shock. He hadn't ever considered that particular scenario before. Then he suddenly thought his silence could be construed as him knowing something. 'Err, I've no idea if he has Lee. You'll have to ask him yourself.'

'Rest assured, sir, I will. And could you let everyone know we are coming to interview people, we'll start from tomorrow. I'd hate to just turn up unannounced.'

'Yes, of course, I'll brief everyone,' Craig said, feeling pleased his call had at least prompted some action. But was annoyed at himself that it needed a kick from Mike Goddard to jolt him into reacting.

Craig called a staff meeting at three o'clock that afternoon in the boardroom to update everyone about the coming police activity. It was a three-line whip, no excuses and everyone came—even Adriana, albeit she was late. To a person, they all looked shocked when Craig explained the imminent police presence. Outspoken groundsman Jamie Peters complained. 'Oh, come on Craig, it's a bloody deer. They get hit by cars all the time in some places and none of this nonsense goes on. Shouldn't the police be doing something better with their time?'

The group nodded in unison, agreeing with Jamie's dissenting analysis, but none of them were brave enough to speak out. Craig gave a wry smile that wasn't a smile at all, 'The problem is this wasn't an accident, Jamie.' The tone of his voice rose, and he became more authoritative. 'Now none of you are to repeat this OK?' He looked around the room for affirming nods, then said uncomfortably. 'This wasn't some chancer looking for venison, or a cranky cult of some sort, either. The police reckon the killer was careful not to leave clues and knew how to dispatch a deer quickly and cleanly. So, make of that what you will, but we will all be interviewed again and we shouldn't rule out home visits either.'

There were gasps of disbelief mixed with tuts of frustration around the room. Craig uncharacteristically lost his level-headed patience. 'Look, we need to find the bastard who did this, get them nicked, and put it behind us. Otherwise, none of us will have a bloody job. Now help the police as much as you can—meeting over.'

The muttering and grumbling staff all dispersed, and Craig felt vindicated he had very publicly ramped up the pressure on finding the deer killer and played his part in the latter—but, of course, he already knew who was behind it.

At seven thirty that evening, an English mobile phone chirped into life. A look at the screen showed an overseas number dialling. The call was answered, and a male American caller's voice spoke in a commanding tone. There was no response and no pleasantries. The man just gave a simple and stark message before hanging up. 'Do what you gotta do to make this deer problem go away.'

17

Occasionally Craig would ask Charlie and Tim to have a round of golf with a new member or a special guest. It was to help the player get a feel for the course and know where the pitfalls were. Play them in, he'd call it. And he had asked them to go around the course with a chap called Gideon Wells and a companion. No apparent reason why any guidance was needed as it would appear the man was already a member. It was just one of those inexplicable favours that Craig asked of them from time to time.

The round turned out to be on a glorious Wednesday morning in early August. The kind of day that seemed to stay warm and light forever, and twilight looking over the golf course from the clubhouse terrace was as idyllic as a visit to the golf club ever got. It was about seven a.m. when Charlie and Tim arrived at *The Sycamores* car park. As they gathered their clubs from the boot of Charlie's car, they could hear the hum of petrol mowers out cutting the greens. The fairways were still short due to the recent hot spell and very playable if a little dry. Groups of magpies chattered raucously on the ground searching for food as the men walked towards the first tee. While a fox, late to his bed was barking in the distance. At the tee they found two men waiting for them, but strangely, with only one set of golf clubs between them. Craig had arranged the game as always, but this time it was earlier than normal and with a long-established member they both vaguely recognised but had never met.

'Morning chaps,' a tall and upright man in his late forties with a friendly face said in an upper-class English accent. He was dressed in long socks plus fours and a sleeveless sweater with thick, unkempt greying brown wavy hair falling across his face. He thrust out a hand to greet them enthusiastically. 'Gideon Wells, delighted to meet you gentlemen, and thanks for getting up so early. Which one of you is Charlie and which is Tim?'

Charlie shook Gideon's hand first. 'I'm Charlie, the good-looking one.'

'And I'm Tim, the golfer.'

Gideon laughed and gestured with an open palm towards the other man, who had remained silent with a golf bag strapped across his broad shoulders. The man was in his mid-thirties, well over six feet tall and looked physically fit, like a sportsman. And on a hot day, he was wearing a jacket over his casual golf wear and a stoic expression. 'Gentlemen, this is Daniel, and he is actually a very good golfer but will purely be my caddy today.'

The man nodded and spoke with a confident air. 'Gents. It's Danny. Only Gideon and my mother call me Daniel.'

Charlie and Tim looked for a handshake, but Danny stayed firm, and by doing so, announced his clear intention not to engage with them. They gave each other a sideways glance. Neither had played against someone who used a caddy before, especially a caddy who looked like Danny. And they were keen to find out what made Gideon Wells so different.

‘So,’ Gideon said, pushing his Harry Potter style glasses back up the ridge of his nose with an index finger. Then adjusting the floppy cricket sun hat he’d extracted from his golf bag and theatrically dropped on his head. ‘Craig tells me you two are useful. Play off about fifteen, don’t you?’

‘Yes, that’s right Gideon, how about yourself?’ Charlie asked.

‘Oh, on a good day, maybe nine.’

Tim nodded out of respect to a single figure handicapper. ‘We’ve got a game on our hands with you then, Gideon.’

‘Let’s get to it chaps, shall we?’ he said, rubbing his hands together in an excited childlike fashion.

The smell of freshly mown grass was everywhere. The green keepers had been out early and the whirr of sit on mowers and rollers could be heard moving busily from green to green. ‘Odd or Even?’ Gideon asked Charlie with two outstretched clenched fists.

‘Even,’ Charlie replied.

Gideon opened one fist and looked at a number stamped on a golf ball. ‘It’s odd, just like me,’ he laughed. ‘Odd or even Tim?’

‘Even.’

Gideon opened his other fist. ‘It’s odd again, doubly odd. Even more like me, eh Daniel?’

Danny was entirely unmoved and didn’t bother to reply.

‘Ok, I’ll go first, then Charlie, then Tim. Game on chaps. Pass me the driver, please, Daniel.’

They each stepped up to the tee in turn and sent reasonable shots down the first fairway. Gideon went slightly towards the right and enough to make him peel away from Charlie and Tim briefly.

‘He seems down to earth for a toff, doesn’t he?’ Tim said.

Charlie smiled, ‘A bit different isn’t he? We could have some fun here today.’

They played out the par four hole with everyone taking five shots and finishing one over. 'So how do you get to play golf mid-week Gideon, obviously got an understanding employer?' Charlie suggested.

'Yes, I pretty much have a free rein, but I work damn hard when I'm there, so I don't feel guilty in the slightest. And Daniel here is a sweetie. He looks after me whatever I get up to and sometimes he has to turn his head in some of the dubious places I take him.' He chuckled, 'We went to a blues club in Soho last night and I got into a bit of a scrape when I fondled one of the waitresses. Just so difficult not to I find. But Daniel intervened and saved the day. Sadly, we were asked to leave the club, though. I love the blues, don't you? You know that deep south American blues borne out of suffering. Some say it's depressing, but I find it so moving.'

'Sorry, not my cup of tee, Gideon,' Tim said. 'But my friend here is a Clapton freak, so he might well agree with you.'

Gideon's eyes lit up. 'Ah Eric Clapton, probably the finest British guitarist that ever played the blues, truly world class, but he's just an imitator of the originals. I'm sorry, Charlie, a white boy from Surrey doesn't quite have the culture to feel it like the old bluesmen did.'

Charlie looked surprised, 'I'm impressed you know he comes from Surrey though Gideon.'

Gideon smiled broadly. 'The definition of an expert, Charlie, is someone who knows more and more about less and less. My entire being revolves around only four things: my work, golf, the blues—and sex.' He roared with laughter, and Danny's eyes looked skyward as he shook his head.

'So, what is it you do for a living, Gideon?' Tim asked quickly trying to change the subject.

'I work for the government, chum.'

'In what capacity?'

'I work in research.'

'What branch of research?'

Danny gave a smile with a definite hint of menace behind it. 'Too many questions gents, why don't you just concentrate on your golf.'

That rebuff was enough to confirm to both Charlie and Tim that Danny was a little more than a caddy—and Gideon was substantially more than a civil servant.

On the fifth hole, Charlie hit a momentous slice deep into the bracken at the edge of the fairway. 'Oh, hard lines chum,' Gideon said, knowing his ball was resting safely in the middle of the fairway.

Charlie threw his golf bag over a shoulder and started to walk off towards the bracken. 'Don't worry Gideon, you'll find that we know our way around this course with our eyes closed.'

Danny's calm but confident south London accented voice came from behind Charlie. 'You'll have to play another ball mate and take three shots off the tee as a penalty.' He pulled a brand-new golf ball out of Gideon's bag and lobbed it gently towards Charlie. 'Here use one of these. I don't want you diving around in the undergrowth where I can't see you. Anyway, you couldn't play your ball from out of that stuff.'

Charlie, concerned by Danny's distrust, hit a much better shot second time, and Gideon almost felt the need to apologise for Danny's curt intervention, 'Nice shot chum, it's just that I need to keep moving, got an extraordinarily busy day after this.'

'No problem,' Charlie said with his brain racing into overdrive.

All the way round the course Gideon was dropping unnecessary, and often cringeworthy, sexual innuendo into the conversation, usually about Adriana. And the challenge for Charlie and Tim was no longer about golf but keeping his conversation above the waist. 'So, are you married, Gideon?' Charlie asked innocently.

Another uncontrolled laugh escaped from Gideon. 'Good heavens no Charlie, I couldn't tie myself down to one woman.' He chuckled again, 'Well let me rephrase that, I could tie myself to a woman—and often have—but never for life. Oh no, I like to play around far too much, and I don't mean golf.'

It quickly became evident to Charlie and Tim that Gideon was frighteningly intelligent by the speed of his responses and opinions about current events thrown into the parts of their discussions that were polite. It seemed likely that he was the product of a public school and Oxbridge education, but in amongst all that undoubted intellect, he was definitely off the wall. They drew the rapid conclusion that the fine line between genius and insanity was a tightrope Gideon teetered on every day.

On the fourteenth hole while Gideon and Danny were searching in the light rough grass for a golf ball, Charlie commented, 'He's got to be doing something pretty bloody serious Fev, to have a bodyguard like Danny.'

Tim nodded. 'He's Protection Command from the Met by the looks of it Flinty. They obviously need to keep Gideon safe for some reason.'

Charlie pondered, 'And the club having Japanese owners probably makes his employers a bit twitchy about him playing here,'

After the round, as was tradition, the men all shook hands, all except Danny, who made no attempt to move or speak. 'Buy you chaps a drink?' Charlie asked, 'You beat us fair and square today Gideon. Even if your handicap is a bit suspect.'

'A lovely thought Charlie, but Daniel and I have to get changed and go to work for the day. Plus, I really must try to get a glimpse of Adriana before we leave. What an enchanting little thing she is. And I am totally under her spell.'

Gideon and Danny disappeared down the concrete path from the eighteenth green towards the clubhouse and the showers. While Charlie and Tim walked to the pro-shop to pick up any jobs that might have come in for them.

'No, you're ok gents,' Ben Tillman said at the shop counter, 'Nothing outstanding for you to do. But could one of you do me a favour, please? Paul, the electrician we've got working in the male changing area, reckons someone has been pinching some of his stuff. You couldn't go and have a word with him, could you?'

'Yeah, I'll go,' Tim said. 'You head back to the shed and get the kettle on Flinty. I won't be long.'

'Good idea Mr Plod, see you back at the ranch,' Charlie replied.

Tim found Paul the electrician halfway up a stepladder running cables in the corridor ceiling void outside the changing room. 'Hello, I'm Tim,' he shouted. 'I understand you've had some things stolen, Paul. What have you lost, exactly?'

Paul came down from his stepladder, 'Well to be honest Tim it wasn't much, I nipped into the clubhouse to get a cup of tea, and when I got back, I'd lost a box of clips, a pack of large cable ties and a screwdriver. Someone wanting to do some DIY at home, probably?'

Tim groaned in disbelief. 'Yes, you're probably right Paul, it's a bit hard to believe in a club like this, isn't it? Now, I have to ask if you want me to call the police and report this.'

Paul shook his head. 'Nah, it was my fault for leaving my

gear out, just thought it would be safe here. I should have known better. Just annoying though, if they'd have asked I probably would have given them what they wanted - why do people have to steal things?'

Tim frowned, 'I don't know mate, I spent a whole career trying to work that one out. Now you're sure that you don't want to take this any further? We will, of course, circulate a message to the members. And we have had some visitors today who we will contact.'

'No, it's alright Tim, but thanks for coming over. Just thought I ought to report it.'

Back in the executive shiny shed, Tim relayed the story to Charlie, and then continued with some excitement in his voice. 'I left Paul and walked into the changing room to check on the notice board for competitions coming up, and while I was there, I spotted Gideon coming out of the shower. You won't believe it Flinty, that a bloke like him would have a large tattoo on his back.'

'Really? He's full of surprises, isn't he—what was it?'

'Couldn't see it close up and didn't want a bloke that weird to think I was paying him particular attention while he was half naked. But it was some kind of scene, and in the middle was a bloke carrying a guitar case.'

'Obviously a blues homage thing.'

'Yeah, blind howling muddy lemon or someone, probably.'

'Shut up, you philistine.'

Tim laughed. 'But the other thing is that Danny was sitting in the hot and sweaty changing room waiting for Gideon, and still wearing his jacket. And do you know why he's wearing a jacket Flinty?'

'Go on, surprise me.'

'Because he's carrying a gun.'

18

It was a sweltering twenty-eight degrees at eleven thirty out on the golf course, while Ben Tilman stood alone in the proshop. Willis Martin had taken yet another of his trips abroad and James Cole was out on the practice range giving golf lessons to a group of enthusiastic junior players on their school holidays. On such a warm day Ben didn't mind being on his own in the cool air-conditioned environment. Particularly as, for once, he knew James was doing his job and not with Adriana. He knew that because Mrs Willis Martin had just walked into his empty shop. On that day she hadn't breezed in with her normal egotistical air of importance dictating instructions to her subservient assistant Kate. She was on her own and looking absolutely gorgeous in a body-hugging black dress and high heels, which hadn't escaped Ben—even though he pretended it had.

Ben was leaning his elbows heavily on the glass counter intently studying his computer screen while doing his best not to stare as he timidly looked up at Adriana's perfect smiling face getting closer. Although she had been into the shop many times to see her husband, Adriana had never really spoken to Ben before, and he was rather hoping it was going to stay that way. He wanted her to disappear into the back office, grab some paperwork, then leave with her nose in the air as she normally did when the shop was busy. As she approached the counter, he began to feel hot and embarrassed. He knew if she asked him something he was going to stumble over his words like a shy and clumsy schoolboy not worthy of speaking to such a beauty. Ben had never been good with girls. The truth was he hadn't had much experience, and always hid himself away within a golfing career. He knew he could never rival James in the looks department, plus he lacked self-esteem and the confidence to develop relationships with the opposite sex. As he moved to stand upright, he lost all concentration and his elbow slipped off the edge of the counter causing his chin to smash into the glass countertop like an unintended slapstick moment. Pain seared through his face and he desperately wanted to grasp his chin and swear loudly, but he resisted and gave a sweet forced smile for Adriana's benefit. His awkwardness in her presence was so very obvious—and she knew it.

Ben could feel himself blushing before he uttered a word. He just couldn't control his bashfulness and thought Adriana must surely think him completely stupid. His heart rate was rising fast and even in the chill of the room he felt perspiration rolling between his shoulder blades causing his polo shirt to cling uncomfortably to his body. 'Oh, err, good morning, Mrs Martin, what can I do for you today?' he stuttered.

Adriana placed both hands on the countertop and seductively positioned her face no more than twelve inches from Ben's, now paralysed by fear and glowing cherry red. She spoke softly in a cut glass English accent, that he always found so sexy but hadn't dared tell anyone. 'Oh, stop it silly, my name is Adriana, no need for formality. I want us to become friends and I'm so sorry for not coming to see you more often. Whatever was I thinking.'

Ben was rooted to the spot. No matter how uneasy he felt, moving in any direction just wasn't an option. It would only lead to more clumsiness. He knew someone as glamorous as Adriana had no interest in him but was beginning to enjoy her closeness. He didn't care that her slow, deliberate and perfectly formed words seemed contrived as he inhaled the sweet fragrance of her perfume. Not cheap and overpowering like something that might be used by some of the older women in the office, but subtle and sophisticated. As she spoke a tingling sensation crept across the top of his head numbing his senses, he could have just closed his eyes and listened to her heavenly voice forever. Ben didn't quite know what to say to Adriana for fear of making a fool of himself, but he had to say something. 'Oh, that's alright. I'm usually pretty busy most of the time anyway,' he said through a forced smile.

Adriana reached over and gently stroked the smooth skin of his face with the palm of her hand, it felt cool and soft against his hot cheek. 'Yes, bless you darling. While my husband is doing whatever it is he does in America and the far east you are carrying most of the burden back here for him. Especially while that lazy charlatan James wastes his days chasing after me and anything else in a skirt.'

Ben suddenly lost some of his clumsiness and started to focus when James was mentioned, delighted to hear that the sordid boasts of Adriana's infatuation with him were untrue. And he had to discover more. 'Oh, I'm sorry I thought that you and James were—'

'Sleeping together?' Adriana said without flinching. 'Well yes, I suppose so.'

Adriana turned away from the desk and started to feel the material of some golf sweaters that she had no interest in. 'Well, he is not without his charms but he has no substance. He's just an infantile pretty boy with an inflated opinion of himself and I'm exhausted by his persistent attention. I was just toying with him for my own amusement but he is becoming obsessive. Trouble is I've broken my own rule really darling, I never get involved with people I can't trust.'

Ben's emotions were fast turning from embarrassment to anger, anger towards James who had surely been lying about this beautiful woman who was showing him warmth. 'But what about Willis?' He asked.

Adriana gushed a laugh and turned back from the sweaters towards Ben. 'Oh darling, Willis and I famously have what they call an open relationship. We both do whatever and - whoever - we wish. He drifts around the world shagging golf groupies, and I entertain myself here. Anything goes with us. There are no recriminations, no jealousy, no questions and the public only see a happy couple and that's how it's going to stay. Now getting back to that trust thing, Ben darling.' She walked the few paces over to his side moving her hips like a catwalk model and he started to lose control of his mind again. He could feel the blood surge up his neck and move throbbing into his head, this woman oozed sexuality, in her every movement and every word. And as much as he knew her outrageously flirtatious behaviour would lead to nothing, Ben was praying no-one would enter the shop to spoil his brief voyage on cloud nine.

Adriana gently leaned her body sideways into Ben's, she stroked his forearm softly and whispered, 'I understand from the pretty boy that you are a very good DJ when you are not working here?'

'Oh, I get it,' Ben said, stepping away abruptly and feeling hurt that the attention, however delicious, was only for long enough to get something she wanted. 'You want me to come and DJ for you.'

Adriana saw his offended body language and heard the wounded tone in his voice and realised she needed to quickly recover the situation. Nothing new, or difficult, for a woman as controlling and resourceful as her. Adriana simply made eye contact with Ben. Sucking him in with her deep chestnut eyes, until he started to melt all over again. 'Yes darling, that is true, but let me explain what I have in mind. You see, I throw lavish parties at our house now and again where I need to have good quality music provided. Of course we know lots of rich and famous people who like to let their hair down—and this is where the trust comes in. The parties can sometimes get a little racy, if you know what I mean darling.' She looked at Ben to test the level of shock on his face, he was still mesmerised and hanging on her every word. 'We tried just playing pre-recorded music, but it was a little flat, besides the person that does it for us has fallen ill at the last minute. Then we thought a competent DJ would provide a little more atmosphere and get everyone going. Anyway, I can't just pick some random DJ off the internet who thinks it might be a good idea to run to the tabloids once they see who is attending, if you get my understanding?'

'I do.' Ben said, rapidly falling in and warming to the idea of mingling with celebrities who could hear what a good DJ he was. And might even offer him a route to fame and fortune.

'So darling, if you think you could do that little thing for me discreetly, then you would be very well paid.' She moved the few paces towards Ben slowly with every step full of lust and her arms raised signalling an embrace. She wrapped her arms slowly around Ben's neck, her bright red full lips were within an inch of his face. 'And if you are interested, I can arrange a little bonus for you. How does that sound, darling?'

Ben's hormones were on fire. There was a knot twisting in his stomach. His head was dizzy and he could hardly speak. 'Mmm,' he mumbled as Adriana slowly forced her tongue into his mouth for only a second.

Adriana leaned backwards gently rubbed the flat of her hand across Ben's chest then erotically coiled a leg around him purposely exposing a stocking top. 'Of course your bonus will be me,' she said, licking her lips provocatively. Ben's eyes were spinning as though he had been drugged. 'Do we have a deal darling?' She whispered erotically in his ear as a shiver ran through his entire body.

Ben was hypnotised like a cobra by a snake charmer. 'Yes, we have a deal, and you can trust me,' he whispered submissively.

Adriana took Ben's quivering hand and placed it down the top of her dress and rested it on her breast. 'Yours whenever you want to take it,' she murmured seductively. Ben closed his eyes in a moment of ecstasy until he heard the click of the shop door opening. He swiftly removed his hand and glowed red again hoping he hadn't been spotted. Unlike Adriana who had no remorse and walked from the shop grinning triumphantly. 'I'll be in touch darling,' she said, knowing that poor gullible Ben would now do absolutely anything she asked.

19

At one o'clock, Craig Galbraith was standing behind the counter in the clubhouse's terrace bar working a gleaming chrome coffee machine that was hissing and spitting steam while making his usual double shot cappuccino. Craig was a creature of habit, he always took something to eat from the kitchen and the same coffee back to his office and locked himself in at lunchtime - even though he continued to work he liked to eat in peace. With coffee in hand he was headed for the kitchen, but before he got anywhere near collecting his lunch Charlie and Tim were waiting to ambush him. Had it been anyone else Craig might have been offended by the interruption to his routine, but he always seemed to welcome their company.

As Craig stepped out from behind the bar and took a polite sip from one of the club's best china cups Tim asked, 'So what's with this Gideon bloke you set us up with today then Craig, that's got to be the weirdest round of golf we've ever had?'

Craig smiled knowingly through a foamed milk moustache, 'Ah yes, Professor Wells, he's an interesting character, isn't he?'

'Professor?' Charlie said in disbelief. 'He didn't tell us that. But we knew he had to be someone pretty senior to have a minder.'

Craig clinked his coffee cup back into its saucer. 'No -one really knows what he does and he never talks about it. He's been with us from the opening of The Sycamores and is only listed as a civil servant on his membership form. All I know is he lives locally, loves to play golf and gets here as often as he can. Usually he plays on his own, well I say on his own with his bodyguard, I mean caddy, is always with him.'

'Yes, wouldn't want to upset Danny would you, he looks like he might be ex-SAS or something,' Tim interrupted.

'Exactly,' Craig replied. 'Gideon likes to play against different people now and again but is very particular who he plays with. He has declined members I have suggested before so I thought with your credentials you two were a safe bet.'

Charlie grinned, 'And that's why they didn't once ask what we used to do for a living or our family background, you had briefed them and they checked us out.'

'I can only presume that must be the case Charlie, I just gave him your names. Anyway I've had no complaints so I suspect he'll want to play again sometime, that ok with you?'

'Sure,' Tim said, 'no problem. He is a bit eccentric but quite entertaining.'

Craig tipped his cup to his mouth and drained it of coffee. 'Only problem is that Willis can't abide him, calls him a wacko.'

Charlie scoffed, 'You mean he doesn't like peculiar upper class English people? So why did he marry one?'

They all laughed, and Craig said, 'Reading between the lines, I think that is Willis's problem. I could be wrong, but our professor is rather fond of the ladies, and I think he may be more than a little bewitched by Adriana. And Willis has taken exception to it.'

Tim nodded in agreement. 'Yes, Gideon did mention something about wanting to drink her bathwater earlier.'

Charlie said caustically, 'Ha, that's bloody rich of Willis after allowing his wife to throw herself at anything in trousers. Why should Gideon be any different?'

Craig shrugged his shoulders and turned back towards the coffee machine, 'Don't ask me, you two are the detectives. You work it out. I'm only interested in running the club and keeping everyone happy. Now if you don't mind boys, I'm going to get another coffee. That one was cold.'

Exactly one week later, Charlie and Tim were en route to the shiny shed for lunch. They walked past Ben who was practicing on the pitching green. They were perfectly content to have the usual raised hand as an acknowledgement from a distance and get back for their break. But Ben wasn't having any of it. He was buzzing about something and with a golf club still in his hand ran over in an animated fashion clearly wanting to talk.

'Hello Gents, are you ok?' Ben asked excitedly, obviously hoping to prompt the same question in return.

Tim replied in kind, 'We're fine mate, how about you?'

'Brilliant, I'm just brilliant.'

'Excuse me for asking Ben, but are you on drugs by any chance?' Charlie asked flippantly, intrigued by the permanent grin on the young professional's usually depressed face.

'No,' Ben said quite seriously. 'Never touch them. But I did a private gig last night that was way better than drugs and I've got to tell someone about it, and you are the only people I can trust.'

'So how do you know it was better than drugs if you've never tried them?' Tim asked.

Undeterred by Tim's well intended nit picking Ben replied, 'Oh, you know what I mean.'

Tim cast Charlie a frustrated glance. 'Flinty, did you ever think all those years of fighting criminals would have led to us becoming agony aunts? Come on Ben, let's go to the shiny shed and hear your story. This had better be good though to interrupt our lunch break.'

'Oh, don't worry Tim it is,' Ben replied.

Charlie unlocked a brass padlock on the shed's door which creaked on its steel frame as it swung open. The smell of stale dried grass from the mowing equipment next door filled the room. 'Take a seat at the boardroom table in one of the high backed executive leather chairs Ben,' he said. But the humour was wasted on the young golfer who was just itching to tell them his tale. Charlie and Tim both assumed this unusual behaviour was just the exuberance of youth and would be something to tolerate and smile sweetly through, while being completely underwhelmed.

'Okay Ben, the floor is yours,' Tim said. 'What's on your mind?'

Ben was so excited he sprang to his feet. 'I know I shouldn't be telling you this, but only a couple of days ago Adriana asked me to do some DJing for a party at her house. She had told me there would be famous people there and in the nicest possible way that I should keep my mouth shut if I saw anyone I recognised. Well, I got taken to Eagle House, where her and Willis live. It's like a mansion way out in the country, it's a really fantastic place. Anyway they shut me away in a spare bedroom to set up and plug into their sound system, so I was doing the gig blind. I guess that was so I couldn't see what was going on around the house, cos she said it sometimes got a bit saucy. But I noticed a couple of celebs on my way in and out.'

'Really?' Charlie said, taking more of an interest.

'Yes, that bloke who does the holiday programmes was there and a couple of famous politicians, oh and the weatherman who is on late at night. They were just hanging about waiting for transport. That was all I saw really, as I was escorted in and out by big scary security blokes and driven home.'

'And you didn't see what was going on during the party, then?' Charlie asked.

'No, they kept me locked in and brought me food and drink until it was time to go.' Ben tapped his nose to indicate he'd worked out that all may not have been what it seemed. 'But they wouldn't keep me out of the way all night if it was a normal party, would they? They paid me about five times what the job was worth and booked me for the next one whenever that is—October, I think they said. And what a house. Wow, it was amazing, like something from the movies.'

'Yeah, we get the picture. You're rambling now, mate,' Tim said, rapidly losing interest.

Charlie glared at his friend for being insensitive. 'So you didn't see Willis or Adriana then Ben?'

'No, not once. The security people dealt with everything. I'd better go now and let you get on. Sorry if I'm being boring, it's just that I've never experienced anything like that in my life before, and it was just killing me not being able to tell anybody.'

Charlie said, 'Sounds like a great night Ben, maybe you'll see more on the next one. Perhaps they were just giving you a trial on your first session, eh?'

'Yes, hadn't thought of that,' Ben replied, grinning from

ear to ear. Almost as an afterthought, he turned and said, 'And you won't say anything, will you?'

'Of course not,' Tim replied a little more tolerantly as Ben almost skipped out of the door. With the overriding thought in his mind that he still had Adriana's bonus to cash in.

Tim walked across the room and took a pre-packed sandwich from a small fridge on a workbench. 'I'll tell you what Flinty, there were obviously some very famous people at that party. Too famous to risk young Ben getting a glimpse of and based on him singing like a canary to us, just now they were right to keep him locked up. Just lucky they didn't have a fire, eh?'

Charlie flicked down a switch on the electric kettle and said, 'Especially as we now know where Willis's cocaine must be going.'

Tim nodded. 'Yes, and we can have a pretty good guess where young Pom and all his Thai friends fit into the operation, too.'

20

The affair that James Cole was having with Adriana Martin continued to be the talk of the club. She could easily manage any gossip and carry out her responsibilities as normal. Conversely, James was becoming more infatuated by the day, to a point where nothing else in the world seemed to matter to him. Members were regularly being let down and Craig was getting complaints about James that he simply couldn't put off dealing with any longer. Especially after previous friendly informal chats had fallen on deaf ears. But before he could send out a letter formally inviting James to a disciplinary meeting Adriana had plans to deal with the matter in her own way. She did not enjoy the attention James's obsession was attracting, or his inability to deal with the situation. Particularly as it was affecting the club, and now her husband Willis was back in the country.

E-mail from Adriana's office computer to James in the pro-shop at 10 a.m: We need to meet.

James's immediate reply: Absolutely. What did you have in mind? I've got plenty of things in mind.

Adriana: I'm busy today so you will have to stay late, I'll meet you at six in the admin office.

James: I'll be there, and I'll be ready.

Adriana: I simply want to have a conversation.

The tone of Adriana's communications were always kept entirely professional. Unlike James, who could never quite shake off his immature lothario image, even when using e-mail and text.

August had been hot and the inevitable thunderstorms brewing for days, and this was the day they arrived with a vengeance, stopping all activity on the course. Throughout the day and while confined indoors, James became preoccupied by Adriana's message wondering what it might mean. Could she be wanting to move their relationship to another level perhaps? She certainly wasn't anything other than enthusiastic with him the last time they met. And the brusque tone of her e-mail was just typical of her professionalism at work and nothing to be concerned about. Not able to concentrate on any kind of work, James wished away the hours until six. He was desperate to hear what surely must only be good news from his lover. James had convinced Ben that he needed to stay on and catch up on paperwork, and Ben didn't need telling twice to have an early night, even if he was highly suspicious of James's motives. After spending ten minutes in the washroom checking his hair and using fresh breath spray, James ran the short pathway to the clubhouse to avoid the worst of the heavy rain. He arrived in the clubhouse at just before six in the evening and walked past The Terrace bar where Willis Martin was busy schmoozing clients and knew the famous golfer would be there for hours. While his wife would be alone and available upstairs. James sprang eagerly up a single flight of hardwood open tread stairs two steps at a time to the admin office. The office had a desk in each corner and ivory-coloured vertical blinds at the windows that were half closed to the sun. The room smelt of stale coffee, copier paper and a subtle hint of an expensive perfume he recognised immediately. The area was flooded by fluorescent light and empty of people, apart from the woman he was besotted with. She was sitting at the furthest desk behind a computer screen and surrounded by professionally taken pictures of *The Sycamores* hanging on the walls. As always, Adriana looked immaculate wearing a black trouser suit and with her hair up. 'You wanted to talk,' James said excitedly.

'Yes, thanks for coming,' Adriana replied impassively, and with a totally blank expression. She removed her large black rimmed reading glasses, 'Have a seat.'

'Bit formal, isn't it?' James replied.

She glanced up from her screen, gave him eye contact and said casually, 'We're done, darling.'

James turned his head sharply like an intrigued dog. 'Sorry?'

'We are finished, over and done, at an end, no more, finito, kaput. Put it however you want darling, but our little arrangement is terminated forthwith.'

James gave a disbelieving smile. 'You're kidding—right?'

'No darling, I absolutely am not kidding. Willis is back and its run its course. So no more silly messages or childish innuendos in public. Please, put it behind you and move on.'

James wasn't used to getting the brush off from women, that's what he usually did to them. He was often brutal with his rejections and seemingly derived some kind of sick pleasure while retaining complete control. Uncharacteristically, he had fallen for Adriana in a way he never had with any woman before. He protested, 'But we were great together. You could never get that from Willis. Leave him and move in with me.'

Adriana roared with laughter. 'Don't be ridiculous

darling, you are completely incapable of giving me the kind of lifestyle I crave. We were just a passing moment, that's all, and I could never be exclusive to anyone.'

James was in complete denial. This just wasn't happening to him, it never happened to him, and he wasn't taking it without a fight. 'OK, I'll have to learn to deal with that somehow, but I don't want to let you go.'

'This really isn't up for negotiation, darling,' Adriana said, as she slipped her glasses back on and her focus moved back to the computer screen. Her body language indicating that the subject was closed.

James placed his hands on the desk and leaned towards her hoping his closeness might make her weaken and change her mind. He was convinced she had to be steeling herself to resist him and finding the conversation terribly difficult—she wasn't. Without moving her gaze from the screen, she said, 'If you don't mind, darling, you are invading my space and I am rather busy.'

James backed away suitably rebuked. He was filling with emotion and for the first time in his life prepared to beg. 'What have I got to do, Adriana? Just tell me and I'll do it. I really can't bear to live without you.'

'Oh, don't get dramatic darling, it's so unbecoming. What you've got to do is grow up, get out of here and stop bothering me—right now.'

James was devastated by Adriana's abrupt and insensitive rejection, and his complete inability to reverse her decision. His pain quickly turned to anger and thoughts of retribution. 'Ok then,' he said confidently, 'I didn't want to do this, but if you really won't see me, I'll go to the police and get them to investigate whatever Willis is doing with his imported golf clubs. I'm not stupid you know. I can see what's going on. And I'm sure you don't want coppers crawling all over your mansion. Willis in prison would make you both front page news, and you wouldn't want that, would you?' James had a smug grin on his face like he was just about to declare checkmate. 'So, I think you really need to reconsider your position, Adriana.'

Adriana didn't move her concentration from the computer screen for a moment, and said calmly, 'I think it's you that needs to reconsider darling, you are way out of your depth here. A spurned lover, with no evidence, trying to convince the police that an international sports legend, with expensive lawyers, might just be up to no good—really? Your name would be ruined, and you would never work again. And let's not forget how annoyed the Japanese owners would be to have their golden boy upset. Not a fight anybody sensible would want to pick, is it? Now just go away, or do your worst. You are getting tiresome.'

James was fuming inside realising his knee-jerk threat was far from checkmate after all, and he was nowhere near brave enough to call Adriana's bluff. But he had to retain some dignity after his very first agonising taste of being dumped by a woman. 'Ok then, but you will live to regret this,' he said, prodding a finger aggressively at her.

'Are you still here darling?' Came from behind the computer screen.

James took a slow and disciplined walk out of the office and down the stairs past the bar where Adriana's husband was still charming his fawning clients. Once out of sight, James ran at full tilt from the clubhouse through the teeming rain into the car park, and furiously kicked at a fibre glass waste bin on the way. Then with drenched clothes clinging to his body, and fuelled by adrenaline, he sprinted into the empty darkness towards the practice area. He was oblivious to the sound of rain bouncing off the steel sheds or a gutter that was overflowing noisily on one of the outbuildings. James stopped to gather his breath for a moment, then picked up some practice golf balls and threw them as hard as he could across the open grass expanse of the driving range. He bellowed, 'Biiiiitch,' several times at the sky before collapsing to his knees into the sodden turf and bursting into a fit of uncontrollable sobbing. He was impervious to the unrelenting rain soaking his shuddering body while he repeatedly shouted expletives to the heavens. He was going to make Adriana pay.

21

Ben Tilman was a conscientious individual. He had been in the pro-shop since seven thirty and was busy booking in customers when Adriana Martin sashayed in holding an envelope at nine o'clock. She gently placed it on the glass topped counter in front of him mouthed, 'for you,' blew him a kiss and left glancing over her shoulder and smiling as she walked out through the open glass door.

'Aren't you a lucky boy,' one of the middle-aged visiting golfers said to Ben as he looked down at the bright red imprint of a perfectly formed pair of lips across the seal of the envelope.

The colour deepened in Ben's cheeks. He felt embarrassed and didn't quite know how to respond. Then he realised the man had assumed the elegant enchantress who had just breezed in was his sweetheart. He was about to make light of it and say, 'Oh, it's just the boss's wife. She's a bit of a wag.' But instead he decided to revel in the moment, knowing he was unlikely to ever see the man again, and particularly not in Adriana's company. He gave a half smile and said, 'Yes, she's alright isn't she, but I've told her not to pester me when I'm busy.'

The man laughed as he took his score cards and turned to walk towards his waiting friends outside. 'She could pester me any time she likes,' he said.

As the shop cleared, Ben gazed longingly at Adriana's ruby coloured kiss on the envelope meant just for him. He hated to destroy the perfect and delicate symmetry of her lips but was desperate to find out what was inside. Carefully he eased open the triangular section of the envelope, thinking he might just keep it forever. It revealed a folded notelet that she had unmistakably sprayed with her hallmark floral perfume. With great anticipation, he pulled out the note and flipped it open, in blue fountain pen ink it read. *In Confidence - As discussed, date of next party October 25th. More of your brilliant music please—and don't forget to tell me when you want to claim your bonus!*

Ben's mouth went dry, and he flushed again but this time with excitement, only to have to quickly fold up the note and envelope thrust them into a trouser pocket as another wave of golfers entered.

James Cole walked into the shop late, as usual, looking like he hadn't slept all night and with his normally immaculate styled blond locks decidedly wayward. He had not shaved or showered but managed to change out of his muddy clothes. And if Ben's sense of smell was correct, he had been drinking heavily the night before.'

As the last of the golfers left the shop heading for the first tee, Ben cast a disapproving glance towards his dishevelled colleague. 'You'd better get some coffee in you before Willis gets here—you stink of booze.'

James gave Ben a disdainful look. 'Yeah Willis, bloody Willis, so what gives him the right to breeze in at whatever time he likes and criticise me for having a few beers last night then?'

'Well, how about being a household name on the

international golf circuit. And having a contract that says he would have to kill someone before the Japanese owners might ever think about sacking him?'

James grunted as he walked into the back office, filled the electric kettle with water and flicked it on. Cups and spoons rattled in the background and the boiling water stopped bubbling in the kettle. James suddenly stopped what he was doing and stepped back into the shop looking alarmed. He sniffed the air inquisitively, then turned towards Ben. 'She's been here hasn't she? That bitch has been in here, I can smell her perfume.'

'Search me,' Ben replied flippantly, thinking lying would be better than entering into an argument. 'But it is her husband's business, so she has every right to be here.'

James walked back into the shop and leaned forcefully towards Ben's face. 'She's been in here talking about me, hasn't she.'

Ben simply turned away, refusing to react. 'You're getting paranoid mate, just drink your coffee.'

But James wouldn't let it go and tugged on Ben's shoulder forcing him to turn back. 'That cow has been in here slagging me off, hasn't she—what did she say—tell me?'

Inside Ben felt quietly pleased that pretty boy James, who found life and girls so easy, was suffering, and he enjoyed the moment of sweet retribution. Nonetheless, he was starting to get irritated by the increasing aggression and physicality towards him. He lifted James's hand from his shoulder and glared at the broken man before him. The reason for his appearance and irrational behaviour was now patently obvious. 'Oh, I get it, she's dumped you hasn't she, and you can't deal with it.'

'Piss off.'

Ben had a sickly grin on his face as he revelled in saying,

'Well some days you're the pigeon and some days you're the statue.' Knowing full well that James had never once been the statue until he got involved with Adriana. Then he so vividly remembered that brief sublime kiss with Adriana and the sensual touch of her breast from a couple of weeks before. It had really happened, it wasn't just a dream men like him have. He could still taste and feel her. And if he could only have Adriana for the briefest of moments then that would be enough for him, and he would surely handle it so much better than James. But now James was being disrespectful to the woman who had taken control of his heart, and his head—and he didn't like it. 'Just get over it, James. Start doing your job, and you'll soon move onto someone else. It was never going to last was it?'

But anger and humiliation were making James lose control of his senses and he started to cross the personal boundaries between them. 'How would an ugly little sod like you ever know how to get over a woman like Adriana?'

'Don't push your luck, James, just man up, will you.'

'What was she in here for?' He demanded.

'She came to see me about my deejaying stuff, that's all. She seemed interested.'

James sneered. 'She isn't interested in you, you muppet. Why would she be—she's only interested in what you can do for her.'

'That's not how I saw it,' Ben said, remembering the wonderful feel of Adriana's warm soft flesh again, and her promise of intimacy.

'Yeah, anything you say mate, but she'll make a fool of you then spit you out when she's done. I was just her bit of rough for a while. That woman doesn't have rules, and she'll get into your head.'

Ben smirked. 'You're just jealous that she likes me.'

James laughed sarcastically. 'I've told you Ben, she

doesn't like you at all. She's just using you. Why on earth would she ever be interested in a creature like you?'

Ben couldn't contain himself any longer. 'I've warned you, James. And if you must know, she thinks you are boring and immature, and she was sick of you always pestering her. That's obviously why she dumped you.'

Just then the door to the shop clicked open and in walked Charlie and Tim to check on course activity as they did most days. They were met by the sight of the two men squaring up to each other ready to fight and so pumped up they were unaware they had company.

'You lying bastard,' James shouted as he threw a punch at Ben's head that he easily dodged.

In his temper James had lost sight of his normal lover not a fighter mindset, and also that in a skirmish his tall, slight frame would be no match for Ben's more stocky and muscular physique - not forgetting his martial arts training. In one deft movement, Ben span his body through ninety degrees and smashed his right fist square between James's eyes like he had been saving it up forever. There was a sickly wet crunching noise, a scream, and James immediately went down. Ben followed up quickly with a hand clasped tightly around James's throat, pinning him to the floor.

'What the hell's going on here?' Tim shouted as he and Charlie ran behind the counter and pulled Ben off. 'Pack this up before anyone sees you. What is wrong with you two?'

'Piece of shit!' Ben exclaimed while struggling against Tim's solid grip and wanting to inflict more damage on James.'

Charlie helped James up from the floor. There was blood streaming down his face from a broken and swollen nose and both eyes were starting to bruise badly. 'Go and clean yourself up quickly before anybody comes in. What on earth are you two fighting about?'

'Adriana.' James said, wiping the blood from his nose on the back of his hand. 'That bitch Adriana.'

Charlie gave Tim a knowing look as James left with a wad of tissues clamped to his face while Ben was shouting, 'Not so pretty now, eh. Next time I'll kill you.'

22

Ben and James were back at work the next day, both ashamed and prepared to lie through their teeth about their altercation and the very obvious damage to James's face. They had been instructed by both Willis and Craig to be at the course early as there was an important event taking place with many local dignitaries and businessmen participating. This was the long-awaited day for the veterans annual grudge match between teams from *The Sycamores* and local club *Woodland Lakes* competing for the *Stanley cup*. It was a serious contest but involved even more serious after match socialising, and it was *The Sycamores'* turn to host the event. As course marshals, Charlie and Tim were going to have to be on their toes to keep everyone moving, because the overriding motivation was to get everyone back for the lunch and no-one wanted to be late. Plus Willis was lined up to do an after lunch speech and present the cup, complete with local paparazzi in tow. It was a legendary fixture, with wives, friends and taxi drivers all on standby to pick up inebriated contestants at about three o'clock before the roads got busy with school traffic. The first call of the day for Charlie and Tim was a message on their radio from one of the groundsmen that smoke was drifting across the fairways adjacent to the twelfth green. Tim looked at Charlie and they said in unison, 'Nathan,' as they started off from outside the clubhouse in their buggy towards his favourite bonfire spot.

The green keepers had asked Nathan to go out extra early and collect any fallen debris from trees off the fairways and greens after high winds overnight, and he had taken it upon himself to burn them. From a distance, Charlie and Tim could catch the sweet odour of fruitwood smouldering and see clouds of grey smoke from burning wet timber drifting in the light breeze of a warm but overcast summer's day. Tim stopped the golf cart abruptly on the path behind the twelfth green and the two men went searching for a recognisable figure in green overalls stoking a fire. They waved smoke away from their faces and saw the familiar silhouette before them. Coughing loudly for effect, Tim said, 'Blimey Nathan, you've been watching those bloody cowboy films again. Who are you sending smoke signals to this time?'

Nathan laughed out loud. 'That's really funny Tim.'

'Better put it out, mate,' Charlie said. 'We've got the entire Sioux nation coming over that hill in a moment and they are all going to be moaning at you.'

Nathan laughed again at Charlie's analogy and then lowered his head and looked remorseful. 'Sorry, I was just getting rid of the stuff that I picked up, didn't want it to build up everywhere.'

Tim put his large right hand on Nathan's shoulder, 'We know you were mate. Come back to it later in the day when the old buggers are all drunk and the course is quiet. You did a great job of clearing up the course, by the way.'

Nathan's eyes widened, and he looked thrilled to bursting by the simple compliment. 'Ok, no problem,' he said as he smiled and merrily set about dousing the fire while Charlie and Tim walked back to their golf buggy and slid inside along the padded vinyl bench seat.

Charlie sniggered. 'He's a boy, isn't he, any excuse to have a bonfire.'

Despite the early fog on the course, courtesy of Nathan, the annual match went pretty much without a hitch, apart from Tim and Charlie having to stop people wasting time in the woods looking for lost balls. At the after-match lunch in the clubhouse, Willis was busy being Willis, posing for selfies signing golf balls and generally working the crowd. Meanwhile, sitting at his table in the function suite was a man in his fifties that no-one recognised. Everyone seemed to be speculating if he was another golf professional, perhaps an agent or specialist coach, or possibly a medic of some description that Willis had known when he was on the circuit and remained friends with.

But the man didn't have the look of a sportsman about him. His appearance seemed too precise in a businesslike way. He was no more than five feet eight tall, wiry with slicked back dark brown hair that was so even it had obviously been coloured. He was expensively dressed wearing a light grey shiny suit, white shirt, and a burgundy tie. He was clearly happy to take a low profile in Willis's presence, but was smiling amiably and shaking hands like someone who was comfortable with their own position in life.

Charlie and Tim were casually drifting past the function suite on the first floor of the clubhouse after the match, curious to establish what kind of alcoholic carnage had occurred to the veterans during the afternoon's lunch and presentations. A pair of double oak doors swung open just ahead of them and out walked Willis and the man in the shiny suit walking side by side towards them. Willis raised his hand in a clumsy kind of way that suggested he may have taken wine with the meal. He spoke even louder than his normal extrovert tones when he said, 'Hey guys, how was it out there today? Seems like everyone enjoyed themselves, kept them all in line, eh?'

Charlie was first to reply with due reverence, as he considered the man with Willis might be connected to the Japanese owners. 'Yes, the course was good, the weather was kind, and everyone behaved themselves. Couldn't have been better.'

'Great, great,' Willis said, as though Charlie's answer had been completely irrelevant. He turned to the stranger in the shiny grey suit and said, 'Guys, I'd like you to meet a really good buddy of mine who is visiting us from New York - Carmine Ricci. Carmine, please meet two of the best course marshals I have ever come across, Charlie Flint and Tim Featherstone.'

Carmine gave a broad smile, exposing a set of teeth that were just too perfect to be natural. Then stuck out a hand sporting far too many garish gold rings in welcome and said, 'Hi guys, wonderful to meet you,' just like an insincere game show host. 'Great little setup you've got here. I'm impressed.' The man spoke in a broad Bronx accent, like a hardened character from an American TV crime show. He seemed bored and impatient with idle conversation and had an underlying menace in his sharp features that coloured the men's view of him.

Charlie and Tim were very much aware this man could well be someone Willis was trying to court to gain some kind of advantage in the golf world. But with what they knew about Willis's criminal activities, both were highly suspicious of him. So they chose to remain rigidly professional. Charlie said. 'Yes, we work like a family here, Carmine. Everybody does their bit, and we all help each other,'

'That's nice,' Carmine replied while faking a contented nod.

'So what brings you to the UK, Carmine?' Tim asked. 'Just wanting to catch up with Willis? I wish I could catch up with Willis on the course.'

Carmine gave a half smile and exposed the gleaming white teeth again that must have cost a fortune. 'Well, it's always nice to catch up with my buddy, but he's also one of my business partners. I have an interest in his country club out in Thailand and one we are developing in Florida, so I'm just using the opportunity to visit and talk turkey at the same time. Plus, my missus gets to melt the plastic up in Knightsbridge.'

Charlie sensed there were no personal reasons for Carmine's visit at all, and he might inadvertently shed some light on Willis's devious manoeuvrings if he could get him alone. 'Well, if you fancy a round sometime Carmine, without being humiliated by Willis, we'll gladly take you out.'

'Thanks guys. I appreciate the offer, but I don't play anymore, can't afford to lose half a day on anything right now.' He turned to Willis and threw him a look to indicate his conversation with Charlie was over and he needed to move on. 'Okay, let's go see James,' he said. Then Carmine felt the need to explain his comment to Charlie and Tim. He held a finger to his lips and said, 'Don't say anything you guys, but we're gonna see if James wants to be a head pro out in Thailand for a while.' Then Carmine and Willis were off down the stairs in deep discussion.

'Sounds like a terrific experience for him,' Tim said as the men disappeared below first floor level.

Charlie wasn't convinced. 'I'd say it sounds more like they are trying to get James away from Adriana.'

'Maybe Flinty, but it still seems like a great way out of

the problem for James, and he can still retain some dignity in the process. Willis could have just found a reason to sack him, and the Japanese would have backed him to the hilt. He was screwing the man's wife after all.'

'Yes, I agree Fev. But we know Willis is a complete mercenary and must be up to something. I want to see what James's reaction is when they ask him. Come on, let's follow them.'

Willis and Carmine moved along the carpeted corridor from the stairs to the front of the clubhouse and then up the short path and into the pro-shop, where they stayed for five minutes. Then they left with Ben still serving at the counter.

As gunmetal grey clouds were starting to build and threaten rain, Charlie and Fev watched Willis and his visitor from the safe distance of the practice range. They were chatting constantly, and Carmine's hands were becoming extraordinarily animated as the pair walked down a long concrete path towards the service area at the back of the clubhouse.

'How weird Flinty,' Tim said. 'They are obviously going to meet James there to discuss this Thailand thing with him. But why would they do that when it's about to rain and there are nice comfortable air-conditioned meeting rooms inside the building they could use. Doesn't make sense.'

Charlie reached into the pocket of his waterproof jacket, fumbled around and found his small rangefinder telescope. 'It's ok Fev, I don't need this to tell me the yardage to a hole today. We can find somewhere safe to watch them from a distance. Let's get round the back of the kitchens. We'll hide behind the bins and get a view from there.'

'Good idea Flinty, let's get there before James does. He must be out on the course somewhere and on his way back.'

After the function the large steel mobile bins at the back of the kitchen were overflowing and starting to develop a distinctly sour aroma. But they were perfect cover and just the right distance from Willis and Carmine. Charlie nestled between the metal bins and raised the rangefinder to his right eye. 'Got em,' he said, 'and here comes James walking down the path still looking like he's done a couple of rounds with Mike Tyson.'

Tim was jostling for position behind Charlie while trying to squint at the men who were little more than a blur to him. 'What's happening Flinty, I can't see a bloody thing from here?'

'Well, Willis is talking and waving his arms about like some sort of strange swimming stroke. Now he's smiling and putting his arm around James's shoulders. Wait a minute, James is pulling away. The boy is looking totally confused—no change confused to worried.'

'Ah, so they must be making him the offer, then. Does he look happy about it, and ready to say he'll take the job.'

Charlie said nothing for a while, transfixed by the images he was getting through his magnifying device. Then calmly he spoke, 'Well, it's difficult for him to say anything at the moment Fev—Carmine has got him by the throat.'

23

As a couple of days passed, James's injuries made him look more and more like he'd lost an argument with a bus. His ego still wouldn't allow him to admit that the plaster on his twisted nose and eyes several shades of black and blue were as a result of losing a fight to Ben. 'Occupational hazard,' he would shrug and say to anyone who asked, or stared at him in disbelief. 'Got too close to a backswing when I was teaching.' But that didn't explain the thumb imprints and bruises around his neck, and people were suspicious of his explanation knowing the tension building between him and Ben. All only exacerbated after gossip had spread of Adriana ending their affair and James reacting very badly.

Ben also wasn't prepared to own up to the truth, embarrassed that he had allowed himself to be goaded into a fight, but he couldn't bring himself to apologise to James. But more importantly neither of the men wanted to face disciplinary action from Craig. Charlie and Tim were never going to spill the beans about the brawl but had lectured both young men about putting the incident behind them before they both got dismissed. Ben seemed to take their advice on board but James arrogantly behaved like he didn't need to be lectured. His pride was in tatters and he just wanted to shut himself away.

'That bloody woman is poison,' Tim said to his friend. 'You just know this won't be the end of it, don't you?'

Charlie nodded in agreement. 'I sense that Ben genuinely regrets the incident. But James is full of anger and out for revenge. That boy has never lost at anything in his life. He's just biding his time.'

'Yes, and we both know Ben won't back down if he's pushed again. Trouble is we might not be there next time, and that boy is a lethal weapon.'

'I'll speak to him again,' Charlie said in a fatherly way.

'You're the man for the job Flinty,' Tim sniggered.

Charlie waited for Ben to be out of the clubhouse and alone. He caught up with him practicing in a late overcast and humid afternoon on the putting green. 'Look Ben, you can't allow this business with James to drag you down or affect your career. And Adriana is a very beautiful woman I know, but she is what's known in the trade as a femme fatale. A woman who ruins lives without ever thinking twice or having regrets. My advice is to leave well alone, mate. She is just trouble.'

Ben nodded graciously and smiled as though he was thankful for the well meaning advice. But he was never going to admit to anyone that he had thought of little else other than Adriana's visits to his shop and her promise. He had busted James's nose for daring to disrespect her. And despite warnings about how dangerous she might be he fully intended to cash in his wonderful bonus, how could he not? It was just a case of plucking up the courage. Nonetheless, he needed to convince Charlie he was absorbing the sincere and friendly counsel. 'Yes, I know you're right Charlie, and I've been very stupid. To be honest, Adriana only came to see me about deejaying at another party and James was trying to twist it into something else. He was hopping mad after she had just dumped him and he couldn't handle it, so decided to take it out on me.'

Charlie gave a half smile. 'Not his smartest move, eh.' But all the while he was feeling a sense of justice that smug and privileged James had finally learned a valuable life lesson.

'Probably not Charlie,' Ben replied. 'But I just got sick of him behaving like god's gift and constantly using me. It all came out in that moment. About time he got some of his own medicine, though. I've heard him being really nasty to girls in the past, nice girls too—and he seemed to get off on it. He's had a few angry boyfriends, brothers and fathers come looking for him afterwards as well, and he's still managed to escape a good hiding. I do feel bad about hitting him though, but he just pushed me too far. I will apologise to him at some point, even though I know he won't apologise to me.'

'That's very mature of you Ben, and you will feel better for doing the right thing. Now don't take this the wrong way, but if you ever feel the need to talk rather than lose your temper again then here's my mobile number give me a call anytime.'

Ben took the scrap of paper with a mobile phone number written on it. 'Thanks Charlie, I really appreciate that, but I'll be ok now.'

Charlie and Tim left the course for home and a quiet evening with their families. At around seven thirty, Charlie was relaxing in his lounge thumbing through a golf magazine, while Ruth was in front of the TV watching her favourite soap when his mobile phone resting on the coffee table rang. 'Oh, who is that, Charlie?' Ruth asked intolerantly while reaching for her husband's phone and looking at the incoming number.

Charlie yawned and stretched his arms above his head. 'It's probably Fev forgotten to tell me something about the society that are playing tomorrow.'

'No, it's definitely not Fev, it's a number your phone doesn't recognise. Could be one of those scam calls.'

'Here, let me look,' Charlie said, reaching for the phone just as it stopped ringing. 'Can't have been important or...' The same number rang again almost immediately, 'Well maybe it is,' Charlie said as he swiped towards the green phone symbol to answer. 'Hello?'

What Charlie heard was a terrified and trembling young male voice. 'Charlie. Charlie. You've got to help me. I don't know how this has happened. Please come quickly.'

Charlie dropped his magazine and sat bolt upright. 'Is that you Ben?'

'Yes, yes. You must come Charlie, it's horrible. You told me to ring you. I don't know what to do.'

'Ok Ben, just calm yourself down for a minute and tell me what's happened.'

But Ben couldn't speak any more. He just squeaked and sobbed hysterically. All he could say that was remotely intelligible was, 'I'm at James's flat, please come quickly.'

'Alright Ben just stay calm. I'm on my way. I know where James lives I've dropped him off a few times on my way home. I'll be there in fifteen minutes - please keep calm. OK?'

'Ok,' Ben said in a voice filled with trauma. 'But please hurry.'

Charlie ran to get his shoes, a coat and car keys and said to Ruth, 'Gotta go love, young Ben is in some kind of trouble. I might be late.'

Ruth looked annoyed. 'I hope you're not getting yourself involved in something you shouldn't, Charlie Flint. Just leave it alone if it's got nothing to do with you.' Then her caring nature kicked in as it always did. 'And you just be careful now.'

Charlie kissed his wife on the cheek and laughed. 'Don't you realise my best friend is an ex- policeman—and he's coming with me. Don't wait up, I'll be fine.'

The evening was warm and the humidity was increasingly oppressive as another summer storm was building. It was still light as Charlie called Tim from the car. He answered tersely, 'What do you want at this time of night, Flinty?'

'Charming. Haven't got time to explain Fev, but Ben has just called me, he is in a hell of a state round at James's place and I'm on my way to pick you up. Be there in five minutes.'

Tim took an exaggerated breath. 'I hope they haven't fallen out again and Ben's not done some serious damage.'

'Exactly my thoughts Fev. I'm turning into your road now.'

Tim turned to his wife Louise. 'Sorry Love, Charlie is coming to pick me up, our young golf professional is in some sort of difficulty, and you know Flinty he just has to help.'

Louise looked up from her novel, 'And don't you try to pretend you're not the same. Remember you aren't a policeman anymore and you don't get paid for putting yourself at risk.'

'I know love, but I couldn't let Flinty face this on his own, could I?'

'I sometimes wonder about you two.'

Tim slid his hand across his wife's waist and kissed her on the lips, 'You've got no worries in that area my sweet. I might be late.'

Louise grinned. 'You just be careful now, whatever it is you've had too many years of taking chances, let the police deal with it. Remember this is our time now.'

'Understood my love. I'll try not to wake you when I get back - or maybe I should?'

'Get out of here and take care.'

On their ten minute journey in Charlie's car, the two men speculated on the possibilities of Ben's situation, trying to find some simple answers to whatever Ben's dilemma might be. But still they both feared the worst. The car slid noisily to a halt in the gravel car park of the small block of eight modern well maintained up market flats, set in perfectly manicured gardens. A fitting place for a merchant banker's only child to live for a few years as a bachelor. They didn't wait for a lift in the lobby but sprinted up the terrazzo tiled staircase to the second floor and found the front door to James's flat wide open. Breathing hard and with bodies sticky from the humid evening, they looked at each other with trepidation before walking across the threshold into a brightly lit hallway. Ben had obviously switched all the lights on in the entire flat trying to lose the darkness.

'Ben! Where are you?' Charlie called. 'It's Charlie and Tim.'

'In here, came a trembling reply echoing around the hard surfaces of the bathroom.' Tim gently pushed on the door to witness Ben sitting on the white WC pan, shaking, head resting in his hands with sunken eyes and looking ashen. The two men winced and turned their heads away as the overwhelming smell of sour puke in the air hit their nostrils and they could see splashes of vomit up the walls and on the floor.

'What has happened here Ben?' Charlie asked in a calm, non-judgmental voice, trying to pacify the quivering wreck of a young man before him.

'In there,' Ben said, pointing towards the lounge where a TV was showing a premier league football match at full volume. 'I just found him like it. Our fight had been bugging me and I came here to apologise. I thought it would mean more to him that way. The door was open so I walked in and found him like that. They'll think it was me, won't they?'

Tim touched Ben's arm. 'Just wait here and get your breath mate. We'll go and have a look. Hold on here until we come back.' Tim feared that Ben might decide to run and make whatever the situation was so much worse.

'Ok,' Ben whispered before starting to retch towards the handbasin again.

Charlie and Tim walked past the open kitchen door. The room looked like a picture from an expensive home improvement magazine. Next to an open microwave oven, there was an empty M&S microwave pasta container on the expensive worktop. But apart from that, the room was spotless and not what either man expected of a bachelor pad. Gingerly Tim pushed on the walnut veneered door into the brightly lit lounge until it was open wide. From the doorway, they saw another immaculate and expensively furnished space. Stepping carefully inside, they felt the deep pile beige carpet beneath their feet, noticed the silver and chrome ornaments resting on modern polished wood furniture and tasteful modern art prints on the walls. In a high backed plush velvet armchair with scrolled arms facing the TV, they could make out James's head tilted backwards. The top of his skull was open and his trademark shock of blond locks were red and thick with congealed blood and brain matter. During their respective careers, they had grown accustomed to gruesome sights but neither of them wanted to walk around to the front of that armchair. Tim was the first. 'Oh shit,' he said as the vision of James came into his line of sight.

Charlie swallowed hard and followed. 'Oh my god,' he said as the gut churning image came into view. James was sitting upright in the chair, his still battered face was covered in blood that had cascaded from the top of his head and there was a look of sheer terror fixed in his eyes. The chair and surrounding carpet looked as though they had been caught in a shower of blood, fragments of bone and grey brain tissue. And between his thighs was the butt of a crossbow, his thumb still on the trigger and the bow pointing under his chin.

'Up there,' Charlie said, jerking his head upwards. 'There's a crossbow bolt embedded in the ceiling. It went straight through the brain and out of his skull.'

Tim reverted to detective mode. 'And I've got money that says this is the same crossbow that killed the deer on the course.' He reached into his pocket, took out a handkerchief and found the TV remote on the coffee table and switched off the loud and distracting football match.

'That's better,' Charlie said as he walked across the hallway and into the large master bedroom. Like the rest of the flat, it was surprisingly fresh and well ordered. Must be the work of a professional cleaner paid for by his dad, he thought. He pulled a perfectly smoothed duvet away from the king-sized bed, then removed a crisp white cotton under-sheet and took it back to the lounge. He and Tim carefully covered the chair and James with the sheet, then Charlie called Ben into the room.

Ben was reluctant at first, but slowly and deliberately took one step at a time into the lounge. 'That sheet does nothing Charlie, I know he's still under there and that look on his face will haunt me forever.'

Tim slipped an arm around Ben's shoulders and asked softly, 'Have you called the police, mate?'

Ben shook himself out of Tim's grasp and became animated and irrational. 'No, I haven't. I just called Charlie. They'll think it was me, won't they? Everyone knows me and James had previous, even you heard me say I was going to kill him in a fit of temper. And the CCTV in the shop will have caught me punching him. All the evidence points to me. My DNA is all over this flat. They'll put me away.'

'I've got to call them,' Charlie said, pulling a mobile phone from his pocket and dialling the number as he walked towards the front door. 'I'd better phone Craig too.'

'No, no, please, I'll go down for it.'

'But you didn't do it—did you?' Tim asked directly, with just a hint of doubt in his mind.

'No, of course I didn't, but no-one will believe me. I need to get out of here before the police arrive.'

Tim clamped both of his large hands firmly onto Ben's forearms and looked into his terrified, bloodshot eyes. 'Now you listen to me son,' he said assertively, 'This isn't the movies where we wrap a body up in a carpet and dump it in a lake at two in the morning and nobody suspects a thing. If you try to run now, they'll find you within hours—and then they really will think you are as guilty as hell.'

'I'm not guilty, Tim, I'm not,' Ben protested.

'Well, this looks to all the world like a suicide, doesn't it? Seems as though James wanted to end his own life,' Tim said, not believing a word of it. 'Look, there's even a note on the table next to his phone,' Tim picked up an A4 sheet of white copier paper and read the brief message aloud. *I am so sorry that I killed the deer. I had to do it to get noticed. I just wanted to be loved.* 'Pretty basic, but this is his handwriting, isn't it?' He held the note up for Ben to read as Charlie came back into the room.

'Yes, that's definitely his handwriting, big and bold and flowery. No mistaking it.' Feeling confused and with a deep sigh, Ben said, 'I can only hope the police think the same as you, Tim,' resigning himself to face whatever music was coming his way.

In the distance they heard the sound of sirens cutting

through the still night air. Ben seemed calmer. Somehow his mind was more content knowing he was doing what was right. He said, 'There's something I need to show you. After I was sick, I went to get a drink from the fridge to wash my mouth out and lose that horrible taste, you need to have a look at what's in there before the police get here.'

Charlie and Tim followed Ben into the ultramodern kitchen with glossy cream-coloured units, glittering quartz worktops and a white porcelain floor. He walked over to a large American-style fridge with an ice machine in the front and pulled the large, curved door open. The fridge smelt clean but was virtually empty except for some butter, cheese, milk, eggs, a few bottles of beer and a half pint plastic container with a sealed lid part full of a dark liquid. 'That container on the top shelf,' Ben said, pointing. Charlie reached up for it. 'No—don't touch it!' Ben shouted. 'My curiosity stupidly got the better of me and it's already got my prints all over it. What do you think is in it? I thought maybe some kind of cooking stock, soup, sauce or perhaps an energy drink.'

Tim walked into the kitchen and over to the fridge. 'Well, based on the crossbow out there, I'd say it's almost certainly deer blood.'

24

From the Kitchen of James's apartment Charlie, Tim and Ben could see pulsing blue lights coming through the lounge window and hear the sound of people running up the stairs and into the hallway. And so could all the other residents who were at their front doors wondering what on earth was going on in their exclusive little block. 'Paramedics,' came the cry from a petite girl in a green uniform with her dark hair in a ponytail. She was purposeful, in her early thirties and carrying a defibrillator and medical pack.

Charlie and Tim walked out to greet her and an older male colleague, who had followed less enthusiastically up the stairs. 'Are you the man who made the call?' the girl asked.

'Yes, that's me. Charlie Flint. And my colleague here is Tim Featherstone.'

'Ex-Detective Chief Inspector Featherstone no less,' a slim young, scruffy and perspiring police detective in a crumpled suit and open-necked shirt said. He was in his late twenties, with a shock of auburn hair and a confident attitude as he walked through the doorway with a couple of uniformed officers.

'Do I know you detective?' Tim asked curiously.

'No sir, not yet, but I am Detective Constable Lee Watkins. I am also investigating the deer mutilation at The Sycamores, and you are on my list of people to speak to. Oh, and I think my DI might know of you from the dim and distant.'

Tim knew a lot of people from the Metropolitan police force who would have remembered him. But he was too wrapped up in the moment to explore connections from the past. He surreptitiously gave the young detective the once over. D.C Watkins was one of those unfortunate people who didn't wear clothes well. Even if he was dressed by Hugo Boss, he would still look like a tramp. And to Tim, that might mean he had an untidy mind and was someone who might just miss details. He was beginning to easily slip back into the persona of the job that he had done so well for many years. 'Well Lee, if you are involved in the deer incident, this is going to interest you.'

He turned his attention to the female paramedic as she began unpacking her bag. 'I don't think you are going to need any of your equipment or your skills here, young lady. A man named James Cole is under that sheet. I warn you though, it's not pretty.'

'James Cole? One of the professional golfers at the club?' the astonished Watkins asked.

'Yes, and I'm another,' Ben added, as if a load was being lifted from him. 'Ben Tilman. I found him like this.'

The female paramedic stepped across the room, gazed into Ben's still ashen face and gently grasped his wrist to take a pulse. 'Are you ok Ben? I think you should sit down for a while and drink some water.' The girl led Ben to a cream-coloured fabric couch, instructed him to sit and left for the kitchen.

Ben was taken by the paramedic's kindness and professionalism, and for a moment started to consider his own condition. He felt weak, nauseous and had the headache from hell. He wanted to lean back into the sumptuous couch, close his eyes, and pretend none of this was happening. But Lee Watkins had a job to do.

'Ah yes, Ben Tilman. I understand from previous conversations with Mr Galbraith that there was no love lost between yourself and Mr Cole.'

Charlie interrupted. His sense of justice irritated by the police officer's immediate implication of guilt. 'I think that's a bit strong detective. It was well known that there was an imbalance in workload when the head professional was away. I think we would all be a bit put out with that, wouldn't we? Hardly grounds for murder though, is it?'

The detective gave a disdainful look towards Charlie, 'And you are, sir?'

'Charlie Flint. I work with Mr Featherstone as a marshal at the club.'

It was Tim's turn to interrupt in support of his friend, 'And he's an ex senior detective too Lee. But he was in insurance rather than policing.'

The young policeman quietly took stock of the information he'd been given, then said. 'Well, Mr Flint, I will need to take a statement from Mr Tilman down at the station.' He stopped mid-sentence. 'Bloody hell!' he exclaimed loudly as the paramedics removed the white sheet from the chair. Charlie studied the detective's face, curious to see how experienced he was with the vision of brutal death. He didn't flinch as the horrific image of James's body was fully exposed, pushed back into the armchair by the force of a crossbow bolt passing through his head at point blank range.

'You'll need to get that bolt out of the ceiling,' Tim said indifferently.

'To check for a match with the one left in the deer.' A smug grin crept over Lee Watkins' face as he spoke. He could see the closure of a difficult case in sight.

Charlie added, 'And in the fridge there is a container of what appears to be blood, probably deer's blood, but obviously you will need to check it out.'

One of the uniformed officers that had arrived with the detective spoke out of turn. 'It all seems to be adding up, doesn't it? Maybe we've found our deer killer. And this looks like a suicide to me. His thumb is still on the trigger and there's a note on the table.'

Lee Watkins crouched and took a closer look at James's face, then said disappointedly, 'Except he didn't beat himself up before firing a bolt through his brain. Look at his face.'

'I did that,' Ben said without hesitation.

The detective ignored Ben's remark initially, then crouched again and leaned left and right to get a better angle of James's injuries. 'Looks very recent to me.'

Ben spoke as though it was obvious the facial damage was in no way connected to James's death. He pre-empted the obvious question. 'We had a fight at work a couple of days ago.'

'About what?'

'A woman.'

'So why are you back here tonight?'

'I came here to apologise. I was out of order, hitting him. I should have kept my temper.'

Lee Watkins pulled a small black notepad and a pen from the inside pocket of his creased grey suit jacket and scribbled notes. Without looking up, he said, 'And remind me, Mr Flint and Mr Featherstone, why are you here this evening?'

Tim didn't consult with his friend as to who should

answer. 'We are here detective constable because young Ben was in shock when he discovered the body and he called us.'

The young detective was getting more irksome with every word he spoke. He was the kind of young officer that might once have quivered in Tim's presence and wouldn't dare think of being so disrespectful, but times had changed. 'So let me get this straight,' he said with a sarcastic tone to his voice. 'Mr Tilman here beat up Mr Cole recently and came back to his flat alone tonight to say he was sorry, found him dead, then called you and not us?'

'What you are inferring simply doesn't make any sense detective,' Tim said, now frustrated by the young man's arrogance.

Watkins gave a self-satisfied grin. 'I'm not inferring anything sir, and with respect Mr Featherstone, may I remind you that you are no longer in the force.'

Looking equally smug, Tim replied, 'Understood, Lee, but as you say, some people still remember me—like your boss.'

Lee Watkins thought better of continuing that particular exchange with Tim and got on with the formal process. 'Ok we are going to take statements from yourself and Mr Flint, then you can go. I will take Mr Tilman to the station to answer some questions. Meanwhile, this flat is a crime scene and our people will be crawling all over it shortly, so I would suggest we step outside.'

A uniformed police officer took statements from Charlie and Tim, which were little more than they had witnessed a disagreement at the club the day before, and came to James's flat at Ben's request. As they stood on the top landing of the stairwell, Ben was walked past by DC Watkins. Ben was in a complete daze, with foul smelling vomit splattered over the front of his clothes. He peered at Charlie with forlorn eyes and said, 'Can you let Craig know where I am. I don't want to lose my job.'

'Of course,' Charlie replied with a knowing nod. 'Don't worry, you'll be out of there soon.'

Lee Watkins threw Charlie a *mind your own business* look as he escorted Ben down the stairs to the waiting police car. Then they were whisked away down the tree-lined avenue towards the local station.

Charlie and Tim walked down the staircase past male and female officers doing their best to pacify concerned neighbours, without divulging all the gruesome detail behind the frenetic police activity in the block.

As the two men moved back to Charlie's car, and people in white disposable coverall suits entered the building Tim said, 'Well my friend, what do you make of that?'

'I'll tell you what I make of that Fev. First, Ben had nothing to do with it, and second, it sure as hell wasn't suicide. James was murdered to conveniently tie up some loose ends by someone.'

Tim nodded in agreement. 'Spot on Flinty, and once a sensible detective at the station gets a hold of this, they will draw the same conclusion. Did you notice the freshly broken and swollen left jaw?'

'I did, and that can't have been Ben because he is left-handed and would have naturally swung at his right jaw.'

'Exactly, and James must have known his killer, because there was no sign of forced entry or any kind of struggle. Plus, James was the most unlikely hunter I have ever met—well unless he was stalking women of course.'

Charlie laughed, 'Can you imagine him waiting for his prey, laying in the wet and cold getting his designer gear grubby?'

'Yeah, he probably would have spooked the deer when

he combed his hair.' They chuckled more through nervous energy than humour.

Charlie pressed the unlock button on his car key fob, the electric locks clunked open, the indicator lights flicked orange, wing mirrors swung out and the door handles were illuminated. 'Blimey, that's a bit flash isn't it Flinty?' Tim said.

'That's what a life in insurance and a decent pension can do for you.' Charlie grinned.

'Yeah, fair point mate. Now there's just a few things still bugging me about tonight. What was that note all about? Obviously designed to look like a suicide note—and clearly James wrote it himself. But we both know somebody was welcomed into his flat, knocked him out, and killed him with a crossbow.'

'Yes Fev, and that person took the CCTV camera and recording device from the shelf by the front door on the way out.'

'So if James knew his killer, then there's a chance we might know them too Flinty.'

Charlie sighed, 'Well, if it's a golfer from the club, it could be any one of the 600 members.'

Tim nodded, 'And knowing the way James put it about, it could equally have been an ex-girlfriend or a disgruntled husband looking for revenge. Ben said he had a few of them after him.'

'It had to be someone very clever to set him up though, someone well enough prepared not to leave a trace of DNA anywhere—possibly someone who had done it before, I'd say.'

As they slid into the cold leather front seats, thunder rumbled and lights flashed across the night sky. Charlie said, 'That isn't the only storm that's breaking tonight. All a bit too obvious for me. And the deer blood. That was clearly planted to try to tie the whole thing together. Why on earth would James want it?'

'He wouldn't—but conveniently no one can ask him now, can they?'

Charlie took in a deep juddering breath, exhaled loudly and pressed the car's start button. 'I'm just worried about young Ben.'

'Trust me Flinty, they'll let him go fairly quickly. Even that dopey kid detective will work out Ben is innocent. But this is more than someone trying to frame our young professional for killing a deer. That was only a useful coincidence. No, somebody wanted James dead for another reason.'

Charlie started to move the car away from the apartment block and into the street as large rain spots hit the windscreen. Without looking at his friend, he said, 'And I hope that detective we saw in London with the cocaine was right about us being safe. Because there's a sadistic killer in our midst and I'd hate for us to be next on their list.'

25

At around seven thirty a.m. on a warm windless late August morning, Charlie and Tim were at *The Sycamores* eagerly awaiting Ben's return. Fortunately it was going to be a quiet day at the course, with mainly members and a few visitors playing. And none of the staff were going to feel much like working once they heard the news about James.

Ben had sent them a text late the previous evening to say he had been released by the police. And that he was ok and would meet them at eight o'clock the following morning as normal. But this was going to be far from a normal day. Everything about the course felt sombre and grey despite the cloudless azure sky. Neither of the men had slept well after James's death. And they had to deal with both of their wives, whose grave fears from the night before had been realised, which left them with a personal mountain to climb. They wanted to get into the golf course early to meet Ben and Craig to offer whatever support they could and hear of Ben's experience with the police. They arranged to meet him in the car park and as they both stepped out of Charlie's car; they were immediately drawn by a pungent smell all around. They sniffed at the air and were picking up the familiar scent of burning brushwood along with the distinctively acidic tang of something plastic melting. They looked at each other and frowned. 'Nathan!' they both exclaimed.

Charlie grimaced, 'Oh, we can do without him sending clouds of smoke across the greens this morning. Think we might have to split up or we'll miss Ben. Tell you what Fev, I'll go and sort Nathan out and you take Ben into the shiny shed when he arrives and make him a coffee. I won't be long.'

Charlie jumped into golf buggy number twelve parked in its bay and drove out towards Nathan's adopted bonfire site near the twelfth green. Sure enough, there was a thick-set figure in green overalls poking at the remnants of a large fire with a garden fork. As he saw Charlie approach, he turned fork in hand and gave a huge beaming smile. 'Hello Charlie, it's OK. I got up early as I had a lot of stuff to get rid of. Wanted to do it before anyone arrived to play. All done now.' From the childlike self satisfied look on Nathan's face, he was clearly expecting praise for his hard work and consideration. Charlie didn't have the heart to admonish him, he had been thoughtful after all by starting early. 'Yes, I can see you've done well to get it finished before the first people get out.' Nathan grinned and looked delighted to think for once he might have made a good decision.

Charlie twitched his nose in an exaggerated fashion. 'But what have you been burning mate, that's not just bits of tree and bracken I can smell, is it?'

'Well, I suppose it must be that box, Charlie.'

'What box would that be, Nathan?'

'Well, a man walked across the course really early when I'd first lit up, gave me a tenner.' Nathan pulled a folded ten pound note out of his overalls pocket and held it up towards Charlie.

'Why did he give you a tenner, Nathan?'

'To burn his cardboard box.'

Charlie started to worry, 'Who was this man?'

Nathan shrugged. 'Don't know never seen him before. I tried to talk to him but he couldn't speak English much, just shoved a tenner in my hand and threw the box in the middle of the fire. He hung about for ten minutes to watch it burn, then left.'

'Did you see what was in the box?'

'No Charlie, it was all taped up, smelt like there was something inside soaked in petrol and it really went up a treat.' He laughed. 'You and Tim would have gone mad if you'd have been here.'

Charlie walked up to the embers and peered into the glowing pile of charcoal. It had obviously been a large and very hot bonfire. 'Nothing left Charlie,' Nathan said. 'Did I do wrong?'

Charlie sighed, 'No, you're alright, mate. What did this man look like?'

'He was about my age, skinny and dark with scruffy clothes. You know, like those car cleaner blokes, but he wasn't one of them—I know those boys.'

Charlie was deep in thought. Was it coincidental that only the night before James had died, and now a mysterious foreigner was tricking Nathan into disposing of unknown items on his fire? Charlie never trusted coincidence.

Nathan startled Charlie out of his trance. 'Can I keep the tenner, Charlie?'

Now fully alert, Charlie slid into the bench seat of his buggy. He questioned whether he should break the news of James's death to Nathan, but thought better of it. Craig would be calling a briefing soon and he wasn't convinced that the boy would deal with the news well in isolation. 'Yes, you can keep the money Nathan, just make sure that fire is properly out will you, I've got to get back.'

When Charlie arrived back in the shiny shed, a tired-looking Ben had arrived and was talking openly to Tim about his police questioning from the night before. There was still something nagging in Charlie's mind about James's death that he had to ask the young professional golfer. 'So Ben, did the detective ask you if you knew of anyone that might want to kill James?'

'Yes, he did. And I told him that maybe only Willis, because of Adriana, but of course he is out of the country again.'

'What about those angry brothers and fathers you told us were after James in the past—were any of those mad enough to want to kill him?'

'A couple at the time definitely seemed to be, but I don't think they would have actually gone through with it.'

'Would James have known any of these people?'

'Yes, a couple really well. They are members at the club.'

'And you didn't tell Lee Watkins that?'

'He didn't seem interested. It was like he had already made up his mind.'

As Tim anticipated Ben had been released from the police station after a couple of hours of intense questioning by DC Lee Watkins, whose next port of call was *The Sycamores* the following day. Strangely, that was always going to be the case, but he was now investigating the death of a golf professional, and not the mutilation of a deer. Tim suspected the young detective was going to do his best to lay the blame for both acts at James's door—especially if he could get more statements to support his case.

Most people at the club the detective interviewed that day didn't have a bad word for Ben, saying he was a genuine, likeable and a hard-working boy. And it wasn't fair the way he was permanently carrying James during his affair with Adriana. Then he got to speak to Adriana.

Craig had allowed the police to commandeer the club's very grand board room for their work, with its long polished oak table, plush carpet and panoramic views over the golf course. Adriana Martin was predictably late for her appointment, just to make her belligerent point. She tapped gently on the boardroom door. The detective constable sitting in his opulent surroundings felt a real sense of power as he uttered, 'Come in.' But the truth was he was simply there gathering information for more senior officers who would be heading the case. Adriana eased the door open and slinked seductively into the large and grandiose room. She was, as always, immaculately turned out and looked like a mannequin from a Bond Street window in a short-sleeved blue polka-dot summer dress and stiletto heels. There was a definite look of intent about Adriana, with her hair pinned up, focused brown eyes, a thin smile, and an air of confidence that said she was ready to draw Lee Watkins under her sexual spell. She was surprised he was such a young man, but that was likely to make things easier for her, as she was so very good at manipulating young men.

Lee Watkins looked up from the paperwork he had spread untidily across the gleaming board room table, as his eyes met with Adriana's, her beauty took him by surprise. He had just made a tick against *Adriana Martin, head professional's wife and event organiser*, on his list of staff to interview. He thought this would be yet another mundane statement for him to take that day. He gestured towards a leather-backed chair on the opposite side of the boardroom table. 'Please take a seat, Mrs Martin, and thank you for talking to me today. I am Detective Constable Watkins.'

'Not at all,' Adriana said as she positioned herself delicately in the chair and angled it directly towards the detective. She placed her handbag gently on the carpet, leaned back and crossed her slender legs very deliberately.

The young detective had to steel himself to remain professional and not gawp at the adorably sensual creature before him. He rested his forearms on the table, leaned forward, and chose to avoid eye contact. He concentrated only on the blank sheet of his notepad, while delicate waves of Adriana's exquisite perfume teased at his nostrils. 'So, Mrs Martin...'

Adriana interrupted, 'Oh, do call me Adriana darling.'

The young detective was immediately subjected to her mind games. 'I'd rather not, if you don't mind, Mrs Martin. So, can you tell me what your relationship was with James Cole?'

Adriana leaned back in a leather meeting room chair and crossed her smooth, shapely legs provocatively once more. 'Well, he worked as the senior professional to my husband Willis, his second in command if you like. He was a bit put out it would seem, because he thought he should have been the head pro at the club—I mean, really.'

Watkins allowed himself to glance up briefly at the sultry vision before him, then quickly down to his notepad again before he turned into a pillar of salt. 'And has there ever been any friction between your husband and Mr Cole?'

'No darling, my husband is often away, and James knew it was best to keep his mouth shut on any views he might, or might not, have. Who wouldn't want to have, *working as understudy to an internationally renowned golfer* on their CV?'

'So did Mr Cole get on with most other people at the club in your view?'

Adriana deliberately crossed her legs in the other direction and laughed, 'Ha, if you wore a skirt, he did. You see darling, James was a very attractive young man, tall with a lithe physique, naturally blond hair and piercing blue eyes that would make many women melt. He was a Casanova and quite arrogant with it, so men tended to tolerate him rather than like him.'

The detective cleared his throat and moved uncomfortably in his chair. 'And err—I don't quite know how to put this, Mrs Martin.'

Adriana roared with laughter. 'Did I sleep with him?'

Watkins was relieved that he didn't have to say the words, 'Well yes.'

'Of course I did, darling. I'm sure many people have already told you. Yes, even I found his charms irresistible for a while. And before you ask, I am completely open about these things with my husband, so I can assure you there would be no recriminations from that direction.'

Still without moving his glance from the table, Lee Watkins said, 'So when did this arrangement between you terminate?'

Adriana sat upright and gazed out of the window towards the golf course as though bored and disinterested. 'Oh, the night before last, I think. Frankly darling, I simply see these things as a bit of fun, just a dalliance, but James was infatuated and became an absolute pain. He even wanted me to leave Willis—how ridiculous is that—so I had to get rid of him for my own sanity.'

'And how did he take it?'

She turned to face Watkins, who was still scribbling notes and managing to avoid her stare. 'Very badly darling, he told me he didn't want to live without me—all a bit dramatic at the time, I thought. But the CCTV system caught him running out of the clubhouse like a mad thing, kicking waste bins and howling at the moon. After which, I suspect he went home and drank himself senseless. Stupidly he came in the next morning and in his frustration picked a fight with poor little Ben and wished he hadn't.'

Something sparked in the detective's mind and instinctively he looked directly into Adriana's dark, sensuous eyes with a quizzical expression on his face. She leaned in towards him and even from the other side of the table, her hypnotic eyes and slightly open mouth made him feel awkward enough to move himself back in the chair. 'So do you think when Mr Cole said he didn't want to live without you, he was suggesting he might be considering suicide?'

Adriana replied, 'At the time I thought his reaction was all about shock and loss of control. He felt he had to say something theatrical. You see, this was unknown territory for James. He simply didn't know how to cope with the rejection.' Adriana reached into her Louis Vuitton handbag and plucked out a black mobile phone and seemed to play it like an instrument with her damson-coloured thumbnails. 'But if you are looking for something a little more definite, darling, then read this message James sent to me from his phone last night - I can only presume it was tragically just before he took his life.'

The detective reached over and took the phone and tilted the screen away from the glare of the artificial lights. The message read, *'If I can't have you Adriana my life is not worth living. I love you, goodbye.'*

'Of course, one of your people will have picked that up from his telephone already, darling, won't they?'

The detective passed the phone back across the table. 'Did that message not alarm you, Mrs Martin?'

'Well, I was rather busy last night darling, and didn't pick it up until this morning. But if people are going to do it, then they are going to do it, aren't they?' Leaning forward again as if she wanted to be discrete, Adriana whispered,

'But I do have something that troubles me greatly about James and his mental stability.'

Lee Watkins smiled inwardly, thinking this case was becoming more and more like one of those open and shut versions everyone refers to in TV dramas. 'Please go on, Mrs Martin,' he said.

'Well, during our brief fling, he felt the need to bare his soul to me quite regularly about certain things. Like past girlfriends, how his father constantly tried to buy his affection and losing the chance to be the senior professional when The Sycamores owners installed Willis.'

'Forgive me, Mrs Martin, but I think we have already covered that point. Was there something else?'

Adriana gave him a sweet disarming smile and for a moment Watkins cursed himself for not looking at this divine woman for longer. 'You are such an impatient bunny,' she said as though she were about to tell him something entirely insignificant. 'After one of our more intimate moments, James confessed to me he slaughtered the deer in the woods.'

The detective sat bolt upright. 'But why would a golf professional with everything going for him want to do something like that?'

'Well, in his own way he was quite insecure, so it was just to feel the power of making everyone squirm, darling. And he said the blood thing was to spook people even more. Didn't tell me any more apart from that he felt terribly remorseful about it.'

'Would you be prepared to swear to all of that under oath in a court of law, Mrs Martin?'

'Absolutely darling.'

26

Detective Constable Lee Watkins spent the entire day shut in the board room interviewing people from *The Sycamores* team, but none had anything to say that he didn't already know. Apart from Adriana Martin. And in amongst the mind-numbing boredom, she had given him a reason to feel smug.

The next day, the regular morning case meeting at the local police station was chaired by his detective chief inspector, but Lee Watkins had top billing. Round a full meeting room table DCI Stevie Lawson said, 'Ok Lee tell us what you've got from The Sycamores on the death of golf professional James Cole.' She was a DCI who was keen on developing her team and encouraged junior officers to take ownership and speak up.

Lee Watkins had been rehearsing what he would say for half the night and wore a suit and tie for the occasion. He had to remain professional at all costs, but as an ambitious individual, he wanted to get all the kudos he felt he was due. Opening his notebook, Lee cleared his throat nervously. 'After taking statements for most of yesterday up at The Sycamores golf club, I have established some more solid evidence regarding James Cole's death.' He cleared his throat again, like a man unfamiliar with the spotlight. 'It was all pretty mundane stuff until I got to Adriana Martin, wife of head professional Willis Martin, who was openly having an affair with Mr Cole. Two nights ago, he sent her a text message implying he was going to end his life after she finished their arrangement. I've checked Mr Cole's phone, and it was definitely sent from there around the time of his death, according to the pathologist. I have also looked at CCTV footage from the club showing Mr Cole behaving very irrationally the evening Mrs Martin terminated their affair. And I have numerous accounts of Mr Cole being totally besotted by Mrs Martin to the point of distraction.' Watkins thumbed through a few pages on his notepad. 'In terms of the outstanding case of the deer killing and mutilation, forensics has now confirmed that the crossbow bolt used on the deer is identical to that which killed Mr Cole. At this stage we can perhaps deduce that the same crossbow was used in both cases and only Mr Cole's prints are on it.' The detective closed his pad and gave his DCI eye contact. 'Plus, of course ma'am, we have a short-written confession to the deer killing in James Cole's own handwriting.' He left a brief pause for effect before playing his trump card. 'And Mrs Martin is prepared to say under oath that James Cole admitted to her he killed the deer. So with respect, ma'am, I would suggest we have some fairly compelling evidence to suggest our deer killer was James Cole, and he has now tragically taken his own life.'

In keeping with the traditional feel of *The Sycamores,* the main office had a perfectly crafted set of polished small oak boxes that held messages or letters for the staff. These were well constructed pigeonholes that looked like furniture. And this was where Charlie and Tim collected their day's instructions without having to bother Craig. Early one bright and busy September morning, they were picking up the normal details like the course activity, schedules and any special requests from the large building contractor who was taking over the course and hosting a golf day. Unusually there was an envelope marked *FAO Charlie/Tim. Private & Confidential* in Craig's handwriting. 'How bizarre,' Tim said. 'He's never done that before.'

'No, not like him at all Fev. Let's go somewhere quiet and open it just in case. After the business with James, who knows what it could be.'

Tim followed Charlie out of the clubhouse and down the path towards the golf buggy charging points to check the vehicles were ready for the builders. They had a quick scan of the area and Charlie peeled open the envelope. He read aloud, '*Get the builders out on their golf day, then meet me in the pro shop at ten. Thanks, Craig.*' Charlie shrugged his shoulders and passed the sheet of golf club headed paper to Tim. 'That's all it says.'

'All a bit strange and clandestine isn't it Flinty? Why wouldn't he want to meet us in his office?'

'Well, he's only got Ben in today and the builders have paid for a professional to go round with them. So, I suppose he's having to check people in himself.'

Neither of the men really understood the logic, but Tim said, 'Ok let's get cracking and be back for ten, we'll find out soon enough, Craig is not a time waster.'

Five minutes before ten they reached the professionals shop which was in complete darkness. 'There's your answer, Flinty,' Tim said, pointing to a sign on the door that was directing golfers to the clubhouse. 'He's having one of the girls check the players in and they've got their own reception set up.'

Charlie cupped a hand against the large plate-glass window of the shop to cut the glare from fluorescent lights in the corridor. He peered inside past the new clubs and golf clothing, looking for movement. A light appeared at the back of the shop as a door to the small office cracked open. 'Here he comes,' Charlie said, 'And by the look on his face I don't think he's about to tell us he's won the lottery and is retiring to the South of France.'

Craig unlocked the glass door and beckoned the two men inside. He immediately locked the door behind them and started walking through the shop towards the back office without uttering a word. The friendly slaps on the back and throw away jokes seemed to have been forgotten in his rush to get out of the public gaze. In fact, his normally genial nature seemed to have evaporated entirely, and something was patently wrong. Charlie looked at Tim and they shared a confused expression. Tim whispered, 'Maybe it's understandable when one of your professionals was found dead and another may still be under suspicion for his murder.'

'Come inside boys,' Craig uttered quietly while ushering them into the office and pulling the door closed. 'Have a seat please,' he said with a voice devoid of emotion and without any movement in the pronounced laughter lines around his deep blue eyes.

Charlie shuffled uncomfortably in his seat. 'Something doesn't feel good about this, Craig.'

Tim was also quick to spot the anxiety behind Craig's unusual stoicism. 'Come on mate, tell us what it is that's troubling you so much.'

Craig slumped into an office chair, leaned his elbows on a wood grain laminate desk top buried his head in his hands for a moment then fell back in the chair. He shook his head and exhaled theatrically. 'Well firstly, thanks for coming boys, and sorry for all the secrecy.' He sighed again. 'Even the simplest of things seem to be difficult today.' Craig slid himself upright in the chair and took in a long breath. 'You two are the people I trust the most in this place and with your backgrounds I feel safe in saying that. But I'm going mad here and I've got to share something, and maybe ask your advice.'

Tim interrupted. 'Before you tell us anything Craig, please be re-assured that despite being retired we are still discrete and professional - and we're with you.'

Craig's shoulders seemed to lose some of their tension and his eyes became distinctly moist. 'Thank you, Tim, Charlie. I had already drawn that conclusion and soon you will learn why I am being so mysterious today.' He looked up towards the acoustic ceiling tiles with a vacant gaze. 'That poor boy's parents are distraught. He had everything to live for. I spoke to them this morning, and it was awful.' Craig's bottom lip started to tremble and his eyes welled with tears. 'Never did I think I would ever be dealing with something like this in my career. The whole thing seems like a living bloody nightmare. I know this really isn't the sort of stuff that you used to deal with but...'

It was Charlie's turn to cut in. 'We were both in fraud Craig, and much as people might think we were sitting in our warm offices pushing paper, there is no end to the evil people will commit to make money. I'm afraid this is nothing new to us.' He reached across the desk to grasp Craig's forearm as a gesture of support, 'so in your own time.'

Craig nodded graciously, as if confirming to himself that he had made the right decision to take the men into his confidence. 'Shit, where do I begin? Well, for starters, the police have now concluded that James committed suicide, and he also killed the deer.'

'Bullshit,' Tim growled. Someone has set him up to take the rap and you don't believe suicide any more than we do Craig.

'No, I don't, Tim, and whatever the police might have decided about the deer, I know different.'

In a more sensitive tone, Charlie asked, 'You say that as though there is something else going on here that isn't obvious?'

Craig nodded and looked relieved to immediately have the men on the same wavelength. 'That's exactly right, Charlie.'

'If it makes you feel any easier, we had both drawn the same conclusion,' Tim added.

'It does, thank you. But the reason I know the police conclusions are not right is because I've had people put the frighteners on me about Willis's activities.'

'The Japanese?' Charlie suggested in disbelief.

'No, nothing to do with the Japanese. Apart from their visit, I hardly ever hear from them.'

'Carmine Ricci?' Tim interjected. 'Has to be one or the other.'

Craig started to wring his hands and move clumsily in his chair. 'Yes, he seems to be Willis's protector. I met him in the early days when Willis was first appointed and he left me in no doubt that I should not poke my nose into Willis's business activities or give him a hard time. But it's not in my nature to sit back and say nothing when I have responsibility for the course and its people. Willis and I had some royal battles when I realised what he was up to, and I threatened to sack him. To hell with the consequences and how famous he was. I wasn't having people think I was involved with his shenanigans.'

Tim exclaimed, 'You knew about the cocaine?'

'Of course I did. He is hardly subtle with it, is he? James knew too. He came and told me about young men who knew nothing about golf, regularly turning up in expensive cars to take away sets of clubs. And, what's more, if Willis had his way, all the staff working here would be the young Thais that he brings over too.'

'So the frighteners you refer to came after you challenged Willis?' Charlie asked.

'Yes, that was after I threatened to dismiss him. I got a call from Carmine one day. All he said was, I told you to back off Willis, now I'm going to remind you of the organisation you are dealing with. And that night the deer got butchered, it was meant as a warning for me.'

'How can you be sure?' Charlie asked. 'It could just have been coincidence. What about the illegal immigrant story, and the car cleaners. We know it's highly unlikely, but you can never be sure, can you?'

Craig sprang to his feet nervously and started to pace the room and wring his hands again. 'I'm ashamed to say that both were merely smoke screens put up by me.' Craig stopped and leant both palms on the desk firmly. He shook his head and said despairingly, 'They threatened my family. I had to do something.' He stood upright again, closed his eyes, and tilted his head skyward, obviously lost in a world of disturbing thoughts. He opened his eyes, looked down at them and said, 'The reason I can be absolutely sure it wasn't coincidence Charlie is that the missing deer's head appeared on the bonnet of my car in the early hours one morning, when it was parked in my driveway at home. And without putting too fine a point on it, I'm fearing for my life.'

'Bloody hell, real godfather stuff,' Tim exclaimed.

'Precisely Tim, that was the point. And that's how I would know what organisation I was dealing with. Carmine

Ricci called me the same day and asked if I got the message he sent—and then enquired if my family were well. So I can hardly go to the police can I?'

'And what about the deer's blood?' Charlie asked.

Craig shrugged. 'Well, I guess that was just to make it different so I knew it was them when it happened, and not some random poacher.'

'You must be beside yourself Craig. Does Kirsty know about all this?'

'No, not a thing Charlie. I've managed to keep it from her. Well, apart from me telling her that Willis is an arsehole. But she'd worked that out for herself.'

Tim grimaced. 'Not only is Willis an arsehole, but a completely untouchable arsehole.'

Just then the phone rang, and Craig listened to the caller without speaking. He hung up and said, 'Got to go boys, but there's more. Meet me back here at one o'clock.'

27

Out on the course, Charlie and Tim were driving around killing time in a golf buggy. In the weak September sunshine, they could barely concentrate while discussing the bombshell that Craig had just landed on them. Charlie shook his head. 'Poor bloke, I can't believe he's remained so composed and cheerful with that hanging over him.'

'Suppose he didn't have much choice, Flinty. If he started to behave differently, people would want to know what was wrong, and that could be a downward spiral.'

'Yeah, and it's not a total surprise that Willis has links to the mob—is it? What else do you think Craig wants to tell us at one o'clock, Fev?'

'Well, one thing's for sure, it's not going to be good news, is it? And I'm beginning to wonder what we've got ourselves into here Flinty.'

At ten minutes to one o'clock, they were eagerly waiting outside the locked pro-shop doors. Just as before, Craig emerged from the back office and walked through the gloom of the empty shop. He unlocked the door. 'Take a seat in the back-office lads,' he said with a marginally more good humoured face than before. As Craig held the office door open, Tim spotted Adriana's assistant Kate Austin sitting behind the desk looking businesslike, wearing a grey trouser suit and seeming decidedly ill at ease. He and Charlie gave each other a *what's this all about* uneasy glance but didn't question her presence. Both thinking that Craig must have had a good reason for inviting her.

'Hello Kate,' Charlie said politely as Craig closed and locked the office door.

'Hello Charlie, Tim,' Kate replied with her usual enthusiasm and cheery smile. 'I know you must be surprised to see me here. I'll save Craig the time in explaining as I have to do this in my lunch break, otherwise Adriana will be looking for me and asking difficult questions.'

Charlie and Tim still looked bewildered, but said, 'Okay,' in unison, both eager to understand what was going on.

Kate leaned her forearms on the desk and took up an authoritative position, and quite the opposite to her normal subservient image as Adriana's lackey. 'Craig tells me I can trust you both and I don't have time to do in-depth checks on you. But my gut and initial intelligence tells me he's right, so I'm happy to talk to you now.'

Tim interrupted. 'Excuse me for asking Kate, but...'

Kate cut him short. 'I'm coming to that, Tim. As you have probably guessed, I am not what I might at first appear. I am an embedded agent working for British intelligence. When we knew Willis Martin was coming here, Craig was instructed to take me onto the team. We have been on to Willis right from the start. He has strong links to one of the Mafia families in New York and we are playing a waiting game with him. Suffice to say being at this club suited him very well, but I can't tell you why at the moment.'

'But whatever it is will finally make sense of why such a

famous golfer wanted to be at this little club.' Charlie suggested.

'And the reason we were told to back off by the police when we discovered his cocaine smuggling caper?' Tim added.

Craig looked astonished. 'And you two knew about the cocaine smuggling, too?'

'We had him bang to rights Craig. Sniffer dog and hard evidence, enough to put him away for a long time.'

'Sorry boys, I had underestimated you. I had no idea.'

Kate sat upright and was very conscious of her time restrictions. 'You are both exactly right. But we couldn't afford to lose the big prize for the sake of a tuppenny ha'penny drugs scam that we already knew about.'

Charlie seemed hurt, as though his and Tim's detective efforts were being dismissed as worthless. 'I can't understand why everyone thinks this is peanuts. I would have thought it's making him 100k for every set of clubs he brings in - hardly small beer, is it?'

Kate realised she'd touched a nerve. 'It probably is that much, Charlie, and having solid evidence gives us something incredibly useful to fall back on. We are tracking his supply and distribution networks right now to identify the bigger players for when we are ready to make our move. But what we are working on with the U.S. government has the potential to be worth billions and change the face of drug trafficking worldwide.'

'Whoa, that's a bit out of our league Kate, I see what you mean,' Tim said with his professional policeman's mindset.

Craig chipped in. 'But Kate thinks you two could be valuable in nailing Willis and these people once and for all.'

Charlie huffed and looked astounded. 'How could we possibly help with something on this scale?'

Kate turned her left wrist inward and checked her watch before taking over the conversation again. 'The thing is chaps, the people we are dealing with here are very sophisticated, and any clumsy attempts to expose them will get picked up immediately and they will disappear into the woodwork. So we have to be completely joined up. I have managed to gain Adriana's complete trust, so much so that she allows me to help with her personal arrangements. To cut a long story short, I need to employ some waiting staff for her next party. The individuals will need to be security vetted by us and sign a non-disclosure agreement for complete secrecy.'

'Yes, we've heard about Adriana's parties,' Charlie said with a raised eyebrow.

'Good, so you will understand the importance of absolute discretion. Now the next party is in October, and it's the big one where we believe things are going to happen. All the previous events have just been warm-ups for this, lulling everyone into a false sense of security.'

'Can't you just drop a couple of your agents in as waiters?' Tim asked.

Kate shook her head and dismissed the suggestion. 'No, they'd be on to it like a shot. Truth is, we don't know who they've got on their payroll that might be privy to our activities. This is big, and we are too close to cracking it to take silly risks.'

'Oh, I get it,' Tim said. 'And a couple of old wrinklies like us won't cause any suspicion?'

Kate smirked. 'Something like that. But more like using people I know they haven't got to, who will be a much safer bet. And particularly those I can rely on. And the good thing is that Willis trusts you, especially after the bust up between James and Ben when you didn't say anything. And you seem to have made a good impression on Carmine too. Plus, from our point of view, you would both be very credible witnesses when it comes to it.'

Witnesses to a major international crime? Charlie thought, how the hell are we going to explain that one away to Ruth and Louise—we are dead men for sure.

Kate looked at her watch again anxiously as Charlie asked, 'So what are you expecting to happen, and what part do we have to play in it?'

'I can't tell you that at this stage, I'm afraid. I will give you a full briefing on the night if you agree to help - so do you agree?'

Charlie and Tim didn't need to consult. Their makeup and drive to do the right thing was so strong and similar. And besides, they had caught Willis once, so they absolutely had to be part of nailing him for good. Tim nodded at Charlie, and Charlie nodded in return. 'We're In Kate,' they said together.

Craig gave a huge sigh of relief knowing that the end of his constant misery might finally be in sight. He slumped into his chair and allowed some of the tension to release from his taught body.

'Thanks chaps,' Kate said in a matter-of-fact fashion. 'You could make all the difference to this operation. I will confirm the date with you through Craig. It will be in a few weeks, and I'll send a driver to pick you up at 6.30 from here on the day. You will get paid, but make your excuses at home because you will be out all night. A uniform will be provided but wear trainers, and don't bring mobile phones or any other communication device as they will be taken off you. Leave your valuables at home too, and you won't need money for anything.'

Tim smiled knowingly. 'Understood. But just one question. Are these people you are after responsible for killing James? Because based on what you've just said it would also satisfy MI6 to have everyone think his death was suicide, wouldn't it?'

Without flinching, Kate replied, 'Yes, I agree it would be very convenient for us, but that's not our style. The people who are controlling Willis Martin were almost certainly behind James's death - but we don't know who yet. However, right now it suits us to have everyone think the case is solved, so please leave it alone and don't make any waves. Now I really have to go before I'm missed.'

'But why would they want him dead?' Tim asked. 'He was just a mixed-up kid who was never going to be a threat to anyone.'

'There may be other reasons, but I suspect they needed to take the attention away from the deer problem, too much unwanted attention from the police at the club. They had to find a culprit to take the heat out of the situation. And of course he was also on to Willis and the cocaine smuggling. Now I really have got to go.'

'But we've still got a murderer on the loose,' Charlie exclaimed brusquely. 'And we knew about Willis's smuggling too.'

Kate pushed her chair backwards. 'Yes, I know that is a real possibility, but it's more likely our killer is now long gone and was just brought in to do a job.'

'Let's hope so. And are the Thai kids that Willis is bringing over also involved?' Tim asked.

'That will all become apparent,' Kate said, rising to her feet.

Everyone stood as Craig left the office and made sure the coast was clear for Kate to leave the shop without being seen. As Kate walked towards the open office door, she turned back to face the two men and gave them potent eye contact in turn. 'I'm really very grateful for your help chaps and I'm sure I don't have to remind you both not to discuss this with another soul. In fact, if any of this should leak, we'll know the source and will come looking for you.'

28

The police activity tailed off, and everything functioned as normal at the golf course for the remaining days of September and into October. The nights drew in and evenings were getting noticeably cooler as Autumn arrived. While Charlie and Tim had to switch off as best they could to Willis's continuing criminal activities. But at least they had the comfort of knowing justice for him was in sight. And they knew retribution would likely come on 25th October. The closely guarded date was when Adriana's next party was being held, and they had already acquired this privileged information courtesy of her resident DJ Ben. Needless to say they acted suitably dumb when Craig gave them the official word from Kate.

They were apprehensive and excited in equal measure at the prospect of discovering what villainy Willis was really up to, and what they might be faced with at the party.

'What did Ruth have to say about you being out all night at a bash that we know nothing about?' Tim asked his friend.

'Oh, you know Ruth, she reminded me that the last time

we got involved with something, there was always a dead body waiting for us. I told her this was different, just a bit of fun being waiters, and the police thought the golf professional's death was a suicide anyway. But she still wanted to know why we have to work all night for a few quid that we don't need. Then, as always, she relaxed. And when I told her we would be serving cocktail sausages on sticks and cheese straws to the rich and famous, she seemed more interested. Still thinks we're completely bonkers though.'

'Yeah, and if Ben is to be believed Flinty, it'll be the rich and famous doing unspeakable things that they shouldn't. Louise was much the same as Ruth, gave me huge amounts of grief after the business with James. But she got used to me doing all sorts of weird stuff when I was in the Met. No doubt they will compare notes as soon as we're both home, though.'

'You can bet your life on it, Fev. Hope they don't find out our employer is MI6.'

'Yes Flinty, not your average catering company, are they? Louise did of course remind me, yet again, that I am no longer a policeman. Funny how they can almost sense that you are not being entirely truthful, isn't it?'

'I hate being deceitful, Fev, and I am such a terrible liar. Ruth will catch me out eventually, she always does. And you know if this gets complicated, neither of them are going to be impressed with us.'

'I know Flinty, and that's scarier than anything we are going to be faced with at any dodgy party.'

While working at the course during the day of the event, the men constantly speculated on what Kate might have in mind for them, repeating conversations they had been having for weeks. And each time drawing the same conclusion - they were clearly going to be more than just waiters for the evening.

'Serving food and drinks will only be a front for surveillance of some sort, I reckon Flinty.' Tim mused.

'Absolutely. I would think Kate will have us fitted up with all sorts of high-tech stuff. She is obviously keen to capture something of major criminal importance that is set to happen at the party.'

'Except Flinty, if I was some kind of celebrity or politician, I wouldn't be turning up to a do like that, unless I could be sure I wasn't going to be all over the tabloids the next morning. So whatever she's doing, it will have to be pretty clever if the guests are going to feel safe.'

'Well, I think we're about done for the day here, so we won't have to wait long to find out Fev. I'll pick you up just before six we'll get back here park up and wait for our lift to the soiree.'

Still not quite knowing what to expect, the men arrived back at *The Sycamores* without valuables or phones and dressed casually in chinos, sweaters and trainers, just as Kate had instructed. Charlie locked the car with a press of the fob in the almost empty golf club car park. Only the bar and kitchen staff were parked there, along with the seemingly ever-present Craig, and the club's minibus was in its bay for the night. They walked towards the clubhouse entrance accompanied by the sound of the parakeets' twin shrieks as they flew to the tall trees to roost for the night. At the entrance to the clubhouse, the men waited restlessly for their transport to arrive and felt conspicuous in the strangely tranquil area that was normally alive with activity.

There was a slight chill to the air as darkness started to fall, far more noticeable while they were static and a sure sign that warm summer evenings were another year away. As the time passed slowly, Charlie nervously looked for conversation. 'I wonder what kind of car they'll send for us?

Probably something nondescript, so as not to draw attention, but fitted out with all kind of spooks kit.'

'Doubt it mate, this trip isn't secret, we are just a couple of hired waiters going to a party aren't we.'

'Yes, you're right Fev, maybe it will be something sleek and modern then.'

'This could be it now,' Tim laughed as a battered old grey Skoda estate taxi moved up the gradual curves of the driveway towards them.

Charlie squinted at the car in the fading light. 'Where does Willis live Fev?'

'Somewhere over Guildford way.'

'That's what I thought. If I'm not mistaken, the number on that taxi's sign has a Guildford dialling code.'

The car drew up next to them and stopped. There was a whirring sound as an electric motor powered down the passenger side front window. A young Asian man wearing jeans and a faded pink tee shirt leaned across the car. 'Flint and Featherstone?' He asked.

'That's us,' Tim said.

'Climb in gents. My name is Rav and I've come to take you to a party,' he smiled.

The car turned full lock outside the clubhouse and headed back down the drive. It stopped at the junction with the main road turned right towards the M25 motorway and then onward clockwise to junction ten. Charlie asked, 'So where are you taking us, Rav? We've never been to the famous Eagle House.'

'It's the back of beyond, sir. Way out in the country just North of Guildford.'

Tim leaned forward and asked, 'Have you been to this place before Rav?'

'Yes, sir, a couple of times.'

'Ever taken anyone famous there—you taxi drivers always have a story, don't you?'

'Not me sir, seen plenty of limos going in and out, caught a glimpse of a few people, but I only get to take the plebs - oh no offence like.'

Charlie and Tim both laughed, and Charlie said, 'None taken Rav.'

Relieved that his gaff had been forgiven Rav said apologetically, 'What I mean is I usually take the workers and drop them at the front gate.'

Charlie was keen to draw out any information he could about Willis and Adriana's home. 'So you have never been in to see the house itself then Rav?'

'No, sir, never. Strict security control at the gates. That's where I'm going to have to drop you tonight, I'm afraid.'

The journey continued through picturesque Surrey country villages and hamlets with idle chit-chat about sport, the weather and TV programmes with the driver still giving nothing away about their destination. Then Rav slowed and turned a sharp left into a lane barely wide enough for one car to pass. There were established trees and hedgerows on either side bordering woodland and open fields beyond.

'Blimey,' Tim exclaimed. This is narrow isn't it, can't imagine much traffic goes down here.

'It's a bit tricky,' Rav said, concentrating intently on the road before him. 'But there are a few passing places and only two houses down here, then it's a dead end. So normally you don't meet other cars, but tonight it might be busier.'

They drove down the constricted lane and Rav flicked the headlights on to main beam in the failing light. He leaned forward in his seat to get a better view around the twists of the road ahead of him. Then about half a mile down the lane, the taxi was forced up a bank by an arrogant speeding large dark German sedan with blacked-out windows. Sharp Hawthorn bushes noisily scratched into the taxi's paintwork as Rav cursed under his breath in an Asian language neither Charlie nor Tim recognised. 'I'm sorry about that, gentlemen,' he said once he had composed himself. 'I had to move out of the way. I need to keep this car on the road to make a living.'

Charlie replied, 'Don't let it worry you, Rav. But that obviously gives us an idea of what we are up against. I presume they must be linked to the party.'

'Yes sir, the only other house down here is a farm, and I've never known them to have a do.'

After that incident Rav drove even more gingerly for the next mile or so until they spotted an eight-foot-high ancient weathered red brick perimeter wall with security lights sporadically placed along its length. Some four hundred yards later Rav swung hard right into the semi-circular entrance where curved brick walls met high columns and ten feet tall black metal electronic security gates. Fixed to the wall on the left flank was a large grey slate sign with gold inlaid lettering that read *Eagle House* and underneath were two crossed golf clubs, looking like a tasteless coat of arms. Patrolling the gates were three burly guards who looked like clones. All black suited well over six feet with shaved heads and almost as broad as they were tall.

'This is it, gents, have fun,' Rav said. Charlie reached into his pocket to give Rav a tip, forgetting that he'd left his wallet at home. 'Not necessary sir, all taken care of,' the genial driver said.

'Maybe see you later Rav,' Charlie said, hoping that return arrangements had also been organised.

'Maybe sir. Not sure who's lined up to do the early morning stuff.' Rav muttered while gravel crunched and spat beneath his tyres as he sped off down the lane he had so carefully negotiated earlier.

'Names!' the obvious alpha guard of the three carrying a clipboard demanded.

'Err, Flint and Featherstone,' Tim replied, slightly taken aback by the directness.

The guard ran a finger down his list and resolutely made two ticks with his pen. One of his associates thrust a white plastic box with a flipped open lid in front of them. 'Empty your pockets. Watches, wallets, phones, everything.'

'Really?' Charlie balked.

The second guard breathed heavily through his nose and spoke with a frustrated cockney accent. 'Look mate, I'm not here to debate this, just empty your bleedin' pockets will ya—you are staff, remember?'

Charlie and Tim both realised that getting refused entry at the gate would not be a good story to tell Kate after so much careful planning. So one by one, they dropped whatever valuables they had into the container. Fortunately, Kate's briefing meant this was only handkerchiefs and small change. The alpha guard gave them a ticket with the number 37 on it and said, 'You can collect it at the end of your shift. Ok check them out Mo.'

A large and morose olive-skinned man with a mean pock-marked face walked across to them from the gate. With a thick middle eastern accent he said, 'Raise your arms and spread your legs.'

The comedian in Tim made him say, 'But we haven't even had dinner yet.' They quickly discovered that humour wasn't one of Mo's more obvious qualities, looking at each other in disbelief as the guard roughly patted them down.

'They're Ok Jeff,' Mo said, stepping back to his position on the gate.

Jeff, the alpha guard, swung open a pedestrian gate and

said, 'Follow the path to the front entrance. Someone will meet you there - and stay on the path at all times.'

'What kind of party is this, Jeff?' Tim asked flippantly.

The guard glared at him menacingly. 'It's the kind of party you may never leave if you don't behave yourself.'

29

Charlie and Tim followed the red tarmacked pathway towards *Eagle House*, which was illuminated by floodlights angled up from the lawn and washing the facade with soft yellow light. The house was a large elegant mock Georgian mansion, possibly built in the 1970s using modern materials. It looked like a Disney version of a typically neoclassical English country home. It was double fronted with probably ten bedrooms, large multi panelled white windows and constructed of red brick to match the perimeter wall. Except the perimeter wall was centuries old and doubtless built to surround an original house that had been demolished to make way for the new retro property.

Charlie laughed, 'Don't you think this is all typically Willis and Adriana?'

'What, garish and trying to be something it can never be?'

'Well yes, but beneath the fake exterior it has just a hint of aristocracy—for Adriana at least.'

Over to their right and further into the garden they could see a floodlit golf green complete with flag, and beyond the chain link fencing of a tennis court. This was indeed a very impressive residence, and they could see it must have required an army of gardeners to keep the grounds maintained. A job that Nathan once did before Adriana took offence to him being different, and something that still gnawed at the two men. They arrived at a large white portico with three long Portland stone steps leading up to the main entrance of the house. Fibre glass fluted columns were cleverly disguising the reinforced concrete beneath and supporting a pitched roof canopy. Standing rigidly at the huge double leaf oak doors were another two clones of Jeff the alpha at the gate. Both looking like gorillas in dark suits with hands held crossed in front of their crotches.

'Flint and Featherstone?' one of them asked in an Eastern European accent.

'That's us,' Tim replied, now growing a little tired of the constant scrutiny.

The guard opened one leaf of the doors inward and said, 'First door on the left, go and get changed.'

'Are our uniforms in there?' Charlie asked.

The man laughed. 'Yes, speak to Dino. He will tell you what you are wearing.'

They stepped inside the large hallway where everything seemed to be white and shining. The porcelain tiled floor, polished plaster walls and grandiose, sweeping marble staircase were all gleaming in the bright artificial light and only punctuated by completely out-of-place portraits by old masters in oils. 'Blimey,' Tim said. 'Willis must have had the architect watch *Gone With The Wind* several times before he built this.'

Charlie's facial features twisted with displeasure, unimpressed by the obvious pretentiousness all around him. 'Frankly my dear, I don't give a toss. Let's get on with it.'

They turned towards the door on the left and caught the

sound of repetitive thumping music in the background and the distinct smell of marijuana drifting in the air. Then their attention was drawn by the sudden squeal of a small dark-skinned girl running down the stairs and disappearing through an open doorway. She was wearing only a Venetian mask and in hot pursuit was what looked like an older gentleman sporting a Superman outfit.

'Ahh. That kind of party,' Charlie said to his friend, chuckling.

'As we suspected, mate,' Tim replied.

Dino the guard was yet another clone, only with a full head of hair and a Yorkshire accent this time. He was expecting them and had unlatched the door to their changing room in readiness. As they moved into the room, he said, 'Your things are hanging on hooks to your right. Leave the clothes you are wearing in the bins provided and collect them when you leave. Get changed and I will tell you where to go.'

Charlie and Tim heard the door click shut behind them and scoured the small cloak room for uniforms. 'I don't want to worry you Flinty,' Tim said, 'but the only things hanging on hooks are those two brown bartenders' aprons and a couple of Lone Ranger masks.'

Charlie immediately went back to the door and opened it. Dino turned to face him and glared as Charlie asked politely. 'Excuse me Dino, but we can't seem to find our uniforms. Can you remind me where they are?'

'I told you—' he barked, 'they are on the hooks to your right, an apron and a mask each.' He shook his head. 'I wish they would brief you bloody people. You have to wear nothing else apart from trainers. We need to be sure you don't have anything concealed. Just get on with it, will you.'

Charlie was desperate to avoid confrontation with the

burly guard, but far from happy with the clothing arrangements. 'Ok. Can you call Kate and let her know we are here?'

Dino was fast losing whatever small amount of patience he had. 'I have radioed her already. She is coming. Now get changed or get out.'

Charlie closed the door and turned to Tim. 'That is the uniform Fev, and probably why they didn't ask for our sizes beforehand. Oh, and Kate is on her way.'

Tim shrugged. 'Got to go with it now Flinty. They'll start to smell a rat otherwise.' He started stripping his clothes off, 'Come on mate, don't be shy, there is at least a pocket in the apron to put your hands in if you get cold.'

'Yeah thanks, it's not my hands I'm worried about.'

Five minutes later, there was a gentle tap at the door and a very serious-looking Kate walked in. She was not dressed in her normal practical and frumpy work clothes, but a black cocktail dress and high heels. Her hair was down, her contacts were in, and she had used bright red lipstick of the Adriana variety. 'You didn't tell us about this,' a very self-conscious Charlie said. 'And by the way, you look lovely.'

Kate held a finger to her lips. 'Shhh. Thank you. If I'd have told you how it works here, you'd never have come, and I need you tonight—your country needs you tonight.' She produced a clipboard and said casually, 'Ok, before we start you two need to sign one of these sheets each.'

'What's this all about then, Kate?' Tim said abruptly.

'It's the non-disclosure agreement I mentioned. It's just to say that whatever you see tonight, you can't go to the press or put it on any kind of media. If you don't sign, I can't even get you past the guard on the door.'

Tim looked displeased and had obviously forgotten the requirement. 'So, what else haven't you told us, Kate?'

Charlie had to control the edginess building in his friend

and took the clipboard. 'Ok, Ok, we'll sign we've come too far.' They both scribbled a signature without looking at the documents and passed the clipboard back to Kate. Charlie huffed, 'Now let's get on with it. Tell us what we've got to do.'

Kate moved closer and spoke softly. 'The job is to walk around with trays of drinks, pick up empties and refill at the bar with anything the guests want.'

'And the real job?' Tim asked.

'Keep your voice down please,' Kate chastised.

'Sorry,' Tim murmured as he and Charlie moved closer to Kate.

She lowered her voice to a whisper. 'This is a hedonistic party, hence the uniform. Think of the Stanley Kubrick film Eyes Wide Shut. You will see lots of people you might recognise from the TV in compromising positions with young Thai girls, or boys, mainly. They'll all be wearing masks of some description, and maybe even costumes, but you'll soon work out who they are.'

Charlie pulled a distorted and disapproving face. 'Really?'

'Yes really,' Kate said abruptly. 'And you two must remain completely unmoved by whatever you encounter. Don't comment, or even pull faces like you just did, Charlie.' She gestured for them to shift to the back of the room and away from the white Georgian panelled door where Dino was waiting on the other side. 'Willis, Adriana and their masters are trying to trap someone very high profile here tonight, and certain rooms have been set up for secret filming. They are looking to capture the kind of footage that could ruin someone for life.'

'So, their plan is to blackmail somebody important?' Tim suggested.

'Exactly,' Kate replied. 'But not for money. These people

want an individual to go and work for them—they want to own him.'

'Well, they are going to have to catch him doing something pretty bad to make whoever it is agree to that, Kate,' Charlie said.

'Believe me, Charlie, it will be,' she said with a knowing nod. 'Now we've got to let this thing take place, or we will blow our cover and have no evidence. Then our job is to get hold of the chip from the secret camera that has captured the event before they do. So, here's what's going to happen. You will both serve drinks for a few hours and keep your mouths shut. When I give you the nod, you will follow me without question—understood?'

Charlie and Tim both swallowed hard. 'Understood,' they said in harmony.

'Good,' Kate said without emotion. 'I'll tell you more when I get back. And now we need to start doing our jobs, go and find Jack at the bar in the big room—and remember, no one but us three are in on this. And I repeat, do not look shocked, whatever you might come across tonight.'

30

It was just after eight when, with bandit masks in place and brown cotton aprons hooked over their heads, tied at the waist and completely open at the back, Charlie and Tim cautiously stepped out of their dressing room. Shuffling past unflinching security guard Dino, they moved their white trainer wearing feet tentatively along the grand hallway, feeling very conscious of their bare flesh on display. The area was quiet apart from the low-level party music reverberating off the glossy surfaces. 'Ben's here somewhere, Fev,' Charlie said.

'Yes,' Tim replied, swivelling his head to take in the opulent surroundings. 'Bet they've got him locked away again. Probably just as well. Have you seen some of the signs on these doors?'

On the first large glossy white panelled door they passed was fixed a computer printed sign indicating *Bondage Room* with a picture showing knotted rope and a whip. Further on was another saying *Fetish Room* with a picture of red patent stiletto heels. Then a freestanding sign with an arrow pointing left down a corridor that said *Punishment Room, Dominatrix, and Headmistress.*

Charlie cast Tim an old-fashioned sideways glance. 'Looks like they've thought of everything.'

As they reached the end of the hall, they entered a large open lounge room about fifty feet square with high ceilings and tall Georgian sash windows looking out onto the vast expanse of dimly lit garden. The polished oak floor was covered in places by expensive Persian rugs, and dark reproduction furniture stood around the smooth painted light grey walls. 'Blimey, this is impressive,' Charlie commented.

'Isn't it just,' Tim replied. 'All of it screaming fake, just like Willis. Now, according to Kate, our place of employment should be in here somewhere.'

The room smelt of food being prepared with subtle overtones of garlic and that sweet musky aroma of smoke they both recognised again. 'Someone's got the herbal Woodbines on the go,' Tim murmured with a sly grin.

In the far corner of the room, a bar was being stocked and prepared for the evening's events. As they moved towards it, they noticed several coffee tables surrounded by plush armchairs, deep Chesterfields and the occasional chaise lounge. On each table there were four silver bowls, one containing regular filter cigarettes, another with reefers, the third with every type and flavour of condom you could think of, and the last piled high with white powder. Charlie gave Tim a nudge. 'There you go Fev, straight out of Willis's golf clubs and onto his tables.'

Over at the bar, in a uniform just like their own, a slim middle-aged man with a grey beard and receding hairline was preparing his stock and pouring drinks like he was a professional. The men introduced each other and shook hands. 'I'm Jack,' the man said. 'Have you signed the forms yet?'.

'Yes, all done, and we're Charlie and Tim, by the way,'

Charlie replied hospitably, knowing he was likely to need the man's advice.

Tim smiled, realising the barman was in the same clothing predicament as him. 'You've done this before Jack, by the looks of it. Very organised.'

The man carried on expertly pouring champagne into flutes one handed. 'Yeah, I work nights in a Soho club normally, where some of the guests here tonight are regulars. All sorts go on there too, but you soon learn how to react and keep your trap shut.'

Charlie and Tim looked at each other and wondered quite what to expect, and what Kate might still be holding off telling them. 'You're new, aren't you?' the barman said.

Tim nodded. 'Yes, is it obvious? This is all a bit strange to us, Jack.'

The barman burst into laughter. 'Don't worry, it's a bit strange to everyone, mate. Think of this as a very exclusive gentleman's club where their every sexual whim has been catered for. With city financiers, politicians and top civil servants here, this is a gathering for the older and more influential gentlemen of the country, and the odd celebrity, of course, where anything goes. That's why the security is so tight.'

Tim looked surprised. 'Do you do many of these events then, Jack?'

'Yeah, I've done loads, but only my second here. They're all mostly the same format, never as lavish or well controlled as this though—which tells you something about the type of guests. But I get paid bloody well, so you'll never hear me complain.'

Tim couldn't help probing while the man was speaking openly. 'So, who provides all the stuff in the bowls then, Jack?'

The barman suddenly turned decidedly frosty and gave

Tim direct eye contact. 'I don't know about any of that stuff and never ask questions—nor should you if you've got any sense. We are just here to serve drinks, and that's all.' He leaned towards them and spoke softly. 'Some friendly advice lads, don't ever push your luck with these people.'

'How does it all work then, Jack?' Charlie enquired, trying to move the conversation forward.

The barman's attitude moderated. He smiled, then turned and took a bottle of champagne from a glass fronted cooler cabinet behind the bar. He stood the frosted bottle on the countertop and gave Charlie and Tim his full attention. 'So, the first thing that's going to happen is that some gentlemen, of the more mature variety, will start to arrive in various states of undress—and often in, shall we say, unusual clothing. Plus, every one of them will be wearing masks or face coverings of some sort. The good news is that once you see them, you'll feel less worried about what you are wearing.'

Charlie and Tim gave a nervous laugh as Jack continued. 'There is every chance you might just recognise some of the people. Now whatever you do, don't act surprised or engage them in conversation and definitely don't let on that you know who they are. They have got to feel completely anonymous and safe while they're here. It's part of the experience for them.'

'Got it,' Tim said. 'We've already been warned. What happens after that?'

Jack opened the bottle of champagne on his counter, completely oblivious to the sound or force of the cork being removed. He held the bottle delicately at the base and started pouring again. 'Once the old boys arrive, they normally have a couple of drinks. By the way, I've got everything here.' He tapped his nose with a forefinger. 'Even Viagra if anybody needs it. Or maybe they'll take something else to get them relaxed. There's plenty of it about. Some will wander off into the special rooms you will have spotted when they get the word, and others will hang around waiting for the main party to start. Quite soon after that, several young men and women will arrive, and tonight they are mainly Thais. They'll be wearing outfits to titillate the guests and will have masks on too. They will all mingle in this room for a while before going off to do what they've got to do. And I'll warn you now, it's free rein here so they could be anywhere, apart from a few locked rooms that are out of bounds. You'll find them up to all sorts in any of the bedrooms, the showers, the swimming pool, the greenhouse, cupboards and even in the open areas, so you'd better be broad-minded boys.'

Charlie and Tim both swallowed hard, knowing they were in far too deep to do anything else but comply. 'So anyone goes anywhere and does anything?' Tim suggested.

'That's about the size of it, Tim,' Jack replied. 'And your job is to find them and keep them plied with drinks all night long. As the night wears on, they will swap partners or several of them will gather in one place, and it'll be like a scrum. Then they will come back here for a rest and to take a little something to keep them going. The party will just go wherever it goes all night long and you will have to keep up with it.'

'Really?' Charlie said, looking disgusted.

'Really,' Jack replied in a clipped fashion. 'And as the evening wears on, more drink goes down their throats and white powder up their noses. They really don't care about anything. Just remember you are not here to judge, however unsavoury you think it all might be.' He held the side of a hand to his mouth, grinned and whispered, 'Although we do have a few men from the bench in tonight.'

Their task was starting to become less amusing by the

second for Charlie and Tim, made worse by the barman adding pragmatically, 'Oh, and if any of the guests should proposition you, then politely decline. Don't even think about giving them a slap. If anything turns funny, then security will deal with it, and believe me, they are nasty people who don't stop to ask questions. That's why you two are here. The last waiters are still recovering, along with the old DJ who thought he might get a bit lairy. Anyway, just offer the guests drinks from your trays and keep coming back for top-ups and special orders—that's all there is to it.'

Jack turned his head sharply sideways and gave a well-practiced and insincere smile. He spoke out the side of his mouth and said, 'Stand by your beds. Here come some of them now.'

31

A very familiar male voice with rich educated tones spoke from behind Charlie and Tim as they stood facing the bar. 'I'll have one of your finest glasses of Champagne barman please.'

'Yes of course sir,' Jack subserviently replied, keeping the synthetic smile fixed firmly across his face as he placed a bubbling flute on the countertop

Then another slightly muffled but confident voice said, 'And I'll have a scotch and soda, young man, if you please.'

'Coming right up, sir,' Jack said cheerfully.

When considering the view they were giving to the arriving male guests, Charlie and Tim thought it prudent to turn their backs to the bar so they swivelled to face the two voices. They were taken aback by the vision before them and had to contain an involuntary expletive. One of the ageing men was wearing nothing but a leather thong, straps around his torso, a flat black leather cap and a cat mask - complete with whiskers. And the other a head to toe one piece rubber outfit with only the eyes, mouth and nostrils visible. Tim was working hard steeling himself to suppress a laugh, while Charlie was somewhere between sickened and hysterical. They had seen this kind of thing in films and strange late night TV channels but never in the flesh, and there was plenty of flesh. But they both realised the time had arrived for them to play their part. 'Your country needs you,' Kate had said.

'Evening gentleman,' they both pronounced, doing their utmost to get into the spirit of the party.

The two old men didn't reply. They simply took their drinks, nodded and moved off towards the easy chairs. 'Bloody hell,' Tim exclaimed out loud. 'One of those was a TV reporter. I'd recognise that voice anywhere, and I'm guessing it was the one in the cap. That rubber outfit was probably far too tight around the other one's nether regions for him to speak clearly for very long.'

Jack the barman glared at Tim. 'Remember what I told you now, don't get yourselves into trouble on your first night.'

'Yeah, sorry Jack,' Tim said, glancing at more men of varying shapes and density of body hair. They were arriving in togas, nazi uniform, sailor suits and more than one dressed as a baby, complete with nappy, mop cap and dummy.

'Think one of these is a football manager,' Charlie whispered to Tim, out of the barman's earshot.

'Champagne gentlemen?' Tim said, sliding a flute laden tray off the bar countertop and onto the upturned palm of his left hand as more people approached. Charlie did the same and moved towards the area of the room where a steady stream of men with pale saggy skin were entering, wearing even more ridiculous outfits and masks—and in several cases, just masks. All the while, Ben's background music was bouncing around the walls. Male chatter was getting louder as alcohol, marijuana and cocaine kicked in. A palpable tension began to build among the forty or so men lounging in the easy chairs and sofas - and it was designed to be that way by the organisers.

Suddenly the music stopped and a young male voice came over the sound system. It was Ben. 'Gentlemen, I am pleased to announce that your rooms are now open.'

Tim laughed as they carried trays of empty glasses back to the bar against a flow of older men hurrying towards certain humiliation. 'Young Ben hasn't got a clue what that means. Someone has just told him to say it. But the guests aren't shy about letting us know which are the warped ones are they. Who have you clocked so far, Flinty?'

'I've seen a couple of politicians I recognise, a comedian and a quiz show host. How about you?'

Tim was starting to get blasé, 'A couple of luvvie actors, a singer, and I'm guessing high ranking civil servants, perhaps even some of the judges Jack mentioned.' He looked over to the part of the room where the guests had trickled in earlier and said. 'Look out Flinty, here comes the main event.'

The men that had previously been relaxing in comfortable soft furniture all stood with delighted smiles on their faces. They watched intently as young girls and boys all wearing venetian masks and red devil horns walked towards them looking exuberant and waving excitedly. The old men were sliding their arms around youngsters in skimpy underwear, girls dressed as French maids, serving wenches and schoolgirls or just plain naked. And boys in gladiator garb, thongs or permutations of the Village People. Their youthful tight bodies mingled with euphoric and tactile wrinkled old men just waiting to establish their preference. The room was full of nervous laughter, broken Thai English conversation and elderly men promising to look after their escorts who had doubtless heard the story a million times before. Then, couple by couple, the large room emptied, leaving Charlie and Tim back at the bar wondering what to do next. Barman Jack stretched across the bar for their trays and said, 'Leave it for a while lads, just pick up any empties and give all the guests half an hour before going to find them. They'll be starting to swap around about then. Go and get yourselves something to eat and I'll refill the glasses.'

But Charlie and Tim didn't much feel like eating. They had both been nauseated by what they had witnessed. 'Some of those kids looked really young Fev, didn't they?' Charlie said with a real look of sadness about him. 'I just need Kate to hurry up this all makes me very uncomfortable.'

Tim put a comforting hand on his friend's shoulder. 'Bigger picture mate, but it had better be bloody good. I'd hate for anyone to think we were in any way involved with this. But I'm telling you now I'm going to expose every last one of these sick bastards if MI6 don't.'

'Any thoughts yet on who they're trying to trap, Fev?' Charlie asked.

'Not a clue Flinty. Could be any one of them, couldn't it?'

After re-stocking his bar and getting more drinks ready, Jack beckoned them over. 'Ok lads, take your trays and wander everywhere. Don't worry about disturbing people, they won't care, but brace yourselves,' he laughed scornfully.

Charlie and Tim balanced their trays carefully, took a deep breath, and moved off. Charlie said, 'You go up and I'll go down and we'll swap over next time.' Tim nodded in agreement and with a wry smile, Charlie watched his friend's naked back half climb the grand sweeping staircase. He moved down the hallway and stopped outside a room where he could hear screams of agony from behind the door. With trepidation, he tapped politely then pushed the door open only to see the man he thought was the TV reporter on all fours being dominated by an overweight middle-aged woman in a PVC body suit holding a whip. From the small circular burns, it was clear she had been stubbing cigarettes out on his back, and the skin on his buttocks looked raised and reddened from being lashed. The woman looked up and gave Charlie a half smile while taking a glass from his tray. 'Oh, thanks love, I was gasping. Don't worry about leaving one for him.' The man turned his head in an attempt to glance at Charlie and the woman loudly berated him. 'Did I say you could look?' she shouted.

'No mistress,' the man whimpered in his slightly trembling but still very recognisable voice. Then he yelled in agony as he took a stiletto heel slammed down hard between his shoulder blades.

Charlie left the room, wincing at the thought of the pain and totally perplexed. Unable to understand how anyone could find such an experience remotely pleasurable, let alone risk a successful career for. There were similar stories in the other rooms with men licking shoes and being demeaned by women controlling their every movement and word, whilst seemingly lapping up the experience. Then he moved into the barely lit dungeon room where he discovered the rubber suited man suspended upside down by ropes and with a horse's bit between his teeth. Charlie felt it prudent to just leave a couple of drinks and walk out again quickly, careful not to stare.

'How did it go upstairs, Fev?' Charlie asked as they met back in the lounge area heading for the bar.

Tim exhaled loudly. 'Well one room was like the Blue Oyster Bar from the Police Academy film, but another was like a Roman orgy, they all seem to have piled on top of each other. There was even a naked girl acting as a table, she was covered in food and letting people eat off her. I couldn't watch. I just left the full glasses, picked up the empties and went. Oh, and some old boy in a sailor's outfit touched me up, so I chinned him.'

'You did what?'

'Sorry mate, I couldn't help myself, but it's ok no-one was watching,'

'Nice one Fev, now we'll get thrown out, and Kate's months of planning will be ruined.'

'Don't worry Flinty, they're all off their faces anyway. He'll think one of the others in the tangle of bodies kicked him in the head.'

Charlie shook his head in disbelief as they moved through the almost empty lounge. 'Come on Kate,' he said impatiently under his breath.

Jack took in all the empty glasses and grinned. 'You made it back then, lads. Give them all another break before you go out again. They'll need one before the next round when they start spreading out—it gets better.' He seemed to revel in the men's obvious discomfort, and they were beginning to take a dislike to him.

Tim looked disturbed. 'I'm not being funny Jack, but some of the guests don't look like they are going to last the night, especially being full of drugs and booze as well.'

The barman gave a superior smirk, 'Don't worry Tim, there are plenty of doctors in the house. In fact, we've even got an eminent heart surgeon in here somewhere.'

Charlie and Tim continued to mingle with trays full of wine and champagne plying people in all kinds of compromising positions almost anywhere in the house and grounds. They diverted their gaze at the sordid goings on as they quietly went about their business. Wondering how they might possibly be helping their country by encouraging such depraved behaviour, all the while wishing for Kate to appear. They arrived back at the bar to get refills for the umpteenth time, slipping into a routine and almost forgetting their state of undress. Charlie looked at Tim and said, 'This is just horrible, mate. If Kate doesn't show in a minute, I'm out of here.'

'Not quite as easy as that Flinty,' his old friend said. 'They are not going to let you leave here just because you don't like what's going on. That makes you a risk to them, and you could blow whatever this is all about with MI6 wide open. Stick with it kid, I'm sure something will happen soon.'

Charlie shook his head. He knew Tim was right, but he was struggling with what he had to witness. Then a quiet female voice from behind them said, 'Ok, don't turn around or make a fuss, we are making our move now, just bring your trays and stick close to me and do exactly as I tell you. Nod if you understand.'

They both nodded.

32

Charlie and Tim picked up trays of drinks, wheeled around and followed Kate out of the room and towards the grand sweeping staircase, stepping carefully around wine glasses, discarded clothing and spent bodies on their way. Kate tilted her head downward and spoke. 'They can lip read from cameras, so say nothing and listen carefully. We are about to go into a control room on the premise that you are going to take a security man a drink and ask what he wants to eat. He will not want to let you in, but whatever he says you must force your way into the room when he unlocks it, and I will be right behind you.'

At the base of the staircase while still gazing at the floor, Kate whispered, 'Pay attention. The door to my left is the trophy room. Make sure you remember it. It's going to be very important for you later.'

'Yup,' Tim mumbled, almost without movement of his lips.

As they moved up the staircase, naked old masked men were sprawled out and looking drained, but still with enough energy to lift wine glasses from their trays as they passed. While young Asian men and women wrapped in silk dressing gowns were sitting on the landing drinking bottled water, seemingly exhausted.

'We're going into a room off the next bedroom,' Kate said discreetly. She stopped, turned a brass doorknob and pushed open the large white panelled door. A startled, disrobed man leapt off a king-sized bed in the centre of the room, where everything seemed pastel green. He was flushed and alone but had no apparent reason to be alarmed. Still, he left the room hurriedly and without resistance when Kate said, 'I'm sorry to disturb you sir, but we have to shut this room for security purposes.'

Kate took the key she was holding and locked the door after Charlie and Tim had walked into the bedroom. She rapped loudly with her knuckles on a smaller door immediately to their left and moved backwards out of sight. 'Ready?' She said. 'He won't like it but just force your way in, alright.'

Before they could answer, a slight young man of about twenty with unruly dark hair wearing jeans, a checked shirt and trainers cracked the door open just enough to see inside. He adjusted his steel-rimmed glasses and looked surprised. 'Oh Hi, I didn't ask for a drink. I usually ring down if I want anything.'

Tim thought on his feet, 'Yes, we know, but we hadn't heard from you, and didn't want you to be forgotten, especially as everything is running out down there. You also need something to eat as you must be getting hungry by now. Don't want you passing out on us.'

This boy is a geek, Charlie thought. We were expecting another muscular clone to be with him but this kid is obviously here to do something technical, something specialised with computers, probably. 'Let us in will you mate,' Tim said. 'I'm about to drop this tray and you'd better have a drink soon or you'll dehydrate and I'll get into trouble. I've got water, lemonade and orange juice too.' The young man hesitated and Tim leant his not inconsiderable bulk against the door as Charlie forced his way through the gap between the door and frame. The boy was shocked and uncomfortable with their presence, but they were inside. The room looked like a high security control room full of CCTV and computer screens. There were banks of panels showing coloured graphics monitoring the condition of everything you could think of in the house and gardens. Fire and intruder alarm systems, lighting, temperature, water sprinklers, electrical and gas supply. This was some kind of command centre that they were not intended to see. A place to keep tabs on everyone, and somewhere to gather evidence for blackmail. They placed their trays on a desk and attempted to divert the boy's attention, who was by now wondering why they had been so forceful. 'Sorry, that was a bit dramatic,' Charlie said, trying to appeal to the young man's ego. 'But we've got strict orders to look after you at all costs. You're obviously an important cog in the operation. Now what would you like to drink, young sir? Sorry, didn't get your name?'

The youngster hesitated. 'It's Ryan.'

They were keeping him distracted for as long as they could, all the while wondering where Kate had got to. Tim smiled sweetly and asked, 'Any idea what you might like to eat, Ryan? I'm sure we can get the chef to knock up whatever you fancy.'

Ryan looked at them both suspiciously, he was beginning to smell a rat. 'And where are you going to write my order?' He asked.

'Photographic memory, Ryan,' Tim said smiling while tapping his temple with his right index finger. 'Fire away.'

Ryan had been told by the security team not to let anyone into the room and that any communication to him would only come through the telephone on his desk. So he was feeling very uneasy with the sudden change of circumstances and reached for the handset of the desk phone. 'You will excuse me if I make a call to check this out guys, it's just that I've had very specific instructions not to...'

There were quickening footsteps across the carpet, a dull thud and then a crack. Ryan's eyes glazed over and he hit the ground unconscious with blood trickling from a wound on his head. Kate had run across the floor, leapt into the air and smashed a huge solid glass dildo into his skull. Charlie and Tim looked aghast.

'What?' Kate glared and asked. 'It's all I could find, okay. Now shove his socks into his mouth and use these curtain ties to bind his hands and feet, while I lock the door.'

Charlie grimaced. 'Urgh, now we know why that dirty old sod was so keen to leave. Make sure you wash your hands, Kate.'

They trussed the still unconscious Ryan up like a Christmas turkey, bundled him into a cleaner's cupboard, and secured the door, but not before Charlie had lifted a modern smart phone from the back pocket of his jeans.

Kate moved over to a double row of TV screens set around a semi-circular desk, all showing live footage of whatever debauchery was going on in *Eagle House* that night. Completely unmoved by the images before her, Kate sat herself in a black leather high-backed chair on casters, leaned forward and scanned the screens. 'Right, let's see if we can find the correct room. Ah yes, there it is,' she said, pointing to a screen on the bottom left and using her feet to roll the chair across the floor towards it. 'Camera eleven is trained on the trophy room, and can you see those two people just coming into the picture now?' She turned to Charlie and Tim, looking for confirmation, as she seemed to with everything. 'Well gentlemen, what they are about to do is get captured by camera eleven, and that piece of footage will be what this entire operation is all about.' Kate spun her chair around and stared at them both in turn. 'And we've got to get to it before the mafia does.'

Charlie and Tim sucked in deep breaths to fill their lungs with oxygen, keep their heads clear and concentrate. This was now all very real and very serious. Charlie took a swig of orange juice to deal with his dry throat and waited for instructions. Kate stared into the whites of their eyes to be sure they were up to the task. 'I know you've got a million questions, but we haven't got time, so just listen. The camera sending back those images is hidden in a golf trophy which is standing on top of a glass fronted display cabinet with several others. It's a large silver bowl that Willis won in 1995, the camera is concealed in the wooden base which I saw them testing earlier today. Now, the information is stored locally on the device rather than on a central hard drive, and that's because it's easier to remove and transport quickly. So, once the action is over I need you to get the memory card out of that camera and then carry on about your business as though nothing has happened. I haven't got time to explain now, but it will be obvious what is going on when the performance starts.'

'Performance?' Charlie interrupted.

'Yes, that's right. Just remember, the two people will be acting something out. And as soon as they leave the room, get down there, grab that camera, smash it and take the card. I will arrive and cause a distraction to give you time to do it—are you clear?'

'Err, just one thing,' Tim said, pointing to his obvious lack of clothing, 'what are we supposed to do with this card thingy when we've got it?'

Kate took a last glance at camera eleven's screen and rapidly moved towards the door. 'One of you will have to swallow it. Now there's every chance I may not make it out of here tonight, and if that happens, then someone will be in touch. Lock yourself in, keep watching the screen and get down there as soon as the room is empty - good luck.' Then with a slam of the door, she was gone.

Charlie positioned himself in the still warm chair, Tim locked the door after Kate's departure and then leaned on the desk next to Charlie and focused on the activity being transmitted from the trophy room. 'This is where it could start getting dangerous, mate,' he said as they both concentrated intently as though their lives depended on it.

In the centre of the trophy room stood a long, slender white marble table streaked by the irregular grey veins of a natural material. It was about waist high and supported by a robust carved circular pilaster at either end. Around the table prowled two figures, the slighter one seemingly beckoning the other to follow. They were dressed in full length white satin hooded pagan ritual robes and wearing black feathered venetian masks. From their differing physiques, this was obviously a man and a woman. The womanly figure secured the door and carefully spread a white sheet across the cold marble tabletop. She dipped her hand into an adjacent urn and allowed pink rose petals to tumble delicately from her grasp onto the sheet.

'Bloody hell, what's going on here Flinty?' Tim whispered excitedly.

'Well, I'm hoping it's nothing more than rumpy-pumpy, and the honey trap we were expecting. But I've got a nasty feeling Kate is anticipating it to be a little more than that, otherwise we wouldn't be here.'

'Think you might be right Flinty, the bloke has started to wave a huge scimitar sword around in some sort of figure of eight pattern. We'd better get down there.'

'No, we can't do that,' Charlie said. 'We'll blow our cover, and it's probably just some weird, kinky stuff. Willis isn't into killing people, and remember Kate said it's a performance.'

They both stayed glued to the screen as the woman shrugged off her robe and let it slip to the floor, revealing a young slender, perfectly formed naked body with long dark hair cascading onto her shoulders. She climbed onto the marble table, laid out submissively and removed her mask.

'It's Adriana,' Charlie blurted.

Tim shook his head in astonishment. 'She is one way-out girl. And look, she is pulling the bloke towards her and undoing his robes.'

As the man's robes fell from his body, they could see from the back view that this was a more mature male form, with sagging and creased skin.

Tim almost pushed his nose onto the screen and squinted hard, 'That tattoo on his back, I'm sure it's—Yes, it is—it's bloody Gideon.'

'Let me look,' Charlie said, pushing Tim away from the screen. He carefully studied the back of the naked man, who was now slowly waving the scimitar horizontally above the length of Adriana's motionless body. 'Robert Johnson,' Charlie said succinctly.

'Nope, it's definitely Gideon,' Tim replied.

'No, the tattoo is a man with a guitar case standing at a country crossroads. For a bloke who loves the blues like Gideon, that has to be Robert Johnson.'

'So what's the significance of that then, Flinty?'

'Well, the story goes that Robert Johnson was just an average blues player until he met the devil at the crossroads, then he became a brilliant blues player.'

'And your point is?'

'They say Robert Johnson sold his soul to the devil to get what he wanted. Has Gideon done the same?'

'Holy shit, now you're scaring me.'

Charlie and Tim watched intently as Gideon traced the outline of Adriana's naked body with the scimitar. She appeared to be orchestrating his movements, but the camera's view of her face was obscured by Gideon's torso. Adriana reached up and gently stroking his face, removed his mask, then she patted her left hand on the marble top and Gideon moved around to the other side of the table. 'She's put him there so the camera is getting both of their faces very clearly,' Tim commented. 'Something is about to happen Flinty.'

Charlie looked concerned. 'He's bending forward and making slicing motions with that sword like he's going to cut her throat. Now he's moving back around this side so we can't see her face.'

Suddenly Gideon leaned over Adriana's body and appeared to slice her throat for real. Her arm was visible and reaching for the apparent wound as her body jerked and blood ran off the side of the table and pooled on the floor. For a while her body convulsed, then eventually stopped and lay perfectly still.

Neither of the men panicked. 'Can you see what's happening here?' Charlie asked his friend.

'Yes, this is it Flinty, they are setting him up, that's why they are filming it, and the blood is fake,'

'It's the deer's blood Fev, isn't it? It's all beginning to add up now.'

Tim stood upright. 'They'll edit that footage to make it look like he's killed her in some kind of pagan sacrifice. He's the one they want, and that's how they're going to get him. That footage could be all over the world tonight if he doesn't agree to their demands. Come on Flinty, we've got to get to that camera before they do.'

'Just hold on a second. They haven't left yet, and Kate hasn't shown herself either.'

Adriana lay motionless for a few minutes as Gideon ran his hands over her bloodied body. 'She's making sure they've got the best possible footage to use against him,' Charlie said. 'He is totally besotted with the woman and would have done anything to get to her. She must have trapped him by saying this sort of thing turned her on. What a bitch.'

Finally, Adriana sat upright and Gideon backed away from the table to put his robe on. She slid off the table, delicately lifted the cover sheet and produced a towel to wipe the blood away that was covering her body, then dressed herself in the robe.

'Show's over,' Charlie said. 'We'd better get going can't afford to wait for Kate—that footage is dynamite.'

33

Camera eleven was still rolling and showing the rear view of Gideon and Adriana about to leave the room. Suddenly it picked up a commotion as the trophy room door flew open and Kate's body was thrown across the hard porcelain tiled floor and an aggressive-looking security guard followed her in. Tim pulled on his friend's arm. 'Come on mate, I'm sure this isn't what she had in mind. Let's go.'

Charlie almost leapt out of his chair. 'Yes, and Kate obviously didn't manage to cause her distraction, so before we go, let's cause one of our own. You hit the *Full Alarm* button on the fire alarm panel over there and I'll do the same on the intruder alarm and pull the keys out so they can't be reset. On a house this size in the middle of nowhere with a famous owner both will be wired straight into the local stations, and the noise of the alarms will send everyone running.'

'That should do it,' Tim said as the alarms sprang into life. 'Squad cars and fire engines on the way.'

'And lots of hysterical old boys crapping themselves,' Charlie smirked.

Continuous bells rang, loud irritating klaxons sounded,

and lights flashed throughout the house as Charlie and Tim locked the control room door and ran down the staircase to be faced with a scene of complete mayhem. Half dressed, or completely naked, old men frantically trying to wipe white powder off their faces were bursting out of doors in a state of panic, just like a French farce. Young Thai girls and boys were screaming and bumping into each other, not knowing which way to run. While security men were shouting instructions and doing their best to guide the terrified and irrational to an assembly point on the front lawn - but no-one was listening.

At the bottom of the staircase, Charlie and Tim found the trophy room with the door ajar and a trail of bloody footprints leading out into the hallway and beyond. They gingerly eased the door open and inside the room Adriana was nowhere to be seen, but the huge security guard Mo had a handgun trained on Kate and Gideon. He turned to check on the noise behind him and waved the barrel of the gun at the two men, indicating for them to move across the room with the others. 'Get over there and don't make me kill you,' he said through gritted teeth.

The men complied with the instruction, but Tim decided to mess with the security guard's head. 'What are you going to do kill four of us?'

'Shut your mouth,' Mo growled back. Then he pointed the gun at Gideon in his white bloodstained robes and waved a hand towards himself. 'You come with me.'

Gideon walked casually towards him, looking defiant, 'Why don't you put the gun away chum, you're not going to kill me. I'm too valuable to you.'

Mo pulled his right arm back and slapped Gideon across the side of the face with the gun. He let out a scream of pain and dropped to his knees, clutching his fractured cheek.

'Get up!' Mo screamed, 'and come with me.'

As Gideon slowly got to his feet, holding his face with both hands, blood oozed from a gash below his left eye, then the light from the open door behind the security guard grew dim. Someone had entered the room, but Mo was oblivious to it. Before Gideon made his last few steps, there was a rush of air as a foot in a highly polished black shoe appeared from nowhere and thudded at lightning speed into Mo's ribcage. He let out a grunt as he dropped sideways and then a fist to his jaw knocked him face down to the floor. In an instant, a tall dark figure landed both knees on the guard's back and twisted his oversized shaved head sharply to the right until his neck cracked and Mo was dead. The man stood upright out of the shadows, and they saw his face—it was Danny. He picked up the gun from the floor, grabbed Gideon's arm, and pulled him towards the door and said, 'Get yourselves out of here before the police arrive and before anyone comes looking for him.' He nodded at the floor and Mo's lifeless body. Danny dragged Gideon into the throng of hysterical guests, leaving Kate and the two men in the trophy room.

Kate ran to the glass-fronted cabinet and located the trophy with the concealed camera on the top. From the wooden base holding the silver bowl, she lifted a small black plastic box with a glass lens that was the purpose of the party and all-powerful to the blackmailers. She passed it to Tim. 'You're going to have to smash this, get the card out - and then swallow it. Now hurry, then get yourselves out of here. I'm going to find Ben before he becomes a casualty.' As she stepped around Mo's body, she said, 'I don't know why all these sodding bells are ringing. This was all meant to be a controlled exit. Sorry you're on your own chaps. One of us will be in touch soon—good luck.'

Tim dropped the tiny rectangular box onto the hard and shiny floor tiles, then stamped on it with his trainers, but they were too cushioned and the box stayed intact. Then he jumped on it repeatedly until Charlie said, 'It's no good mate we'll have to find something to break it with.'

Tim reached up and felt the weight of Willis's trophies in turn until he found one that felt solid. It was some car manufactures sponsored tournament in America from back in the nineties. Tim admired it briefly, then smashed it down on the camera. Black plastic splintered everywhere, and the body of the camera slid under the marble table. Charlie dropped to his hands and knees to retrieve it. Tim crouched behind him, just as two naked old gentlemen in masks walked into the room looking to escape the bells and imminent arrival of the police. They scanned the scene before them. 'Oh, so sorry to disturb you,' one of the men said.

Tim raised himself up to his full height, incensed by their implication, 'That's alright sir, you see the gentleman lying on the floor here? Well, he just accused me of being a homosexual, so I had to kill him. Mind you, don't step in his blood on your way out.'

The two men looked horrified and ran back out of the room as Charlie emerged from under the table with the memory card in his hand. 'Here it is I've picked it out of the debris mate over to you to swallow it.'

'Why me?'

'Well, you know how my belly is. The slightest thing upsets me, and we've got to hang onto it for as long as possible. We haven't got time to argue—get it down your throat.'

Tim studied the small card and wondered how he was ever going to swallow the tiny sharp-edged plastic and metal item, let alone get it through the complexities of his digestive system.

'Come on, get on with it, will you. People are prepared to kill for that card. We've already got one body tonight.'

Charlie reached for a nearby urn shaped glass vase, pulled out a bunch of white lilies and said, 'Here, use this to wash it down—just be quick will you.'

'You're all heart.'

Tim placed the card on the back of his tongue, closed his eyes, took a huge swig of the cloudy water from the vase, and swallowed hard. He began to gag and quickly tipped the rest of the water into his mouth and over himself. He swallowed again and held his throat as he finally felt it clear of the obstruction.

Charlie looked on anxiously, 'Whatever you do Fev, don't be sick—now let's go.'

'Thanks for your concern. You are unreal Flinty.'

As they ran for the door to make their escape, the staircase was lit up by blue pulsating light coming in through the windows and they knew they had to get out of the house quickly.

34

Once the initial police response of a couple of uniformed constables had assessed the situation and realised what they were faced with, they called for back-up immediately and closed the lane leading to *Eagle House*. The whole area in and around the house was in chaos. Soon there were police vehicles and fire engines everywhere and nothing the all controlling security guards could do about it. The facade of the house was soon illuminated by throbbing blue lights as famous people ran through the grounds in outlandish costumes, frantically trying to evade capture. The high-profile guests were desperate to dive into their limousines and get whisked away into the safety of the night. But the police had the only entrance and exit well covered. Plus most of the elderly attendees were incapable of climbing the high boundary wall, and trapped within the confines of the estate, just waiting to be discovered.

Charlie and Tim had made their escape from the trophy room through the big communal area and into the kitchen, exiting out of the back doors by the garage block. They thought for a moment about going back for their clothing, or any clothing for that matter, but knew there was no time to delay. They had to get away or get bundled into the back of a Black Mariah with The Village People. There was just no way getting caught at that kind of party would end well, particularly as Kate was nowhere to be seen and couldn't vouch for them. Besides, they didn't want the shame of being taken into custody with dozens of other men protesting their innocence, having to answer degrading questions and maybe even appearing in the media dressed as they were. No one was ever going to believe they had simply been employed as waiters for a second, and it was going to take forever to clear themselves—especially with their already suspicious wives. But apart from all that, once the security guards had checked the CCTV footage around the house and worked out they had the memory card from the trophy room camera, they were dead meat.

As the men emerged through the back doors of the kitchen, the cool and damp October night air bit into their bare flesh. All around there were police and security people, with very different agendas, scanning the grounds with powerful torches. Charlie and Tim surveyed the scene and concluded there was far too much open ground to cover to get to the perimeter wall without getting noticed. They stood fixed to the spot, trying to evaluate their escape options when they heard a whispered voice ahead of them. 'Dis way sir, over here, come now.' The old stable block was about a hundred yards away, across a wide pea shingle path. The door was slightly open spilling yellow light onto the gravel covered ground and in the doorway stood the slight figure of Pom dressed in a grey silk dressing gown with his arms wrapped around himself, looking hollow and exhausted. Once eye contact was made, he unfolded his arms and was furiously waving at them to follow him. 'Come, sir, come.'

Tim grasped Charlie's arm. 'Ok Flinty, time to do your

best Usain Bolt impression, but on the grass and not the gravel. Go!'

The men didn't need asking twice to enter the temporary sanctuary of the stable block. They sprinted on the grass verge to avoid any unwanted noise from the gravel path and were through the open door in an instant. Pom pulled it closed and gave them both a slightly effeminate hug.

Still panting from the run, Tim stuttered, 'Thanks Pom.' He put an arm around the youngster's slim shoulders, 'are you ok?'

'Yes sir, all ok, but you need to go. Police come here soon. Back door easy to road, have to climb wall.' He smiled, 'We do it sometime.' He led them down the central spine of the stable block. The stalls where horses were once housed had been converted into bedrooms by Willis, and Charlie couldn't resist stopping to take a look at what the golfer had provided for his staff. There was no natural light in any of the rooms, only high-level fluorescent tubes, an extractor fan in the ceiling and three sets of bunk beds wedged against the grey painted brick walls. Any areas of wall that weren't covered by furniture were adorned with tourist posters of Thailand and family pictures from home. 'How can you get six people in that tiny room?' He said out loud to anyone who was listening as he fumed at the injustice. 'How many of you live here, Pom?'

'Oh, maybe fifty Thai people sir, very busy and very cold in your winter time, not like Thailand.' He smiled as a comforting image of home ran through his head.

Charlie was angry when he saw more of the sordid accommodation. There was only one small toilet block for everyone to use, two showers, one washing machine and one filthy kitchen with a kettle, microwave and toaster. The conditions were squalid, and the block stank of human occupation and condensation. 'Is this where you stay all the time, Pom? Do you ever go to the house?' Charlie asked.

'Yes sir, just to help Mr Willis with work, he gives here to sleep.' He looked over his shoulder anxiously at the entrance. 'Police find us soon. We all be gone. Maybe we go back home.' There was a look of relief on the boy's weary face and Charlie didn't want to think about what sort of work Willis had Pom doing.

Tim could sense his friend's disgust. 'I know what you're thinking Flinty, and I agree with you, but right now we've got to worry about ourselves. Willis is very soon going to get what he is due, and the whole world will see him for what he really is. The man all the Thai kids thought was their saviour is about to be exposed. And Pom's dream of a better life that became a nightmare will be over.'

Charlie calmed and whispered. 'They came from the land of smiles to this.' But it was at such times that Charlie was thankful to have a genuine friend like Tim, and they were about to rely on each other like never before.

'Hurry sir,' Pom said as he checked outside the open back door of the stables and turned towards them. 'You go now, quick, quick.'

They moved out into the garden onto a small gravel path and area of lawn which were partly illuminated by the open door and almost before they said, 'Good luck Pom, take care of yourself,' he had slammed the emergency exit door shut, the light was snuffed out and they were on their own in the darkness. Their attention was drawn by the loud slap of helicopter blades coming towards them, then immediately overhead. The sound was deafening, and the downdraft moved the trees and bushes like a gale force wind as a light on the undercarriage searched for a landing site. They watched as the helicopter disappeared behind trees half a mile away and landed in a field, then within a minute it was up again and gone into the distance. 'Must be a police helicopter dropping reinforcements off,' Charlie suggested.

Tim smiled knowingly. 'Not a chance Flinty, up and down too quick. Someone is being taken away from here in a hurry. That'll be Danny getting Gideon out. He's had the fright of his life tonight. That little episode should cool his ardour for a while.'

Charlie pointed to a vehicle's headlights running parallel with the perimeter wall about two hundred yards away. 'Look, that police vehicle's moving people out, so the road must be open and it's the lane we came in on Fev.'

'Yeah, I guess they've taken everything inside by now to contain it and probably put a couple of uniformed bobbies on the gate. Using the barriers they've already got—makes sense.'

Charlie huffed, 'Anyway ex-chief inspector, as I was saying, if we can make it across the lawn through that privet hedge and over the wall, we'll be away.'

Tim gave an incredulous look, even though Charlie couldn't see it. 'May I remind you what we are wearing, Mr Flint. And even if we were to make it across the lawn and through the privet without getting spotted, that brick wall looks really high.'

Tim's words of protest were wasted and met with a simple, 'Let's go,' as he saw Charlie's pale naked rear end disappear into the darkness and he reluctantly followed. They ran for the three feet high privet hedge, which seemed to run most of the length of the wall. Once crouched in front of it, they were partially shielded from the house and perimeter lights.

Panting for air, Tim said, 'Are you mad? Let's just give

ourselves up. I've been thinking about it and I'm sure I can talk us out of this. Don't worry Flinty.'

'It's you that's bloody mad if you think you could ever talk your way out of this. Didn't you see what was going on in there? We'll all be tarred with the same brush—guilty until proven innocent.'

Tim thought for a moment. 'Ok, fair point. I'll give you a leg up and then you can hoist me up.'

'Bugger that. How would I ever hoist a lump like you up an eight-foot wall? No, we'll find a brick pier and use it to climb up.'

They pushed through the dense privet in front of the wall and let out muffled yelps and profanities as branches scratched their bare legs. Charlie's hand eventually found the brick boundary wall through the meagre tungsten light from the occasional lamp standards in the grounds. He kept that contact as he walked to find one of the piers that were spaced at roughly twelve feet intervals. 'Did you know that these bricks are called Red Rubbers Fev?' he whispered. 'That's because they are really soft and can be rubbed into any shape. Been using them for centuries.'

Tim rolled his eyes in the semidarkness. 'Yeah, that's fascinating Flinty. What a moment for a bloody history lesson.'

Time, frost and plant life had damaged the original bricks in the piers enough to conveniently provide decent hand and footholds. The two men easily climbed the wall and dropped down onto a narrow grass verge that was bordering the road. Charlie pointed. 'Quick, over the road and into the cover of those trees before we get picked up by the headlights coming this way.'

'It's probably a meat wagon.' Tim shouted.

The men dashed across the narrow road up a small bank,

then ducked down below a wild rhododendron bush to watch a vehicle pass at speed down the lane and away from the house. From their position in the darkness, they couldn't easily make out the vehicle, and its occupants, but it was clear one of the tail-lights was smashed and showing white light. 'Not a meat wagon at all Flinty, but are you thinking what I'm thinking?' Tim asked.

'Yes, it's Nathan in The Sycamores van and we could wave him down and be rescued from all this.'

'Except?'

'Except he's missed the house and going the wrong way,' Charlie said. 'Remember the taxi driver mentioned it was a dead end.'

'But someone must have called him to collect them, and he's got here bloody quick.'

Charlie nodded in agreement. 'My guess it's young Ben, and he's legged it over the wall like we did.'

'Well, if we're right Nathan will soon realise his mistake, turn around and come back.'

'And here come some lights,' Charlie said. 'Let's move closer to the road behind those trees and get a look to see who is in the bus.'

'And not flag him down for a lift?'

'Think about it Fev. Didn't Nathan used to work for Willis as a gardener at Eagle House?'

'Yes, of course, so he should know his way around here pretty well, shouldn't he?'

'But clearly he doesn't, so he may have another reason for being here.'

Tim crooked his neck to look up the road. 'Here comes the van. Let's try to get a good look inside if we can. You check the front, and I'll check the back.'

The vehicle slowed to check a side turning further down the lane, then picked up speed and moved off towards them. But slowly enough for Charlie and Tim to get a look inside as they passed no more than six feet away. Then the minibus cruised off up the lane with one white and one red tail light glowing through the dark night.

Charlie said, 'Definitely Nathan driving, and Adriana sitting in the passenger seat still in her blood-stained robes.'

'Yes, and definitely Ben and Kate bound and gagged in the back.'

35

It seemed totally inconceivable to Charlie and Tim that Nathan could have been involved in something untoward, just not his style to be getting involved in anything confusing and complicated. However, having taken some kind of responsibility for his wellbeing, they knew he was definitely the kind of lad who was vulnerable and could be easily led, especially if he thought he was pleasing someone.

'So, do we think Nathan thought he was doing Ben a favour and has been hoodwinked by that cow Adriana, or is he somehow in this up to his neck?' Charlie asked his friend while still peering at the vehicle's broken taillight in the distance.

Tim's face contorted. 'Well, he wouldn't be the first man to fall under her spell, would he?'

'No, but someone must have bound and gagged the pair of them, and Adriana wouldn't have risked breaking a nail.'

'Unless one of the security guards did it for her.'

'Unlikely Fev, they will have all been wrapped up by the police, and besides, they are on the wrong side of the wall.'

Tim nodded, 'Agreed. But why on earth would Nathan

get involved with Adriana, a woman who had him sacked? And where the hell are they taking Ben and Kate?'

'Well, Ben is an innocent party, but they don't know that. And Adriana has obviously picked up by now that Kate is undercover and thinks her and Ben are in cahoots. No doubt convinced they both know where the missing chip is with the incriminating footage of Gideon.'

Tim rubbed a hand on his midriff. 'Yeah, it's working its way through my gastrointestinal system as we speak.'

'Well, if we're right, they'll be taking Ben and Kate somewhere to get that information from them, and there are some frightening people behind this. That can only mean one thing.' Charlie grimaced.

Tim swallowed hard. 'Yes, they'll be tortured, by the type who take Black & Decker drills to kneecaps.' He started to look around desperately into the blackness for inspiration. 'We've got to get out of here Flinty, and quick, to find Kate and Ben, and we don't have too many options. Definitely can't give ourselves up dressed like this. There would be too many questions we don't have time for. And we can't stumble across a friendly little farmhouse down a leafy lane where they give us fresh clothes, a cup of tea and a lift home like they do in the films either. I mean—what would you do if two semi-naked old men knocked on your door in the middle of the night asking for help—and what could we show them as ID?'

'Quite.'

'But you do still have young Ryan's mobile phone Flinty, so we could call for a cab.' Tim said frustrating himself with the lack of positive ideas. 'Nah, forget that. The minute a taxi sees all the police activity, they'll run a mile in the other direction.'

'I'll phone Ruth,' Charlie said, like it was the obvious solution.

Tim let out a roar of laughter as Charlie started dialling his home number on Ryan's mobile and held a finger to his lips requesting silence.

'She's going to be well chuffed with you at four in the morning, isn't she. By the way hasn't that phone got a security code?'

'Yes, it's 1234. That was helpful of Ryan wasn't it. And of course my darling wife will do it. She's picked us both up when we've been rolling drunk before.'

'Yes, she is a very sweet girl. But it's not entirely the same thing as this Flinty, is it?'

'Shhh—she's picking up. Hello love, sorry to wake you. No. No, we're alright. It's just that the little job we were doing as waiters tonight has gone a bit tits-up.'

Tim clamped a hand to his mouth and sniggered. Charlie covered the phone and told him to shut up before going back to the conversation with his wife. 'Oh, nothing love, just talking to Fev. Anyway we're a bit stranded with no money out over Guildford way.' Charlie moved the phone away from his ear to avoid the shouted response from the other end. 'Yes, that's right, Guildford. It's all slightly complicated, but we need you to pick us up. Yes, I know what time it is, and I'm sorry to have to ask you, but we're a bit desperate—no we're not hurt. I need you to leave right away though love, and bring me some clothes and a few bigger things for the fat boy. Yes clothes, I told you it's complicated. Now here's what I want you to do. Get onto the M25 and go to junction ten, then head down the A3 towards Guildford and Portsmouth. Go past Wisley gardens and look for a turning to Ripley—yes, you're right, we've been there before. Take your mobile phone with you and when you get to Ripley, stop and call me on this number. It doesn't matter whose phone it is right now. When you call, I will give you co-ordinates to put into the sat nav. It will take you down some narrow lanes, but you will find us. It should take you about an hour at this time of night. Drive carefully and thank you sweetheart—you're a diamond. Yes, Fev knows it will cost him. See you soon love—bye and thank you.'

Tim looked at Charlie and was shaking his head in awe. 'Didn't think you'd pull that off Flinty. And how on earth did you remember that we passed through Ripley?'

'Easy, it's where Eric Clapton is from.'

'I might have known, and don't tell me you've dragged poor Ruth there on some kind of pilgrimage in the past?'

'Something like that. Right, we've got an hour to find the road that runs from Ripley to the lane that led us down here. And I reckon it's diagonally across about three fields once were out of these woods.'

'Call me old fashioned Flinty, but how are we ever going to find our way across several fields in the pitch dark and happen across the road to Ripley?'

'Doddle Fev. This phone that I pinched from matey boy has got one of those map app thingies, and a compass. It's brilliant, so brilliant that even old technophobes like us can understand it. I can get a satellite view of the whole area. I know exactly where we are and where we need to be—plus it's fully charged and got a torch. Come on let's go, stay close and watch your footing.'

'I'm not sure I like the view but I'm right behind you.'

They moved deeper into the woods hearing unknown animal scampering out of their path as they crunched their way through fallen twigs, autumn leaves and undergrowth. Then suddenly they were into open ground brushing a hedgerow that was sharp against their skin. 'Brilliant, this phone is absolutely bloody brilliant,' Charlie enthused. 'Just where it said the field would be. Looks on here as though there's an entrance about 300 yards to our left. We'll follow the hedge until we find the gate and walk in the tractor ruts along the edge of the field until we reach the next one.'

Behind them they could hear the sound of sirens piercing the damp still air and pulsing blue light seemed to travel for miles across the open countryside.

Tim said, 'Okay Sherlock I'm with you, but I just want to point out that those maps on Ryan's phone could be based on surveys taken years ago—and keep your eye on the battery you don't want it to run out just at the crucial moment.'

'Good point mate, let's keep our fingers crossed, eh?'

Further along the hedge, they found a five-bar gate, opened it, and entered the field. 'Stick to the edge of this one. It will be easier.' Charlie said, checking his phone map again.

It was simple. They dropped down into uneven tractor tracks and kept walking straight for 15 minutes across the rutted ground with trees to their right and sour smelling cabbages to their left until they reached another gate that they unlatched and closed behind them. 'Now this field is going to be a bit more difficult Fev. We've got to go diagonally across it better hold hands or we'll lose each other.'

Tim laughed, 'If somebody told me I would be wearing only an apron and holding hands with you in a field in the middle of nowhere at this time of night...'

'Well, better me than a complete stranger, eh? You could have been doing this with a highly suspect TV reporter.'

Tim chuckled again. 'Suppose so.' Then his nostrils started to twitch. 'I don't want to worry you mate but I'm pretty sure this particular field isn't used for growing crops. Those cabbages were bad enough but now I get the distinct aroma of cow shit in the air.'

'Yup, and I've just trodden in some.'

'Me too, and it's making me heave.'

'Don't be a tart, it's a healthy country smell. Just keep going. There's only one more field after this one.'

Occasionally they could make out the lights of a car winding its way through the lanes, either night workers or vehicles going to or from *Eagle House*, they thought. In the distance an external security light on a cottage was just visible indicating that they were heading in the right direction. But this was a much larger field and the ground was hard going underfoot so their precious time was being eaten up. Charlie checked the map on his phone again twisting it through several different angles as they reached another hedgerow marking the boundary. They took a breath. 'Can't see a gate on this one Fev, so we're going to have to look in the hedge for a gap and hope we don't get scratched to ribbons.' Charlie scanned the hedge with the phones torch then fixed the bright white light on an opening at low level. 'Hands and knees mate through there, I'm afraid.'

'Must we?' Tim asked with a deep sigh.

'Think of Kate and Ben. We've got to get to them.'

'Ok, let's do it.'

Charlie lit up the gap in the hedge and they crawled through one after the other, both cursing as the hawthorn spiked their bare skin. Through the other side of the hedge they stood upright, rubbed their wounds and got their bearings. 'Looks like a potato field,' Charlie said, sweeping his torch light through 180 degrees. 'We can't cut through the middle of it. We'll just get hopelessly lost.'

'Round the outside in tyre ruts again then, let's go. It's going to be a lot further, the squaw on the hippopotamus and all that stuff eh Flinty.'

Charlie chuckled, 'Yes, and Ruth won't accept Pythagoras theorem as a reason for being late, better step up the pace, stick with me Fev.'

As the terrain dipped and turned the men regularly twisted their ankles and lost balance. Shouting obscenities when their bodies jerked in different directions as they trudged relentlessly across the hard, dark ground. 'I may be wrong,' Tim said, 'but in the daylight this is probably a popular route for dog walkers—as if treading in the cow's poop wasn't enough.'

'Well at least that's a good sign, we must be getting close to civilisation Fev.'

The lane grew ever nearer and the meagre lights from cottages became brighter, which gave them a sense of relief. Having yomped around the vast potato field in an L shape they squatted behind another four feet high hedgerow to recover their breath, conscious to avoid being spotted by any passing police vehicles while waiting for Ruth's call.

Breathing heavily Tim said, 'Something has just dawned on me Flinty, don't know why I didn't see it before.' He smacked his forehead with the palm of his hand.

'What are you going on about?'

'Idiot. Idiot.' He smacked his head again.

'Stop knocking yourself about and tell me what it is.'

'It was just watching you with that map that made it come to me.'

'Will you get on with it.'

'Keep your hair on Flinty. We have established that either Nathan didn't know his way to Eagle House, or had forgotten—right?'

'Right.'

'So either way, to find his way through this maze of lanes he would have had to read a map or put information into a sat-nav.'

'Agreed.'

'But Nathan doesn't read or write, does he. So how could he possibly have found Eagle House on his own?'

Charlie was getting anxious about Ruth's call and not really giving Tim the attention he deserved. 'Well he could have been here recently and remembered it or got someone to enter the address into the sat-nav for him.'

Tim was completely unfazed by Charlie's preoccupation. He had cracked something really significant. 'Yes, well how he got here tonight isn't really the issue.'

'You're now being weird Fev.'

'Stick with me Flinty, and this is the important bit. Everybody thinks that Nathan can't read or write. So if he wanted to write something down, what would he do?'

'He'd get someone to write it for him.' Charlie suddenly became alert to his friend's train of thought—'Like a confession note.'

'I knew you'd get there in the end Flinty. Nathan must have knocked on James's door that night and James innocently invited him in. Nathan was probably saying he wanted to own up to the deer killing and showed James the crossbow as proof. And then asked him to write a note of confession that he could give to Craig.'

'But because it was in James's handwriting, it looked like his own confession. Very clever.'

'Then Nathan knocked James out, sat him in the chair and set up the cross bow to silently put a bolt through his head.'

Charlie was now racing ahead. 'And immediately after Nathan had killed James, he found his mobile phone and sent a suicide message to Adriana. No way a pathologist could be that precise about the time of death, so it looked to all the world like James had sent it just before he took his own life.'

'And on leaving, Nathan removed all the recording equipment, which is probably now at the bottom of the golf club lake Flinty.'

'And do you remember the bonfire the following day Fev, when he was burning plastic? He said that a stranger gave him stuff to burn. But the plastic must have been overshoes, disposable overalls, gloves and clothes from his visit to James the night before. In fact his obsession with bonfires was nearly always to help get rid of evidence. Nathan is our killer, and the whole vulnerable thing is just a very elaborate act.'

Tim took an exaggerated breath. 'Yes, Neanderthal Nathan is a mafia hit man sent to protect Willis, and remove obstacles, while they trapped Gideon.'

Now even more eager to get home, Charlie checked their precise location on the phone and memorised the co-ordinates. Some ten minutes later, his phone flashed and burst into life playing some kind of Ibiza style clubbing mix. 'How very tasteless, Ryan,' Charlie said as he swiped his finger across the face of the phone to the green symbol. He immediately recognised Ruth's number calling and before he could speak, she said, 'Right. I'm stopped in Ripley by the village green, where you told me Eric Clapton was born.'

'Great, well-done love. Now stick these co-ordinates into your sat nav. You'll travel for a mile or so out of the village, then turn left for a couple of miles, then left again and you'll find us a mile or two down that lane. Look for a large metal gate leading to a field on the left.' There was a pause as Ruth absorbed her husband's instructions. Charlie sniggered at a question from his wife. 'How will you find us? Oh, you won't miss us. Just keep your eyes peeled for two naked old blokes wearing only waiters' aprons walking towards you. It will look like a sketch from Monty Python. No, I'm not kidding—see you soon.' Then the phone went dead and Charlie prodded it frantically. 'What's up with this bloody thing? Can't believe the battery has run out already.'

Tim grasped Charlie's forearm. 'Forget it mate, they've

found young Ryan and switched the phone off. We're in Ruth's hands now.'

Crouching back down behind the hedge, Charlie and Tim watched the road from Ripley anxiously waiting for signs of a car. Then Charlie leapt to his feet excitedly. 'Here she comes,' he said proudly, with a broad grin on his face. 'I'd recognise the shape of those Fiat 500 headlights anywhere.' With that, Charlie moved quickly through the galvanised tubular steel gate and stood in the middle of the road with his arms outstretched, looking like a star in the car's headlights. The car slowed to a stop three feet from Charlie's exposed legs.

Tim shouted from behind the hedge. 'Well done Flinty, it's a Ford Fiesta, not a Fiat 500.'

In his enthusiasm, Charlie didn't hear his friend's warning and instinctively ran to the passenger door opened it and started to slide in. It was only then he realised his terrible mistake. As he was confronted by a middle-aged woman who looked like a school ma'am with over permed grey hair and horn-rimmed glasses. 'I'm so sorry madam,' Charlie said shamefaced backing out of the car. 'I promise you this is not how it looks. I was expecting my wife.'

'I bet you were, you bloody pervert,' the woman screamed as she pushed her foot down hard on the accelerator, forcing the door to slam shut as the car screeched up the lane in a cloud of burning rubber.

Tim waved the smoke away from his face theatrically, then leaned on the metal gate like a country yokel and watched the car speed up the lane. 'That's the idea Flinty, keep us below the police radar. Now the coppers will be out looking for a weirdo in his birthday suit praying on women drivers. And there are a million of the buggers just down the road.'

Charlie shrugged his shoulders and held his palms

upwards. 'Who'd have thought there would have been another car coming at this time? Easy mistake to make in the middle of the night when you're tired.' His attention was suddenly drawn to more headlights in the distance. 'Anyway, here comes Ruth now, that's definitely her car.'

Tim ducked below the hedge again and said, 'You'll forgive me if I wait here, won't you Flinty.'

Charlie ran into the road again frantically waving his arms, this time the car pulled into the verge by the gate. He opened the door of the grey Fiat 500 to be met by his wife's concerned face and a barrage of abuse. 'What the hell is going on Charlie Flint, and where is Fev?'

'I'll explain later love. Where are the clothes?'

'There's a bin bag in the back with sweatshirts and jogging pants, thought that might be best.' Then she saw the humour in the situation as Charlie turned and she caught a glimpse of his bare buttocks. 'Does Fev look the same as you?'

'Well not quite as chiselled as me obviously, but dressed the same, yes—back in a sec.'

Behind the gate, the men quickly pulled the thick clothes from the bag and put them on. They felt an immediate and comforting warmth; it was good to have their skin and modesty covered again. And to be walking towards a waiting car ready to take them away from all the madness of the night. Charlie released the catch on the passenger seat to allow Tim access to the back of the car. 'Evening, Mrs Flint,' Tim said as he raised his foot to step in.'

'Wait!' Ruth yelled. 'You are not getting into my car with those shoes on. You both stink to high heaven get rid of them.'

'We had to walk through fields that had cows in sweetheart,' Charlie pleaded.

'I don't care. I mean it, leave them here for a passing

tramp.’ She folded her arms indignantly. ‘I’m not moving until you’ve done it.’

They removed their trainers, dropped them in the bin bag and tossed it into the field then climbed into the car barefoot. Charlie exhaled loudly, ‘Happy? Now get us home quickly Ruth, people’s lives are at risk.’

36

Once the police had entered *Eagle House*, they very soon established it wasn't a burglary attempt, or fire, they were attending. Particularly after finding a dead body, large quantities of drugs and dozens of very young Thais running everywhere. Apart from murder, immorality and use of banned substances, they realised this was a house party illegal on so many levels. And with such high-profile guests the fallout could be so enormous that they immediately put a cordon around the property.

The police were stopping everyone from leaving or entering the house, while trying to establish precisely what was going on. What they could see amongst the many visitors were high levels of well organised private security, alerting them to something particularly secretive taking place in a famous sportsman's private residence. When questioned, the security staff went into self-protection mode, pleading they were just doing what they were contracted to do by Adriana Martin. They denied having any part in the hedonistic activity going on around the house yet couldn't explain why one of their number had been killed, or why some were armed. Meanwhile, senior politicians and media stars were being unmasked and standing exposed in their outrageous costumes while being asked to give statements and their names. The arrival of the authorities had triggered something akin to *The Great Escape,* with guests scattering in every direction. Some had managed to get away, but the majority had been captured within the grounds and surrounding farmland and returned to the scene. Those that managed to evade capture had left their clothes and mobile phones behind, and in some cases even their drivers and cars were still parked in the lane outside. So, in real terms, none of the guests could really escape, as their identity was still at *Eagle House,* even if they weren't. Thus, it was merely a matter of time before they were apprehended and shamed. And within an hour of the alarms being sounded, the press were inevitably jockeying for position outside the gates. With TV cameras and crew soon afterwards, waiting to broadcast sensational tales of revulsion involving eminent people. Someone at the party had clearly tipped them off for thirty pieces of silver and the finger of suspicion was firmly pointing towards Jack the barman.

For a while, the Surrey countryside must have been swarming with famous mature men in costume trying to avoid apprehension by the police at all costs. Each of them was desperate to get home to their wives or partners with some kind of dignity intact. But without the aid of a telephone or normal clothes. Locals who had been awakened by the sirens, helicopter and vehicle headlights knew something big was happening in their area and were keen to get in on the act. Knowing a famous golfer lived nearby, they were out with cameras and mobile phones desperately trying to get a coup they could post on the social media networks.

Those guests that did manage to get away and, against

the odds, made it to their London offices, had just enough time to find a change of clothes, write letters of resignation and phone their bosses, before heading home to face the music. Or in the case of one very senior politician, dressed as a centurion, just long enough to lock his office door, drink a bottle of vodka, and swallow a large handful of tranquillisers.

The police released the dominatrix and all the fetish people that had been hired in. They were doing nothing illegal and no more than it said on their business cards. But the Thais were a very different matter. Many were discovered to be no more than thirteen or fourteen and the police tipped the stable block upside down, keen to find clues amongst the squalid and cramped conditions youngsters like Pom were living in. It became obvious that over in Phuket they had been seduced by the offer of a salary and somewhere to live, thinking they had been given normal domestic employment on Willis's estate. Until Willis informed them, they owed him rent, airfare and the cost of acquiring a passport. A huge sum of money to them as children and one they didn't have a hope of paying back—unless they did favours for his friends. So they were stuck in a strange country without any way of getting home and with enormous debts, and by that time Willis also had them hooked on drugs. So sexual services seemed the only way out for them and for some a way to make extra money for a ticket home. Yet all the while Willis Martin was creating the charade of top sportsman turned good Samaritan, trying to rescue Thai youngsters from a life of poverty and giving them a new start in England.

The police spent the rest of the night taking statements and establishing the main players in Willis's people trafficking operation, while also contacting their Thai counterparts. So by the time daylight broke, people were being arrested in transport hubs, airport lounges and in their UK, Bangkok and Phuket homes. While the media were having a field day. But the cocaine trail still remained untouched, while Willis and Adriana Martin were both missing.

37

Willis had a plan. Willis always seemed to have a plan. But then someone so corrupt with his profile couldn't afford not to have a contingency. Besides which, the man was fundamentally a coward. When he first heard the alarms sound at the party, he was dressed as a highwayman, complete with breeches, silk shirt, mask, and tricorn hat. He quickly slipped inside his bedroom and changed into jeans, tee shirt and shoes that were already laid out on the bed. By the time he picked up the first police sirens in the distance, he was running down the crowded staircase ignoring pleas for help from his panicking guests and knocking them aside without remorse. Willis knew what was coming next, he helped design the alarm systems. He was only thinking of getting himself out before the police and fire service wanted to speak to him as the property owner. Perfectly reasonable and professional under normal circumstances, but not when there was a dead body in your house and lots of famous people high on illegal drugs and having underage sex. Apart from avoiding the law, Willis was running away from his project to snare Gideon Wells. He remained blissfully unaware of the outcome and had left his wife to deal with it. Breathing heavy and with clammy skin, he hurried through the ground floor of the house into the gym and burst out of a set of French doors into the garden and the cool October night air. Turning hard right, he ran straight for fifty yards to a small brick-built building with a flat roof at the back of the garage. He had only a wallet in one back pocket and his passport in the other. Three minutes later, the double wooden doors of the small brick structure eased open, and Willis emerged seated astride a dark blue quad bike with headlights blazing and its cold petrol engine revving loudly. He gently opened the throttle to move away from the house in a controlled fashion and set out across the lawn of his vast garden into the blackness beyond. Once out of the range of house lights, Willis cranked his right wrist to increase his speed. Time was not on his side. The quad bike's wheels span and began tearing tracks across the manicured grass as he drove towards the rear boundary, which was at least half a mile away and not accessible by normal vehicles. Willis parked the quad bike out of sight behind a tall box hedge and lost no time in unlocking a brass padlock on a small, pitched roof timber garden shed that smelt of preservative. Inside the shed hung a leather jacket, and a rucksack holding overnight essentials like a comb, toothbrush, change of underwear and a fully charged burner phone that he had never been used, apart from testing. On the floor of the shed were a pair of Armourite gloves and casual boots with fresh socks pushed inside. All this had been carefully planted ahead of the party, just as he always did before any of his risqué events at *Eagle House,* to facilitate an urgent escape. At the back of the shed on its stand, was a small mud splattered motorcycle trials bike filled with fuel and a key already in the ignition. Willis put on the socks, boots and jacket, slipped his arms through the straps of the rucksack and got it comfortable on his back.

Then he pulled on a black crash helmet with a visor that had been resting on the motorcycle seat. He checked everything in the bag twice, then walked the bike out of the shed and kicked down the stand while he locked the shed door to avoid leaving obvious clues. Willis slid on the gloves, then looked behind him towards the house where most of the bright, blue, pulsing beacons seemed to be—but no-one was coming in his direction.

Willis threw his right leg over the motorcycle and bounced up and down on the spongy suspension a few times to get comfortable before getting ready to press the start button. He patted the fuel tank and said, 'Come on baby, don't let me down now.' The bike sparked into life without hesitation, but this was a ragged and noisy sounding engine designed for producing the kind of torque you need to get across uneven ground quickly and exactly why Willis chose it over the quad bike. He turned to see if the uneven rumble of the rough engine had attracted any attention at the other end of the garden, but the police were occupied, armed with torches and chasing party guests in every direction. Still behind the hedge and parallel to the rear perimeter wall, Willis rode the trials bike to a point two hundred yards away where he stopped. Still straddling the motorbike, he slid back a temporary timber fence panel covering a hole in the brick wall. Then he eased the bike carefully through the gap and into the fields. He had done this exercise a few times before and knew precisely the route to take around and across the fields northwest towards Woking. And he figured that if he kept it steady at around four o'clock in the morning, it would only take him twenty minutes before he hit familiar signs of civilisation on the outskirts of the town. Sure enough, after a fairly bone jarring and animated eighteen minute ride over a dry and rutted landscape, he came to a football field on the edge of a large housing estate. Squeezing the bike through a vandalised chain-link fence, he rode down a long concrete path to a metal entrance gate that was permanently open. Willis stopped outside the park on the grey pavement slabs. He lifted the rucksack from his back, unzipped a side pocket and fumbled inside for a key, kissed it and slipped it into his jacket pocket. He bounced the bike off the pavement onto the road and headed off to find the nearby arterial *Landseer Drive,* on the housing estate where all the streets were named after famous painters. Willis weaved his way through the maze of quiet residential streets, drives and avenues, all full of inconsiderately parked cars and commercial vehicles garishly displaying the names of all kinds of products and services. Until he finally reached *Rembrandt Way* and a nondescript bank of ten garages with galvanised metal doors, all looking exactly the same and sprouting weeds out of the cracks in the concrete hardstanding surrounding them. Willis stopped outside the door to garage number three in the block, put the bike on its stand and admired the new graffiti on the door that had appeared since his last visit. He took the key from his jacket pocket, unlocked the handle, then flipped up the metal door. As the door's spring creaked and groaned, a blue Vauxhall Corsa car in a clean garage was revealed by the yellow glow of a nearby sodium streetlamp. Willis took another key from inside the rucksack, unlocked the car and drove it out of the garage onto the hardstanding. He pushed the motorcycle inside and unhooked a suit carrier from a rusty nail embedded in one of the timber rafters. Inside were a sports jacket, fresh trousers, shoes, socks and a shirt. Another change of clothes, and this time one more befitting of a travelling wealthy professional golfer. Much better than arriving at Heathrow Airport covered in mud and dust from fields thrown up by a trials bike. Willis was shutting down ready to leave as the spring on the garage door overpowered his grasp and it clattered shut, causing lights to come to life in nearby houses. He chuckled to himself as he drove away from the block, because being reported didn't worry him for a moment. The Vauxhall Corsa was a stolen car with false plates, and the police were hardly going to chase him around the county for being noisy. As a renowned golfer shielded from the real world, Willis Martin had been prepared exceptionally well by his masters.

Willis found the London orbital M25 motorway and the airport easily. He had done it as a dry run several times. He drove the car to a short-term car park at Heathrow, parked on one of the quieter upper levels, and then walked into the terminal looking to buy a ticket to New York on the first flight he could get. 'No bags to check in, Mr Martin?' the girl at the sales desk asked.

'No honey,' Willis replied, 'My Mom's been taken ill and I need to get back home quick, no time to pack a case. Just this backpack to take on board.'

'Oh, I'm so sorry to hear that, Mr Martin,' the girl said, not having a clue who he was. She studied her computer screen for a moment and smiled thinking she may just be able to help him out of his dilemma. 'I haven't got first or business class available, I'm afraid sir, but I can find you a seat in economy on a flight to Newark that goes in just over an hour if that helps. But you'll have to hurry and go straight to the gate.'

'That would be just fantastic sweetheart. I'll go through right now.' He paid by card and the transaction was immediately picked up by the British intelligence services, but they were never going to have him stopped. The American Drug Enforcement Agency was going to track his every movement when he landed in Newark and he would lead them straight to his sources, who they already had staked out. They were working on the principle that for a man like Willis, rational behaviour disappears when you are scared witless.

38

Within half an hour of getting home Charlie was showered changed and back in Ruth's Fiat 500 ready to collect Tim and go searching for Kate and Ben. As Tim climbed into the car outside his house, Charlie said, 'We're going to have to deal with the fallout from the girls later, and it won't be good, but we've got to do this.'

'You're not wrong Flinty. I've still not explained why I arrived home stone cold sober wearing your clothes and stinking of cow dung. Let alone going straight out again to catch a murderer.'

As Charlie started the engine to move off, he inadvertently activated the car's unfamiliar infotainment system. 'Sorry about that mate,' Charlie said as he flinched and reached over to turn the volume down on a radio station playing loud dance music. 'Hadn't realised Ruth listened to that kind of stuff. One of the kids must have changed the station for her—bless them. Got any thoughts on where to start looking?'

'Yeah, probably the younger one,' Tim chuckled. 'She's a bit of a handful, like her mum.'

Charlie laughed and scratched his beard stubble. 'You know that awful music has just given me an idea.'

'Go on.'

'Well, if we're right and Kate and Ben are going to be taken somewhere and tortured, it makes sense to hold them in a place where their screams of pain won't be heard right?'

'Yes, sickening thought, isn't it?'

'Well, where better than a soundproofed room?'

'Like a recording studio.'

'Exactly.'

'OK, let's go to Ben's house and put your foot down Flinty.'

Charlie drove with a real sense of purpose towards the house which was around fifteen minutes from where Tim lived. He had dropped Ben there from The Sycamores occasionally when his car had been out of action. At 05.30 am Charlie pushed his luck driving through amber lights at speed. And overtaking people heading for their six o'clock shifts in urban streets while they shook their fists and questioned his parentage. He glanced over at Tim. 'And another thing, Fev. Who knew Ben had converted his spare bedroom into a recording studio or even where he lived?'

'Well, definitely not Kate. She purposely distanced herself from everyone, and certainly not Adriana, all far too tacky for her. So in that vehicle only sweet, helpless little Nathan.'

They turned off a main suburban thoroughfare into *Gordon Road*. This was a street of early twentieth century slate roofed two up two down terraced houses with front doors straight onto the pavement, and small walled back gardens linked by a network of narrow alleyways. Cars were parked on either side of the street banked on the pavements and the road was only passable in one direction at a time. Charlie had to drive two hundred yards past Ben's house to find a parking space, and the golf club bus was nowhere to be seen. Tim turned his head in every direction. 'Must have dropped them off and left the bus a few streets away. Wouldn't want to leave it outside, would he?'

Charlie and Tim threw the car doors open in unison and were careful to close them quietly in the early hours. They walked quickly along the uneven grey flagstone pavement damaged by the constant weight of vehicles. Their route back to Ben's end of terrace house at number 25 was lit by modern LED streetlamps highlighting the narrow space between cars and house walls.

Charlie tutted, 'Modern society, eh? This would be lethal for a blind person.'

Tim scanned up and down the street, then back towards Ben's house. 'It's remiss of the boy not to have an alarm fitted with all that equipment in his place, isn't it?'

'Yes, we'll speak to him about it later, shall we Fev?' The men were simply talking to help deal with their nervous energy and worrying about what they might find inside the house.

Their hearts raced with trepidation as Tim rapped on the front door's glazed panel with his knuckles. Not loud enough to wake the neighbours, but loud enough to raise some movement inside. Maybe someone startled by the noise or crying for help. But the house remained deathly quiet. 'They've got to be here,' Charlie said. 'Nothing else makes sense. But I'm not breaking the glass and drawing attention just in case we're wrong. Let's try at the back.'

They walked down a pitch-black side alleyway and found a wooden latched and bolted gate set into a brick wall. 'Get your shoulder on that big boy,' Charlie whispered to Tim.

'Yes sir,' he replied sarcastically, and gave two almighty shoves against the gate until the wooden frame split and the door swung open. Both of them scanned the surrounding houses to check for lights coming on in case they had woken anyone, but there was no obvious interest.

Most of the houses in the street had been extended in the nineteen fifties and sixties to add a ground floor bathroom. This took up half the meagre garden and left the back door tucked in a dark corner. The wooden bottle green rear door with two slender frosted glass panels had probably never been changed from the original construction and yielded easily to Tim's next shoulder charge. Once inside the house, Charlie fumbled along the walls for a switch and flicked on some lights. In a tungsten glow, the place had all the hallmarks of a young man living alone, a young man without any of the privileges or domestic support James Cole enjoyed. Days old dirty dishes were piled high in the sink, used saucepans and a frying pan sat on a freestanding gas cooker with the congealed remnants of a previous meal inside, and the smell of animal fat hung in the air. There was a hint of bleach escaping from the ground floor bathroom which was trying to combat the sour odour of condensation permeating from the mould covered walls.

'Ben, Kate!' Tim called aloud. 'Are you here?'

There was no reply as Charlie searched through the kitchen cupboards for some kind of weapon. He eventually settled on a large can of fly spray. Tim looked over in disbelief. 'Are you serious?'

'Deadly. I can squirt this into someone's eyes from a distance and disable them instantly.'

Charlie crept into the hall and switched the staircase light on. As the area came into view, there were obvious signs of a struggle. A china ornament had shattered on the floor, wallpaper was torn from the walls, and part of the balustrade had been splintered from a kick. They were even more confident that Ben and Kate were in the house, especially once they caught the distinctive fragrance that was Adriana's trademark.

With a carving knife taken from a kitchen drawer in his hand, Tim stepped onto the creaking bottom step of the stairs. 'As we thought, they'll be in the back bedroom. Flinty, there's a light coming from under the door. I only hope we're not too late.'

As Charlie and Tim reached the landing, muffled groans could be heard through a closed bedroom door, and their hearts sank. They prepared themselves to find beaten and half alive bodies with all kinds of hideous injuries. Charlie grasped the round brass handle of the door, turned it clockwise, and eased the door open gingerly. Illuminated only by a small desk lamp, Ben and Kate were lying side by side on the floor, both apparently unharmed, but with their hands and feet bound and cable tied to chairs with their mouths covered by grey duct tape. Tim cut free their bindings and said, 'I'll let you pull the tape from your mouths—it's going to hurt.'

'Are you both ok?' Charlie asked, intrigued by the flat sound to his voice and drawn by the conical shaped foam tiles fixed to the walls and ceiling. They both sat up on the thick carpet and nodded while carefully removing the tape from their mouths—rather than leaving it to Tim.

'He's coming back for us,' Ben said, nervously rubbing his wrists and ankles. 'Nathan is just going to get rid of the golf club van and he's coming back.'

Tim was following the logic. 'Yeah, a Sycamores van parked outside is an enormous clue, isn't it—not really stupid at all, is he?'

Ben was shaking with shock and unable to control his fear. 'But I don't know anything. All I did was play music in a locked room. I haven't got a clue what this is all about—what do they want with me?'

Charlie crouched next to Ben and put a comforting hand on his shoulder and said softly. 'It's alright, son. He won't be coming back here. You're safe now.'

Kate leaned over and touched Ben's arm and said sensitively, 'Don't concern yourself. Nathan is going to be too busy to worry about us.'

'What about Adriana?' Tim asked. 'What did she have to say for herself?'

Kate struggled to her feet. 'For once she didn't have an opinion on anything, stayed quiet the whole time, let Nathan take the lead on everything, not that he said much either. She's gone with him, probably to make herself an alibi and say she's been at the golf club all night. Did you get the memory card from the camera?'

Tim patted his midriff. 'It's in my personal safe for the moment, Kate.'

'He's going to kill her,' Charlie said casually. 'And she has no idea. Nathan wants her to believe he has to get rid of the van, but really he's taken her away to murder her. He had to get you two safely locked up where no-one could hear you first. Don't you see, she was clearly visible in the film when Gideon was supposed to have cut her throat. Even though she would have been told that editing would make the whole thing look totally convincing.'

Tim interrupted, 'Yes you're right Flinty and if suddenly she's discovered safe and sound, the case against Gideon is shot to bits and worthless.'

'So, she has to die,' Kate said with a macabre excitement in her voice while slotting the pieces together. 'Because this thing with Gideon is much bigger to these people than her existence. The mafia have just been using her, and Willis must have known all along that she would lose her life.'

Charlie cast Tim a glance that spoke volumes and they both moved towards the door. He said, 'We are going to leave you two and head for the course. Maybe we can save her. Kate, ring the police and tell them to meet us there.'

'I will. They'll be quicker than our people, but there's something I haven't told you.'

Tim looked decidedly anxious. 'This is not going to be anything good is it?'

'I'm afraid not. The security guard that was lying dead in the trophy room left an open channel on his radio, so all the guards heard what you did with the memory card from the camera. And people will be searching for you.'

Tim looked skyward. 'Fantastic! So not only is Nathan going to kill Adriana, he is also luring us into a trap because he knows we'll try to stop him. No need for him to come back here and torture you. He knows exactly where the card is. At least he won't be looking for anyone else but me.'

'And your accomplice,' Charlie said, swallowing hard.

Kate frowned. 'Leave it to the police chaps. Let the professionals deal with it.'

Tim checked his watch. 'Right now the professionals are at shift changeover, so it's not going to be a quick response from them, is it—'

'Besides,' Charlie cut in, 'We've got to keep Nathan at the course. It's better we know where he is than out on the streets looking for us.'

'Please take care,' Kate said with real feeling. 'And thank you both.'

Almost as an afterthought, Ben added. 'He's got a knife, one of those huge hunting knives that he was going to stab us with. He's a lunatic, be careful.'

Moving towards the door, Charlie said, 'We will.' He turned to face Kate squarely. 'You've got to tell us now as we're in this up to our necks in it and our lives are on the line—why does the Mafia want Gideon so badly?'

Kate rubbed her wrists to relieve the soreness caused by

over tight cable ties. 'Professor Gideon Wells is a genius, and probably the best in the world at what he does. He can manufacture pretty much any opioid drug you care to mention, and some no-one has even heard of yet. And he can do this to any strength and the best quality—even if it's derived from a plant source. So imagine if an organisation, whose business it is to import and supply illegal drugs on a massive scale, can suddenly cut out poppy growing tribal chiefs in Afghanistan or drug lords in South America. Not only are they in control of their own destiny, and have a much bigger market, but they can remove whole layers of the supply chain and put that money straight on their bottom line. They would have no issues with poor harvests or smuggling problems. They'd build their own factories to produce the stuff, and they already have the infrastructure in place to distribute it. In his day job, Gideon has been working on a range of substitute opioid drugs manufactured in a laboratory to help medical science. But it will also help recovering addicts, and without the risk of people dying after taking lethal cocktails bought on the cheap from overseas or the black web. The mafia have done their research and know that Gideon's work is groundbreaking, and no-one in the world would want to stop him. So if the mob can get him set up behind the facade of a bona fide humanitarian operation, they will also be producing something they will look to get licenced and make perfectly legal. That is until the authorities close the loophole, but by then the bad guys will have flooded the planet with it. Gideon is seen as the man who knows everything on the subject, the best. He could work for any government in the world, the drug companies or illegal operations. They have all approached him many times, but he is fiercely patriotic and refuses to go anywhere.'

Charlie stated confidently, 'And that's why they have to

have something on him so horrific that he has no choice but to work for them. And why Adriana really has to be sacrificed.'

'And it explains why Danny is always with him,' Tim added.

Kate arched her body to try to relieve the stiffness of being bound for hours. 'Exactly. The Mafia had to try another tack, and they cleverly targeted Gideon's weaknesses. They know where he lives, that he loves to play golf and his was one of the first names down to join *The Sycamores.* They also knew of Willis and Adriana's appetite for a hedonistic lifestyle and that Gideon had strange tastes in that direction they could accommodate.'

'Sorry to interrupt,' Tim said. 'Are you saying that Willis was installed at The Sycamores by the Mafia?'

'Of course,' Kate replied. 'He was their trump card. How could the owners possibly say no to someone of his fame?'

Charlie nodded knowingly. 'And to answer your question, Fev, that explains why a man like Willis would come to a tin-pot club like ours.'

Kate rotated her neck from side to side to loosen tight muscles. 'Exactly right. They had all the ingredients and wanted to draw Gideon into a murderous honey trap—using his Achilles heel. Then force him into agreeing to go and work for them, otherwise they would expose him as a sick and perverted murderer, put him in prison for life and bring shame upon his family. Plus, they would tie in some government ministers with blackmail for good measure.'

Charlie looked stunned. 'You mean there were more cameras in the house?'

'They were hidden everywhere, and some people will be feeling very uncomfortable right now.'

Tim smiled a satisfied smile. 'So now you've got enough on that slime-ball Willis to finally nail him?'

Kate examined her red and sore wrists. 'We'll have all the security people in custody by now, and anyone remotely linked to this. But I think Adriana and Willis are now faced with much bigger problems than us.'

Charlie thought of his and Tim's bigger problems in the shape of Ruth and Louise. 'Think we might need you to write us a note to take home to our wives, Kate.' He saw a small digital clock on one of Ben's consoles. 'Better get cracking. What time did they leave for the golf course?'

'About forty-five minutes ago,' Ben said, 'and it's about twenty minutes from here.'

As he left, Tim turned to Ben and said, 'Oh and sorry about the damage, mate, better get yourself a carpenter.'

Ben shook his head in disapproval. 'And it looks like I'm never going to get my bloody bonus either.'

'Sorry?' Charlie asked.

'Nothing.'

'Be careful you two, don't become dead heroes,' Kate shouted as they ran down the creaking wooden staircase and out the front door.

39

Trafficking drugs, or people, were never Willis's core skills, and nor was blackmail. So even with help from experts, he was bound to make some mistakes sooner or later—he was just a golfer after all. But now he was faced with the disturbing prospect of having to explain to his ruthless employers why he had fled the UK to save his own skin. Without even considering he might expose their operation in the process. More importantly, he was going to have to confess he didn't know for sure if the crucial deal with Gideon Wells had been secured. Which was the very essence of the entire operation, and something the organisation had been orchestrating for years. Sitting at the Heathrow departure gate waiting for the Newark flight to board, all kinds of scenarios were running through his head. He checked himself and tried to remain positive. It was no use him running from the family, they would find him wherever he was. Besides, the mock sacrifice had taken place and people in England must surely be taking care of the memory card, so it would all work out. Yet there was no real choice for Willis. He was going to have to front it out with Carmine Ricci, whatever the outcome of the party.

Which is why he called from Heathrow to let him know what flight he was arriving on into New York.

Things rarely went wrong in Willis's world. He'd even been getting away with drug filled golf clubs for ages. And he had totally convinced himself that proceedings in Surrey would get sorted before he landed in the U.S.—Adriana would have seen it through. And he would be in the clear with the UK authorities, because he simply wasn't at the party. He was heading for the states, wasn't he? And ok he must have known about the event, but he would blame Adriana for everything and let her take the fall. So convinced was he that he would escape any charges that he also called contacts in Miami and Phuket. To let them know he would be visiting soon, and it was business as usual. Both calls were intercepted and recorded before he stepped on the plane.

During the seven-hour flight and after Willis's plane touched down in Newark, he had been recognised and was asked to sign a few autographs and pose for selfies with passengers and staff. This was all part of the celebrity existence he enjoyed so much. Yet in the arrivals hall it was still just before eight a.m. in the morning and there were none of the usual paparazzi waiting for him, just family and friends meeting regular travellers. Plus a few drivers waiting for business passengers. Drivers like Lou Ferrone, who was holding a card saying *Mr Martin* that Willis picked out immediately. Lou was an overweight, dark-skinned and weary looking man in his sixties, but immaculately dressed in an open-necked white shirt, dark blue suit and highly polished shoes. He gave a thin smile, then reached out and shook Willis by the hand. 'Hi Mr Martin, it's a pleasure to meet you. My name is Lou, and I am taking you to meet Mr Ricci at his house out in the Hamiltons today. No luggage?'

'That's great, thanks Lou, and I have no luggage.'

As they walked towards the car park and out of the arrivals hall, there were two men leaning against the wall, studying the flight information screens. Lou gave them a long suspicious look, while Willis hadn't even noticed them. When Lou looked back, one of the men had gone. 'Something troubling you, buddy?' Willis asked.

'Nothing really, Mr Martin, just a bit weird for two guys to be waiting on somebody arriving at this time. Usually, it's only one person looking for a wife or partner, unless a whole family comes, or someone like me.' He gave a shrug of his shoulders, 'Ahh, probably nothing.' Lou was ex-operational in the mob and knew it certainly wasn't nothing. He'd have to make a call on the way to the Ricci residence.

As the sleek Mercedes sedan left the airport car park on its eighty-mile journey to The Hamiltons with Willis in the back, there was little by way of chat. Lou was impassive and not particularly impressed that he had a household name from the world of golf in his limousine. While Willis was busy checking his voicemail, which was just coming to life. He sent a text message and wished he wasn't on his way to meet Carmine. Ten anxious minutes passed, and his phone rang. He fumbled clumsily inside his sports jacket, then pressed the receive button and spoke to a male American voice at the other end. Willis screamed, 'What do you mean the security guys didn't get it—where the hell is it then?' There was a pause while he took in more information. 'OK, so they are on their way to you now. And you will get it when they arrive. Make sure to call me just as soon as you have it.'

'Everything alright Mr Martin?' Lou asked.

Perspiring profusely and mopping his brow with a handkerchief, Willis wasn't fooling an old hand like Lou when he said, 'Yeah fine, got any water in here, Lou?'

'In the icebox, Mr Martin, and just to let you know, those

two guys from the airport have been following us for the last half an hour. Agents, I can smell em a mile off. You ain't carrying anything, are you?'

Willis replied indignantly, 'No Lou, I most certainly am not.'

An hour later, the Mercedes glided to a halt outside the gates of Carmine Ricci's mansion in the Water Mill area of The Hamiltons. From inside a small kiosk in the grounds, a smartly dressed guard in uniform opened the tall electric gates when he saw Lou approaching. The car swung smoothly into the property around a paved driveway to the entrance of a huge white weather-boarded New England style house. Lou clumsily eased his bulky frame out of the driver's seat and opened the rear passenger door. 'Up the steps and through the main door, Mr Martin. The maid will take you to Mr Ricci.'

'Thanks Lou. Did you lose the guys from the airport?'

'Yeah, a while back, but their buddies are parked down the street.'

Willis just thought this was another world and people like Lou took care of things that he didn't need to worry about.

Apart from his early days before his talent for sport became apparent, Willis had lived most of his life away from life's realities and things just happened for him. Pulled from a life of poverty within a family of eight children, he was sponsored and protected by the mafia to achieve worldwide success. He lived a fairytale existence of fame and fortune, but at the back of his mind knew one day a favour would be called that he simply couldn't refuse. The time came, and the favour had been called at *The Sycamores.* Now he was about to tell his sponsor that after living a celebrity lifestyle on their coat-strings he had failed to deliver on the one thing they had asked of him. And in his naivety, he thought

Carmine Ricci would probably be annoyed, but understanding.

'This way, Mr Martin,' a short middle-aged Hispanic woman in a light blue uniform with white collar and cuffs said. 'Mr Ricci is waiting for you in the study. Can I get you a coffee?'

'Maybe later honey,' Willis uttered as he looked around the opulent light filled hallway full of expensive contemporary objects d'art before stopping outside a white painted panelled door. The woman tapped twice on the door, pushed it open and said, 'Mr Ricci, Mr Martin has arrived.'

'Thank you, Conchita,' came the reply from a familiar voice.

'Thanks honey,' Willis added, while mentally preparing himself to be at his charming best with a senior member of one of the New York families. With a beaming smile and an outstretched hand, Willis walked into the study where Carmine Ricci was dressed casually and looking dispassionate in chinos and a chunky sweater. Carmine walked across the room with an air of importance, locked the door, then turned to face Willis squarely. Willis was still smiling and offering his hand in welcome, but Carmine continued to ignore it. The Italian American's pointed features pinched as he drew his arm back and delivered an open-handed slap hard on the side of Willis's face, knocking him off balance. 'You were only supposed to come here when you had the footage, you stupid piece of shit, and now you are all over British TV. Reporters will be camped outside my house any time now.'

Willis rubbed his red and stinging face. 'I know Carmine. The cops were coming for me and I had to get out. But we know where the memory card is, and it's coming soon.'

'Yeah, I know. I got a call. But someone has got to cut it

out of the guy first, while you run here like a scared rat and get your stupid ass followed.'

'I'm sorry Carmine, but believe me, we've got it covered.'

'You haven't got shit covered, you dumb assed bastard. Those people you led to my house today are from the DEA. And why do you think the British police haven't had you picked up yet? Because of you, you stupid asshole. They are on to you, and now they've made a connection with me.' Carmine held his head in his hands. 'Why did I ever trust a pussy knucklehead golfer with his brains in his dick?' He looked up at Willis and said incisively, 'I've got to get you out of here, but we are being watched, so I'll have to make this look like we are buddies and you are just visiting. You'll have to play your part and stay here for a day or so. Then we'll get you to Florida for a vacation.'

'Ok Carmine, I'll do anything you say.'

40

As he had done over a hundred times before, Charlie drove up the winding entrance driveway of *The Sycamores.* He took Ruth's Fiat 500 over the irritatingly severe speed humps and past the avenue of sycamore trees lining the fairway of the sixteenth hole, then into the almost empty car park. But he and Tim knew this was going to be like no other day when they had made that same journey.

At six thirty the dawn was showing the first signs of breaking across the vast open space which was heavy with dew in the first light of an October morning. As they left the car, crows fluttered and screeched overhead while the bellowing of restless stags echoed ghostly across the empty course. Vapour from the clubhouse boilers drifted upward and hung in the damp morning air, signalling a building being prepared for occupation. One of the pair of full height double metal doors to the green-keeper's shed was left open and sit on mowers were standing outside ready for their morning's work. The team were always out early, trying to get grass cut and essential maintenance done ahead of the light fully breaking, and eager golfers arriving. Everything seemed perfectly normal, with no obvious sign of a killer on the loose waiting somewhere to trap them. The mini bus with the broken tail light was parked in its bay at the clubhouse end of the car park, and also in its designated space was Craig Galbraith's Jaguar saloon. Craig did insane hours, always the first to arrive and last to leave almost every day, usually wedged behind a desk in his office. As course marshals, Charlie's and Tim's minds had become attuned to noticing anything out of place, and when they reached the clubhouse, they spotted a golf buggy missing from its normal resting place at the charging point bays.

'Nathan will have that buggy, Fev,' Charlie said. 'He gets the keys all the time, and he's probably out on the course somewhere, or that's what he wants us to believe.'

'Nathan wouldn't normally use a buggy this early though, especially when they've all been booked out to a society, it would draw too much attention.' Tim turned his head sharply to the left and said confidently, 'I can tell you exactly where that buggy is Flinty. Someone has driven it into the lake. Look over there, the back of it is just visible sticking out of the water, and I don't think it's kids either, judging by the look on the head green-keeper's face.'

Charlie and Tim walked quickly across the manicured, putting green and the short grass of the fairway to the lake in front of the eighteenth green. The lake had always been one of the main features of the course. It was highlighted heavily on their website, in all their marketing literature and media information, and was the most striking vista from the clubhouse. A fountain pumped water thirty feet into the air, forming a perfectly symmetrical fan shape, and falling cascades played into an elliptical pattern on the lake's surface. Wild fowl swam and scooted around the perimeter of the lake as if it were just an ordinary day, but as they approached the scene, Charlie and Tim knew it was far from ordinary. The back wheels of the cream-coloured electric buggy were resting in the bulrushes on the soft edges of the lake. But the rest of the vehicle was nose down at about thirty degrees, completely submerged. The disturbed mud had coloured the water light brown, which had mixed with clouds of red drifting upwards from the buggy. Head greenkeeper Jason Crosby's face was drained of colour, his eyes were vacant, and he was completely motionless when they reached him at the lake fringe.

'What is it, mate?' Tim asked, placing a firm hand on Jason's shoulder, as if he didn't know the answer to his own question.

Jason seemed paralysed with fear and fixed to the spot. He raised his arm and pointed to the lake behind him while gazing aimlessly into space in the opposite direction. His voice trembled. 'It's Willis's wife. You can just make her out through the water. She was here when I arrived. It's horrible.' Then his body convulsed, he bent double and vomited on the grass.

With the sound of falling spray from the fountain getting louder as the wind dropped, Charlie and Tim walked cautiously to the edge of the lake. Tim looked down at the vegetation at the margin and turned to Charlie solemnly. 'There's a lot of blood here, Flinty. This must be where he did it.'

Charlie looked down at lines of fresh red blood. 'By the looks of it, he went through both arteries, knew exactly what he was doing.'

The men crouched and tilted their heads to get the clearest view through the water they could as a pair of startled moorhens scooted out of the reeds. The churned-up mud was beginning to settle and they could distinguish female manicured hands with bright red nail varnish fixed to the steering wheel by yellow cable ties. The same type of cable ties that Tim had just cut off Ben and Kate's wrists and ankles, and the same as those stolen from the changing rooms. A white gown, made transparent by the water, was covering a seated naked female body and her dark hair seemed to drift back and forth in slow motion with the gentle movement in the lake. Suddenly a stronger breeze disturbed the water, and they saw a pale and terrified woman's face turn towards them, almost in a macabre greeting. It was unmistakably the still beautiful features of Adriana Martin with wide-open eyes and a gaping wound from ear-to-ear surging with blood, which was blending with mud silt and algae. Her bright red lipstick shone through the murky water and even as a corpse, she looked eerily elegant.

Charlie went back to Jason, who was on all fours and still retching. He placed a comforting hand on the small of the distressed man's back. 'When you're feeling ok block this area off from the public if you can mate, we don't want weirdos with cameras turning up. The police will be here soon. Let them deal with it. And get yourself a cup of tea with plenty of sugar. You've had a shock.' Then Charlie and Tim sprinted towards Craig Galbraith's office. They knew there was no time to lose—they were next on the killer's list to be murdered.

41

Craig Galbraith's early morning routine was to get a coffee, then shut himself away for an hour before most people arrived. Just to catch up on anything that may have come in overnight and ensure he was prepared for the day's events. Despite Charlie and Tim's friendship with Craig, they always respected his position as course manager and would knock at his office door and wait to be invited in. But there was no time for pleasantries on that particular morning. His door burst open and slammed back against the wall loudly. 'We need the key to Nathan's flat now!' Tim shouted aggressively.

Craig looked startled and annoyed by the rudeness of the intrusion but was gaunt with worry after just hearing the news of Adriana's body in the lake. 'What the hell has happened now?'

'Key!' Tim barked, holding out his hand.

'Glad to see you're okay after last night boys, have you heard anything from Kate or Ben?'

Tim was losing patience fast. 'Just give me that bloody key will you before we join the body count.'

'Ok, ok,' Craig said looking uneasily at Tim's wild eyes

while fumbling in his desk to find the spare key to Nathan's accommodation.

Charlie could sense Craig's fear and knew he didn't quite know what to do with the total horror he was faced with. 'Craig, we found Kate and Ben. They're both safe and at Ben's house. But we now know that Nathan is the killer, and we have to find him before he kills again, and then skips the country.'

Craig blurted out a laugh, 'Nathan, are you kidding? Some days that boy struggles to tie his bootlaces.'

Tim spoke through gritted teeth. 'Do I look like I'm kidding? He's a mafia assassin no doubt sent here by Willis's mate, Carmine Ricci. And if you think this is in any way funny, go and have a look at what he's done to that girl in the lake.'

'No sorry Tim, I didn't mean—'

Tim didn't let him finish his sentence. He grabbed Craig by the sleeve of his lilac designer golf sweater. 'I know you didn't, but you are coming with us. Get your arse moving. Nathan has come back here to kill me and Charlie, maybe all three of us—come on, run!'

The three men ran out of the building and reached a painted panelled wooden door at the end of a long-tarmacked path at the rear of the clubhouse. In contrast to the pristine entrance of the building, this was back of house. The grass was long and full of weeds. Litter was collecting in the corners of the building. Debris from the kitchens was spilling onto a hardstanding near large steel portable waste bins and the foul smell of rotting food drifted in the air. Craig's hand shook as he tried to enter the key into a weathered and loose Yale lock. Tim pushed him aside and turned the key to release the latch, and pushed the door open hard against the staircase wall. 'Be careful, he might be upstairs,'

Craig said as he stepped backwards to let Charlie and Tim go first.

'Unlikely,' Charlie said, 'This is too obvious and gives him nowhere to run. He'll be out there somewhere waiting for us to find him and not wanting to get caught. We can only hope to find some clues in here.'

Tim ran up the creaking timber staircase two steps at a time, with Charlie and Craig in close pursuit. They entered the ten-by-ten stale smelling living area with nothing more than a single armchair facing a TV on a stand with a DVD player beneath and a stack of vintage cowboy films balancing on it. On a small coffee table were cups full of cold coffee, half-eaten sandwiches, discarded pizza slices and chips, all cultivating green furry mould. Tim poked around busily, like Oscar the dog frantically trying to uncover clues. He moved into the kitchen, which was typical of students' quarters, complete with a fridge with food growing penicillin and stinking of milk gone sour. 'Nothing unusual here,' he said disappointedly.' Let's look in the bedroom.'

Like the rest of the flat, every plasterboard wall in the bedroom was either scuffed, dented or cracked and still in the magnolia paint from the original construction. The room was just large enough to fit a single bed alongside a small wardrobe and it was rank with bodily smells and bonfire smoke impregnated clothes. The bed was unmade with a duvet screwed into a heap and discarded clothing scattered over the floor, while the wardrobe stood empty.

'This is disgusting,' Craig remarked with a disdainful expression on his face, 'I hadn't realised this was how he lived.'

Charlie walked in from checking the bathroom. 'There's a lot we hadn't realised about Nathan. Looks like he left in a hurry. Must have known we were on to him. There are signs of blood in the basin and on the floor. Check under that bed, Fev.'

Tim lay on the floor and slid his arm under the bed frame. In a cloud of dust and fluff, he pulled out a small antiquated square edged suitcase that looked like it was made of rigid brown cardboard. 'Get me a knife from the kitchen Craig, I need to break open this lock.'

Craig brought in a large carving knife and Tim bust open the old-fashioned buckle lock in one swift movement. He reached inside. 'Bugger,' he exclaimed, 'nothing but a sodding notebook with a load of nonsense written in it, no knives, no guns—and no idea who else is on his list, or where he might be.'

'Give it to me,' Charlie said. Tim tossed him the hard-backed A5 book in exasperation. He flipped open the hard black cover and flicked through all the empty pages. 'Only a few words on the front page and nothing else.'

'What do they say?' Craig asked.

Charlie quoted, 'It's a list. 1. Jesse. 2. Fancy Pants. 3. Wild Bill. 4. Wyatt. And a list he's probably forgotten all about.'

'Could be any bloody thing,' an increasingly frustrated Tim said.

Craig chipped in, 'Might be horses that he was going to have a bet on.'

'More like nicknames,' Tim uttered.

Charlie was stretching his brain trying to make any links he could think of. 'They are all cowboy names - except Fancy Pants.'

'Isn't that what Gerry calls Adriana?' Tim added, starting to feel some confidence building.

Charlie suddenly had an Archimedes moment. 'I've got it.'

'Go on,' Tim said.

'It's his obsession with the cowboy thing, isn't it—Jesse is

Jesse James, and James was the first to die. You're right Fev, Fancy pants was Adriana, and she was second. And Wild Bill and Wyatt Earp were what?' He asked as though the answer was blindingly obvious.

'Famous marshals,' Craig interrupted.

'Hang on a minute,' Tim said. 'Don't you think we're getting a bit carried away here? This is a sophisticated and meticulous contract killer who has not left a trace of anything so far, even when he killed the deer. Why would he write a childish list of people he was going to murder and leave it as a clue for anyone to find?'

'Look at the way he lives,' Craig replied. 'There is obviously an element of that brilliant mind that doesn't do order or switch off sometimes. Or maybe he was just doodling to amuse himself one night when he was bored. Either way, your theory adds up to me now. That's why Willis gave me the cock and bull story about him being his gardener, so I would take pity on him and he could get embedded here.'

'And why he didn't know his way to Eagle House,' Tim muttered.

Charlie's thoughts suddenly went to his family. 'Shit, he knows where we live.'

'And we are the marshals, aren't we, Fev—which means?'

'It means Flinty we are definitely the ones he's looking to kill next, and that list confirms he was always going to murder us—memory card or no memory card.' Tim ran for the stairs and out of the building. 'We've got to find the bastard before he finds us.'

42

Charlie, Tim and Craig ran towards the golf buggy charging bay and passed green-keeper George Harris on the path near the kitchens. 'Have you seen Nathan, George?' Craig gasped urgently.

'About ten minutes ago guv,' George replied, looking confused by the anxious faces of the three men before him. 'In the small flatbed heading up the back path by the first, probably on his way to the twelfth to light another bloody bonfire, eh,' he laughed.

Charlie and Tim slid sideways into golf cart twelve's bench seat and turned the key to reverse. As the electric motor whirred and they began to ease backwards, Charlie shouted to Craig, 'You wait here and keep people away from the lake and look out for the police. Nathan must be on this course somewhere and we've got to find him before we walk into a trap.'

Craig called out, 'Be careful boys, watch out for the London cabbies golf society, they've had an early start, and I don't want anyone injured.' But his nervous words seemed to evaporate into the air as the increasing whirr of the buggy's motor took its load and moved the vehicle up the path towards the first tee.

Tim muttered sarcastically, 'Yeah, don't worry about us Craig, we'll be fine. There's just a body in the lake and a homicidal maniac out there wanting to kill both of us. And actually, I'm not so sure the London cabbies would be that keen on playing if they knew what was going on. Where are we going Flinty?'

Charlie replied, 'Odds are George is right, Nathan will be at the twelfth, as that's where his shed is. My money is on him being armed and waiting for us there. He knows that's the first place we would look and is probably using reverse logic, letting us think it's just too obvious for him to be there. We'll leave the buggy at the tenth then cut across the fairway and into the woods behind him and hope we can keep him there until the police arrive. But first we'll pick up that golf bag full of clubs outside the pro-shop we might need them more than the cab driver does today.'

Tim leaned out of the golf cart and scooped up the golf bag full of clubs as Charlie eased past. He pulled out two iron clubs and a few balls and promptly jettisoned the bag out of the cart as it picked up speed. The bag clattered onto the ground with its expensive contents spilling onto the grass. And an angry cabbie could be heard shouting in the distance, using words of one syllable.

After Nathan had killed Adriana and left her in the lake, he went to his flat, cleaned her blood from his hands and changed from the bloodied clothes into the overalls that were his trademark and allowed him to blend into the course. He threw the stained clothes into a black bin bag and carried them out with him. He wasn't as meticulous in his movements as normal, as he only had a couple of jobs left to do, plus some butchery. Then he was going to disappear from the world. As he did most mornings, he had taken a small electric flatbed truck from the green keepers shed to head across the course. Nathan was still keen not to draw attention to himself. He was in control and not yet being followed by the only people that were likely to be onto him. So, with normal golf course etiquette, he politely waited for the society players to take their shots before crossing fairways and stopped while people were driving off the tees, which meant his progress to the twelfth green was slow. So slow in fact, that Charlie and Tim, who were showing no such courtesy, almost knocking over a few cabbies on the way were catching up. Their ungentlemanly progress didn't go unnoticed, attracting loud protests of 'Oi, what are you bleedin' playin' at!' The uproar in the distance reached Nathan's ears and made him turn to witness a golf cart heading towards him as quickly as it could move with two men inside. He smiled to himself. The stupid marshals had fallen straight into his trap. Perhaps a little earlier than he would have liked, but he was only one man in an electric vehicle, so he would move quicker than them and still get where he planned to be in time. He was luring them into the quiet copse near the twelfth green, close to where he had killed the deer. Outside of the clearing where Nathan had his regular bonfires, the area was surrounded by dense auburn coloured bracken, so dense that if a golfer was wayward enough to hit a ball in there, they would never go looking for it.

Nathan's etiquette suddenly disappeared. His carefully considered plan to dispatch Charlie and Tim would have to be adjusted to something less elaborate, but as long as they were dead and he could open Tim up to retrieve the memory card, it didn't matter. He cut across the eight and eleventh fairways, then drove up an uneven track through the three feet high bracken that was beginning to shrink back with the season. He was heading deep into the copse where a groundsman's storage shed was barely visible from the course. He skidded the flatbed to a halt outside the store he often used to while away for hours when having bonfires. Bonfires where Charlie and Tim now realised, he had been burning bloodstained clothing, incriminating DNA and other evidence, all conveniently fuelled by the fallen branches and debris. The store was nothing but an eight by six timber shed with a pitched felt roof, a fixed window in one side and smelt of old grass and nitrogen feed, but this was Nathan's territory, as the cabbies would say, it was his manor.

As the two marshals reached the track to the copse, Tim bawled, 'Hurry up Flinty, let's try to get to him before he can get into that shed.'

'He might already have a gun mate. Think we should keep our distance.'

'No chance. He'd have been shooting at us by now and probably taking out some of Craig's cabbies in the process. If he's got a weapon, it's hidden somewhere in that shed. He's making us follow him there, but if we're quick, we can get to him before he gets inside and gets it. It's a gamble, but we have to give it a try. Forget Neanderthal Nathan. This man is a professional killer and aims to execute both of us.'

As their buggy was rapidly closing the gap on him, they could see Nathan fumbling for a key in the pocket of his overalls and then unlocking a padlock, removing it from a hasp and staple and throwing it to the ground. The door flung open, and he ran inside just as Charlie drew the buggy to a halt outside the shed.

Nathan had a Beretta handgun hidden at the bottom of a sack of granular fertiliser at the rear of the shed behind some gardening tools. He had to find the weapon before the two men were upon him. But he had underestimated their determination and was uncharacteristically losing control of the situation. The door of the shed was thrown open and there, filling the doorway in silhouette, stood Charlie and Tim, holding a golf club each and ready to pounce. But they were faced with a grinning Nathan, now with sharp eyes and without a well-practiced vacant look on his face. He was levelling a pistol at them. 'Back out guys,' he said in a broad Texan accent, 'You don't want to die in this crummy old shed—do you—not very British, eh?' he laughed menacingly.

43

Charlie and Tim raised their hands slowly and moved backwards cautiously from the shed doorway, knowing that before them stood a paid assassin, not somebody nervously, out of their depth who would never pull the trigger. With a wave to the left of his Beretta's gun barrel, Nathan moved them around the building so their backs were toward the flank wall of the timber structure and out of sight of any passing golfers. 'Surprised at the accent, eh guys? Although I thought you might have sussed me, isn't that what you say around here?'

'Thought I heard it slip a few times, but didn't take much notice. Everybody wants to sound like an American these days. Good though, you should have been an actor,' Charlie said grudgingly.

Nathan grinned. 'Good old British TV. I've seen enough of it up in that pokey little box to pick up on the expressions and get a decent accent. I missed a few of yours, though. That's why acting dumb is always so good.'

Tim was more interested in the gun pointed at them in the hands of a killer and tried to reason them out of the situation with their assailant. 'Don't be silly Nathan you won't get away with shooting us, the shots will be heard for miles, the police are on their way so you might as well put the gun down and go quietly while you still have time to escape.'

Nathan chuckled and said in his now pronounced Texan drawl, 'Ya'll really believed I was a stupid redneck, didn't you? People will think the shots are just the farmer scaring birds off his fields, just like he does every day. And when I've killed you both, I'll hide your bodies deep in the bracken. By the time they find you half eaten by the animals, I'll be in a safe house in the states somewhere waiting for plastic surgery and a change of identity.' He laughed, 'So guys, put your head between your legs and kiss your asses goodbye, because I'm about to waste the both of you.' He signalled again with the gun barrel, directing Charlie and Tim towards a large dense bank of four feet deep bracken which was somewhere the deer often hid.

Charlie tried to buy some time by appealing to Nathan's ego and satisfy his own curiosity. 'Before you waste us, Nathan, tell me why James and Adriana had to die. I understand the deer, that was to scare Craig and bring him into line. Plus, of course, to provide fake blood to set up Gideon, but why James—and I thought Adriana was on your team?'

Nathan's self-conceit made him take the bait, and a smile crept over his face, which was no longer the face of a simpleton, but someone focused and threatening. 'The deer was a bit of fun. You know a calling card and let me practise my hunting skills from back home. But no-one expected all the bitchin' from the club and local folks, so I had to shut down the noise - too many cops nosing around that could affect our real business here.'

Tim looked furious. 'So you killed that boy just to give the police a culprit?'

'Yeah, that was part of it, but he was getting way out of line with Adriana, threatening to expose our little cocaine operation if she didn't leave Willis. How do you put it? He was a loose cannon, and we were getting way too close to our main objective to chance it over an out-of-control loser like him.'

'Your objective was Gideon,' Charlie said confidently. 'And then you tried to set up Ben for James's murder.'

'No way. I didn't know he was going to the apartment that night.' Nathan chuckled, 'Ha, lucky he didn't come earlier or I would have killed him too.' He looked at the men's astonished expressions. 'What? Did y'all think I came here to waste people and then hand myself in like an upright citizen?'

'But what about that note James wrote—he did write it, didn't he?' Charlie asked.

Nathan grinned, 'Aw come on guys, y'all are just killing time here. You've got this all sown up. You know James fell for Neanderthal Nathan's story hook, line and sinker. Even the part about wanting to be loved, writing that made everyone think James's heart was broken—he was such a sad pussy.'

'What about Adriana?' Tim asked, 'You had to kill her to make the story fit so you could get Gideon.'

'Ah, that crazy whore she had her own agenda and was way too much of a risk to us, forever pitchin' a hissy fit bout somethin'. I'm surprised your intelligence people didn't whack her before me—she was already blackmailing some of your politicians. But bless your hearts, there you go again. It was clear why she had to die, wasn't it? Once we had trapped the professor with the footage of her sacrifice come hell or high water, your people would have proved it was fake.'

'So you were always going to cut her throat to make it real?' Tim said. 'And Willis must have been in on it.'

'You are surenuff catchin' on, big boy. Once they found

her body, the tape was priceless, and we would have had the professor locked in for sure.' He smiled, 'And Willis? Well, Willis, don't give a damn for anyone but Willis. What kind of guy would set his wife up to have her throat cut for real?'

'So why the golf course to kill her?'

Nathan frowned. 'Yeah, not ideal for framing the professor, but he will be the number one suspect and once that footage is in our hands, he'll be on our team and no mistaking. But fact is I had to come here because I knew you guys would follow me. Your British sense of justice is so predictable. Besides, it was convenient. I'm on my way out of the country and can kill you before I go. But don't worry, you were kind to Nathan, so I'll be kind to you, big boy. I'll make sure you're dead before I cut that memory card out of your guts.' He gave a sickly sadistic chuckle. 'You guys are too smart for your own good. You were figuring it all, so I have to take you out whatever. Now my preference is to kill the big guy first, so both of you on your knees now.'

Charlie nudged Tim and whispered from the side of his mouth, 'Have you seen what's behind him?'

'It's been there for the last five minutes.'

'Ok, I'll distract him, and on the count of three, knock the gun out of his hand and run for the shed. We'll shut ourselves in and leave him to it. One - Two - Three.' Charlie screamed, 'Look out!' As they both turned for the shed. Nathan took a brief, disbelieving sideways glance at the movement behind him, long enough for Tim to take a hard downward swing at his arm with the golf club he was still carrying. There was a crack, then a scream of pain as Nathan's wrist broke and he dropped the gun, falling to his knees grasping his wrist and screaming, 'Son of a bitch!'

Charlie waited for Tim to grab the gun and burst into the shed before slamming the door shut and bolting it. They both moved further inside to a small cobweb covered glass window to watch what was happening outside.

Charlie said, 'I think this could be a fallow deer's version of retribution, Fev. This is the rut, and that stag has been pacing up and down watching us and looking aggressive. He's pumped up and looking for hinds and we were a threat to him getting some action.'

'And Nathan still is.'

The stag repeatedly tilted his head backwards, showing off a magnificent set of lethal antlers and emitting a long and threatening deep throated belching noise as a warning. Nathan didn't know what to do. He was still holding his shattered wrist and deciding whether to run or stay put with his back pushed firmly against the shed as a thirty stone irritable and hormone-crazed stag moved towards him menacingly.

Charlie looked horrified and said, 'The idiot is going to run, Fev.'

'Not a good move with a rampant stag high on testosterone and wanting a fight coming after you.'

'He's making for that big sycamore tree, going to climb it I'll bet—maybe not so stupid after all.'

Nathan reached the tree as the combative stag cantered towards him. He turned to face the bellowing animal with a look of absolute terror on his face and his right hand instinctively reached for a sturdy branch to pull himself up out of harm's way. But his hand was no longer connected to his arm by bone. Before he could change hands, the stag was upon him with head bowed and thrusting a set of sharp antlers into his torso, smashing his body into the ancient gnarled tree trunk. Nathan didn't scream in pain, his body just gave out a sickening grunt as it slumped onto a carpet of fallen leaves and the stag gored him again.

'We'd better get out there,' Charlie said, unbolting the door of the shed.

'He's already dead, mate,' Tim replied in a matter-of-fact fashion.

'I'm sure you're right, but I can't watch this.'

Charlie and Tim ran, waving their arms at the stag to distract him from Nathan's lifeless body. The stag with bloodied antlers gave a condescending sideways glance, as if to confirm he had won the battle and proved his point. He trotted away towards his harem with a superior spring in his step.

Charlie crouched down and felt for a pulse in Nathan's neck. He turned to Tim and shook his head. Tim grimaced. 'Gone through vital organs and arteries, probably pierced his heart.'

Charlie went back to the shed and found a blue plastic sheet to cover Nathan's body just as a police Land Rover Discovery drove up the fairway of the twelfth green towards them.

'Look at the mess they're making of the grass with that bloody car,' Tim grumbled.

The Land-rover drove up the uneven path and through the bracken, as if it felt the need to prove an off-road point. From out of the front seats, jumped two uniformed officers and from the back a plain clothed detective. This was Detective Inspector Gary Sharp, someone who had worked with Tim in one of his many London postings some years earlier. He walked over and shook Tim vigorously by the hand, 'Hello you old bugger, good to see you. Still can't leave it alone, eh?'

'Well, it kind of found us,' Tim said as he introduced Charlie to his ex-colleague.

'So you've got Nathan Jones for us then,' Sharp said,

chuckling. 'Not a very original name for a mafia hit man, is it—obviously a Motown fan.'

'Not with you,' Charlie said, looking confused.

'You know the old Supremes number.'

Charlie and Tim looked at each other and shook their heads. They felt stupid having missed that connection completely. 'So where is he then?' the detective asked.

'Over there under that blue tarpaulin,' Charlie replied.

Sharp looked startled at the pistol tucked into Tim's belt. 'Have you shot him?'

'No,' Tim said, 'he was done for by a rampant stag.'

'And a six iron,' Charlie added.

Tim reached for his growling stomach, and whispered to Charlie, 'Just need to head back to the clubhouse Flinty. Be as quick as I can.'

Charlie looked concerned for his friend. 'Are you ok mate, all a bit much for you?'

'Don't be ridiculous, just a bit of adrenalin kicking in. Not every day you have a gun pointed at you by a killer, is it?'

'Oh, I get it. Time to retrieve Kate's precious cargo,' Charlie sniggered.

'Precisely, and it may take a while to pass security checks.'

44

After news of the deaths at The Sycamores, members left in droves and cancelled their subscriptions. Apart from murders, they didn't want to share their course with a killer stag. Even though attacks were extremely rare, almost never fatal, and only ever during the rutting season.

Following the fallout from the hedonistic party at *Eagle House,* Willis had been shamed by the media, disowned by his profession, and stripped of several titles. With all the events that had happened, it became an impossible task for Craig Galbraith to recover the membership or attract societies with the course's newfound notoriety. Even professional golf staff weren't willing to work there. Inevitably the club's Japanese owners had little choice but to sound the death knell for *The Sycamores,* make the staff redundant and refund all its members.

Charlie and Tim were disappointed to have to attend their scheduled redundancy meeting with Craig. But better him than some faceless human resources person reading from a crib sheet with fake empathy. However, the impact on them was no more than mild inconvenience compared to the others that relied on a salary to pay their bills. They also had other reasons for feeling dismal about their appointment with the club manager. Craig had become a friend and confidant since they were appointed marshals at the course. And in their short working association, they had been through an awful lot together. 'Bet you're not sorry to see the back of this place Craig, are you?' Tim asked, trying to temper the conversation and show support.

Craig seemed resigned to a future without *The Sycamores,* yet obviously saddened by his task. The course manager's office seemed different on that day. There was no air of authority about the place. Even though Craig was sitting at the same desk and the room still smelt of carpet and linseed oil.

'It's a shame,' Craig said, gazing admiringly out at the course through his office window. 'This place could really have been something special, and they were paying me a great salary. But I won't miss all the nonsense with Willis and Adriana. Before they took him on, I warned the owners against turning us into a circus, and I didn't know who he had links with back then. But no golf course in the world was going to turn down the offer of having Willis Martin as their pro, were they?' Craig stood up out of his chair and walked towards the window, he pointed to a half-folded newspaper on his desk left with the back sports page showing. 'And talking of Willis Martin. If you were wondering what happened to the evil drug running bastard who shipped all those kids over here to be exploited and left his wife to die. Well, he's still making headlines, take a look at that.'

Charlie and Tim leaned over, unfolded the newspaper and noticed a picture of Willis in his heyday holding up a golf trophy in triumph, and a headline which read, *Golf Legend Discovered at Sea After Tragic Accident.*

Before they could read further, or comment, Craig said

scornfully. 'Apparently, he was found way out in the Gulf of Mexico. Fell off a boat so they say, although they've not found an empty boat, or any debris yet. He had been in the water for days it would seem, hard to establish the precise cause of death outside of drowning I would imagine.' He laughed. 'Tragic accident my arse. Willis must have upset the wrong man who finally put an end to his charmed life, and I have a very good idea who that man might be.' Craig leaned over and tapped his index finger into the newspaper. 'The newspapers are speculating too. It says here that he was also linked to some big-time drug baron in Miami who was killed by a sniper about the same time.'

Tim sneered, 'Couldn't have happened to a nicer bloke, eh Flinty. I expect Kate was right, and stupid Willis led the police to the drug baron and they both got bumped off before either could talk.'

'Exactly,' Charlie said vengefully. 'I think all those poor Thai youngsters whose lives he has ruined will call this karma. And I'll call it justice.'

Craig slid the newspaper from his desk and placed it into an open briefcase. He walked across and checked that the office door was securely closed, then waved Charlie and Tim closer to him and said, 'Fact is boys, this was always going to happen.'

Charlie looked astonished. 'What, you knew Willis was going to get bumped off?'

'No, of course not. I mean that The Sycamores was always going to close.'

'Now that doesn't make a lot of sense to me Craig. You'd better explain to us two old boys because we're getting a bit slow.'

'That's something you could never be accused of,' Craig said as a backhanded compliment. 'You see, when the Japanese bought this land with the intention of turning it into a golf course, they did a deal with the local authority. This was the kind of deal to encourage them to invest, but also give them an escape route if they needed it.'

'Oh, that kind of deal,' Tim said sceptically.

Craig laughed. 'No, all completely legit. But very attractive to an investor. However, the Japanese had to demonstrate they genuinely wanted The Sycamores to succeed as a top end golf course. Their initial expenditure and getting Willis on board allowed them to fulfil that commitment easily.'

Charlie cut in, 'So why on earth would anyone invest that sort of money and be looking for a way-out Craig?'

Craig shook his head and tutted. 'It'll all make sense if you stop interrupting me, Charlie. Now, if after every best intention the course failed to operate at a profit, and the owners just couldn't make it work after a specified period, the council would allow them to shut it down and sell it off. Well, the Japanese were particularly smart businessmen, and knew that on the outskirts of London and with a station just opposite, they could make a killing by selling the land for housing development. I mean, how many houses do you think they could squeeze onto a site this big?'

'So they were just biding their time before they lost enough money, then they could shut us down. And that's why you panicked when they came over.' Charlie asked.

Craig became quite animated and paced the office. 'That's exactly right,' he said. 'They just needed the figures to stack up for the council to agree. But you know me, I was never going to let that happen. Much to their frustration, we turned it around and profits were slightly up, and all the time we were making money everyone's job was safe.' Craig gave a deep and frustrated sigh, 'Until all this unpleasantness happened. This whole affair played right into their hands, so they weren't even guilty of sharp practice, it just fell into their laps.'

It was all registering with Tim. 'Ahh, I get it. So the Sushi twins had figured out that however much money they chucked at the course, it wasn't wasted. Because builders would pay an absolute fortune for this much land close to the city.'

'Precisely. Their gamble was to keep pushing the fees up until the membership fell away, and they had a builder lined up already. But the good news is that all the staff have taken a package and found work elsewhere, well, all except me. They've given me a good payoff, so I'm going back to Scotland to spend time with my family for a while without any pressure.' He stood between Charlie and Tim and threw his arms around their shoulders. 'I'm really going to miss you two, though. What are you going to do with yourselves?'

'We'll have to find somewhere else to play golf Craig, especially as Tim here has bought a dodgy new set of clubs,' Charlie roared with laughter.

Craig started to move his desk ornaments into a cardboard box ready to ship out. 'You two need to keep your minds busy, much too sharp for cocoa and the allotment yet.' He stopped what he was doing and looked up. 'Do you know what you should do? You should start yourselves up in business. You know some kind of detective agency.'

Tim chuckled, 'Yeah great idea Craig, perhaps you'd like to put that to our wives? They've only just started talking to us again. But I have to admit, it was nice to be using my brain on something a bit more taxing than how long someone should be looking for a lost golf ball in the woods. What do you think, Flinty?'

'I think we'd both need to see a shrink if we went down that road—but it does have a certain appeal to it. I'll grant you that.'

REVIEW

I would appreciate it if you reviewed my book as this would make my day.

Thank You...

Printed in Great Britain
by Amazon

58208572R00172